S0-CPB-050

He had no idea who this woman was, where she was from, why she was here or when she was leaving.

For all he knew she was married. Or had a boyfriend. Or was on the lam.

Besides, if his heart were a neon sign, it would be flashing No Vacancy. He had kids to raise. Crises to avert.

Lisa was holding out her hand, and, not wanting to be rude, Steve took it, grateful that electricity didn't shoot up his arm from her touch. That happened only in those books his sister used to hide in her sweater drawer, anyway. But it had been a long time since he'd held a woman's hand in his, and he had to admit, it felt pretty damn good.

And boy, did he like that smile.

And *boy*, did he have to get the hell out of there.

Dear Reader,

As always, Intimate Moments offers you six terrific books to fill your reading time, starting with Terese Ramin's *Her Guardian Agent*. For FBI agent Hazel Youvella, the case that took her back to revisit her Native American roots was a very personal one. For not only did she find the hero of her heart in Native American tracker Guy Levoie, she discovered the truth about the missing child she was seeking. This wasn't just any child—this was *her* child.

If you enjoyed last month's introduction to our FIRSTBORN SONS in-line continuity, you won't want to miss the second installment. Carla Cassidy's *Born of Passion* will grip you from the first page and leave you longing for the rest of these wonderful linked books. Valerie Parv takes a side trip from Silhouette Romance to debut in Intimate Moments with a stunner of a reunion romance called *Interrupted Lullaby*. Karen Templeton begins a new miniseries called HOW TO MARRY A MONARCH with *Plain-Jane Princess*, and Linda Winstead Jones returns with *Hot on His Trail*, a book you should be hot on the trail of yourself. Finally, welcome Sharon Mignerey back and take a look at her newest, *Too Close for Comfort*.

And don't forget to look in the back of this book to see how Silhouette can make you a star.

Enjoy them all, and come back next month for more of the best and most exciting romance reading around.

Yours,

Leslie J. Wainger
Executive Senior Editor

Please address questions and book requests to:
Silhouette Reader Service
U.S.: 3010 Walden Ave., P.O. Box 1325, Buffalo, NY 14269
Canadian: P.O. Box 609, Fort Erie, Ont. L2A 5X3

Plain-Jane Princess
KAREN TEMPLETON

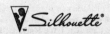

INTIMATE MOMENTS™

Published by Silhouette Books

America's Publisher of Contemporary Romance

If you purchased this book without a cover you should be aware that this book is stolen property. It was reported as "unsold and destroyed" to the publisher, and neither the author nor the publisher has received any payment for this "stripped book."

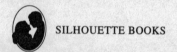 SILHOUETTE BOOKS

ISBN 0-373-27166-2

PLAIN-JANE PRINCESS

Copyright © 2001 by Karen Templeton Berger

All rights reserved. Except for use in any review, the reproduction or utilization of this work in whole or in part in any form by any electronic, mechanical or other means, now known or hereafter invented, including xerography, photocopying and recording, or in any information storage or retrieval system, is forbidden without the written permission of the editorial office, Silhouette Books, 300 East 42nd Street, New York, NY 10017 U.S.A.

All characters in this book have no existence outside the imagination of the author and have no relation whatsoever to anyone bearing the same name or names. They are not even distantly inspired by any individual known or unknown to the author, and all incidents are pure invention.

This edition published by arrangement with Harlequin Books S.A.

® and TM are trademarks of Harlequin Books S.A., used under license. Trademarks indicated with ® are registered in the United States Patent and Trademark Office, the Canadian Trade Marks Office and in other countries.

Visit Silhouette at www.eHarlequin.com

Printed in U.S.A.

Books by Karen Templeton

Silhouette Intimate Moments

Anything for His Children #978
Anything for Her Marriage #1006
Everything But a Husband #1050
Runaway Bridesmaid #1066
**Plain-Jane Princess* #1096

Silhouette Yours Truly

**Wedding Daze*
**Wedding Belle*
**Wedding? Impossible!*

*Weddings, Inc.
**How To Marry a Monarch

KAREN TEMPLETON's

background in the theater and the arts, and a lifelong affinity for love stories, led inevitably to her writing romances. Growing up, she studied art, ballet and drama, and wanted to someday strut her stuff on Broadway. She was accepted into North Carolina School of the Arts as a drama major, but switched to costume design.

Twelve years in New York City provided a variety of work experiences, including assisting costume designers at a large costume house, employment in the bridal department buyer's offices of several department stores, grunt work for a sportswear designer and answering phones for a sports uniform manufacturer. New York also provided her with her husband, Jack, and the first two of her five sons.

The family then moved to New Mexico, where Karen established an in-home mail-order crafts business that she gave up the instant the family bought their first computer. Now writing romances full-time, she says she's finally found an outlet for all that theatrical training—she gets to write, produce, design, cast and play all the parts!

SILHOUETTE MAKES YOU A STAR!
Feel like a star with Silhouette.
Look for the exciting details of our new contest inside all of these fabulous Silhouette novels:

Romance

 #1534 Stranded with the Sergeant
Cathie Linz

 #1535 So Dear to My Heart
Arlene James

 #1536 Doctor in Demand
Karen Rose Smith

 #1537 His Band of Gold
Melissa McClone

 #1538 The Heiress Takes a Husband
Cara Colter

 #1539 His Baby, Her Heart
Sue Swift

Special Edition

 #1411 Courting the Enemy
Sherryl Woods

 #1412 The Marriage Agreement
Christine Rimmer

 #1413 Bachelor Cop Finally Caught?
Gina Wilkins

#1414 Tall, Dark and Difficult
Patricia Coughlin

#1415 Her Hand-Picked Family
Jennifer Mikels

#1416 Millionaire in Disguise
Jean Brashear

Desire

#1381 Hard To Forget
Annette Broadrick

#1382 A Loving Man
Cait London

#1383 Having His Child
Amy J. Fetzer

#1384 Baby of Fortune
Shirley Rogers

#1385 Undercover Sultan
Alexandra Sellers

#1386 Beauty in His Bedroom
Ashley Summers

Intimate Moments

#1093 Her Guardian Agent
Terese Ramin

FIRSTBORN SONS **#1094 Born of Passion**
Carla Cassidy

#1095 Interrupted Lullaby
Valerie Parv

#1096 Plain-Jane Princess
Karen Templeton

#1097 Hot on His Trail
Linda Winstead Jones

#1098 Too Close for Comfort
Sharon Mignerey

Chapter 1

"Please, Princess Sophie—just one more?"

"Oh, yes! Please…please…please…?" went up a chorus of soft voices from a sea of wide, eager, predominantly dark eyes.

"Oh, darlings, I'm so sorry…" Princess Sophie hugged the tiny chestnut-haired girl who'd sat on her lap while she'd read to the children, then set her gently on the playroom's carpeted floor, laughing when the mite knocked her glasses askew. Since it was early evening, some of the younger ones were already in their pajamas, ready for bed. "I'd love to stay, I truly would. But my Baba would scold if I got home late tonight."

She stood, only to immediately bend down, arms held wide, her heart both swelling and breaking as most of the children swarmed into her embrace.

"I have to use the toilet," a tiny blond girl announced, holding out her hand expectantly, and Sophie laughed.

"Well, come on, then, Tiana—"

"Oh, no, Your Highness," one of the staff intervened,

snatching the child's hand from Sophie's. "You needn't bother yourself with that."

"It's no bother, really...."

But off child and caregiver went, the little girl waving shyly to Sophie over her shoulder.

Ah, well...her grandmother would scold, indeed. Sophie said her goodbyes to a staff she'd more or less handpicked ever since the palace had set up the Children's Home ten years ago. No one country—and certainly not one as tiny as Carpathia—could possibly see to the needs of the hundreds of children in the area orphaned each year due to the seemingly impossible-to-heal friction between various ethnic groups that regularly tangled just beyond Carpathia's borders, but one did what one could. And she was proud, she thought as she mounted her bicycle for the ten-minute ride through the village's narrow winding streets, then up the hill to the palace, of how many adoptions, both local and abroad, she'd been able to arrange as a result of her work on the children's behalf.

And for those children not fortunate enough to find temporary refuge here, she spearheaded a half-dozen worldwide campaigns, through an equal number of charities, to secure their safety and happiness.

A never-ending and often thankless task, to be sure. And one, she now feared, that was finally taking its toll on her personal life.

Such as it was.

Dusk had a firm grip on the countryside when Sophie let the bicycle drop by the gate to the kitchen garden, then ran around to the side entrance, bounding up the granite steps two at a time, much as she'd done as a child. Servants curtsied or bowed as she raced through a succession of sparkling, lavishly appointed rooms, until, panting, her chignon disintegrating into a tangled, thumping loop against her back, she tore into her ivory-and-gold bedroom. Ripping off her jacket and blouse, she dived into her room-size closet.

"Sophie!"

"I know, I know," she called out to her grandmother, Princess Ivana, Carpathia's ruling monarch for the last forty-odd years. ''I'm sorry!'' Ignoring the array of glittering gowns in their plastic shrouds behind her, Sophie chose instead a simple, long-sleeved, dove-gray silk. Now overheated, she dashed across the Aubusson carpet, tossing the dress onto the bed's ivory satin comforter. Out of the corner of her eye, Sophie took in her petite grandmother's heavily beaded gown, the understated diamond tiara sparkling in a cloud of pearlescent white hair.

The exasperated set to the elder princess's mouth.

''The only good thing about being eighty years old is that I can no longer say my grandchildren are driving me to an *early* grave. The guests have been here for nearly a half hour!''

Sophie avoided the pair of astute black eyes trained on her. ''I'm sorry, Baba,'' she repeated, carefully, dutifully, her loose hair hindering her movements as she wriggled into a pair of sheer tights, then a floor-length silk half slip. ''The children all had something to show or tell me, it seemed. I just didn't have the heart to disappoint them. Especially as I won't be there again for some time.''

She slipped the dress over her head, reaching around to do up the short zipper on her own as she slipped on a pair of matching silk pumps. A moment later she plunked down at her dressing table, where she glowered at her reflection.

''All your mother's beautiful gowns at your disposal,'' Princess Ivana said softly behind her, ''and still you dress like a little mouse.''

Concern, more than censure, colored her grandmother's words, but Sophie still bristled. After all, the elder princess was still a beauty. As had been Sophie's mother, Princess Ekaterina. And big brother Alek was no slouch, either. On him, the square jaw, the clefted chin, made sense. On her...well, it was hard not to wonder why, considering the genetic odds of her turning out at least reasonably attractive, she should now be facing great-uncle Heinrick's reflection.

Sophie took a brush to her dust-colored hair, her overlarge mouth pulled into a grimace underneath a pair of unremarkable gray eyes—not even silver, like Alek's—half-hidden behind a pair of round, tortoiseshell-framed glasses.

At least the children didn't care what she looked like.

The silver-backed brush clattered to the table as Sophie gathered up her hair, deftly twisted it into a coil at the nape of her neck. "My wearing one of my mother's gowns," she said, "would be like putting weeds in a crystal vase."

"Oh, honestly, child!" Her grandmother's vexation crackled more than the flames in the marble fireplace across the room. Though the calendar said late May, evenings tended to be chilly in the mountains of Central Europe. "I do not understand why you put yourself down so! If only you'd wear a little makeup, your contact lenses…"

There was little point in commenting, so Sophie didn't. A brittle moment or two passed before Ivana said, "Jason Broadhurst called for you this afternoon, so I invited him to join us, as well."

"Jason? What on earth is he doing here?" Sophie inserted a pair of natural pearl studs in her earlobes. "I thought he was in Atlanta, seeing to the new store's opening."

"That was last month."

Two princesses watched each other in the mirror for a long moment.

"He seems very fond of you, my dear."

"We're *friends*," Sophie said, slicking a clear gloss—her only concession to makeup—over her lips. "Nothing more."

"Since he's asked you to marry him, one would assume his feelings have…changed."

"He only wants a mother for Andy, Baba."

"And many a marriage of convenience has led to a love affair."

Sophie stared at her reflection, her mouth set, ignoring the burning sensation at the backs of her eyes as she yanked open her jewelry case, grabbed a string of pearls. "And beggars can't be choosers?"

"Oh, don't be perverse! That's not what I meant!"

Sophie struggled with the necklace's clasp for a moment,

finally ramming it home. "In any case, marrying Jason would put a severe crimp in my work."

"And working for the benefit of everyone else's children is more important than having children of your own?"

Every muscle in Sophie's back clenched. "No," she said softly after a moment. "Not *more* important. But you know as well as I do how many of those children have no one else to champion them."

And her charity work was the only aspect of her life over which she had at least some control, some choice, where she was respected for her drive, her efficiency, her brain, more than her position. Where her appearance didn't matter. Once she married, however, she would be expected to not only continue fulfilling her royal obligations, which were onerous enough, but take on the social duties of a wife as well. And for what? A loveless marriage? Jason's family business interests, including a chain of internationally renowned department stores, would naturally require a wife who was both viable and visible. For heaven's sake—she barely had any life of her own as it was. Yes, marriage to the handsome widower would give her a child to love and help raise—though the prospect of giving Andy any siblings was apparently a slim one, since Jason had made it quite clear he did not wish a bedmate—but as much as she yearned for motherhood, this was one sacrifice she was loathe to make.

Sophie suddenly realized her grandmother had come up behind her to lay her almost weightless hands on her shoulders. She very nearly jumped: while she'd never doubted her grandmother's affection for her or her brother, Alek, the elder princess was not known for her demonstrativeness. "You are very precious to me. You know that, yes?"

Startled, Sophie could only gawk at their reflections in the mirror. "Of course, Baba—"

"So it pains me, when you are unhappy."

"I'm not—"

"You are. You and Alek both. You think I do not recognize the signs, that I cannot tell? First Alek, with his gallivanting hither and yon and his women and his race cars..." She sucked in a sharp, worried breath, shook her head. "And you." Another head shake. "Yes, you do the monarchy proud, with your work. But I am also worried that you are perhaps…hiding behind your speaking engagements and conference calls and committee meetings?"

Knowing a con job when she heard one, Sophie eyed her grandmother again in the mirror. "And you think my marrying Jason would be a solution?"

"I think…sometimes you see only problems, instead of opportunities. Love can grow, child. If you give it a chance."

"Grandmother—"

But the princess patted her shoulders, twice, an enormous pear-shaped diamond ring flashing in the light from the small Baccarat lamp on Sophie's dressing table, then moved away. "We must go down."

Despite a heavy weariness that seemed to rob her of even an interest in breathing, Sophie managed to rise from the bench, glared at her mirrored twin one last time, then followed her grandmother down the stairs, to once again do her duty, be where she was supposed to be, make sure she did nothing to upset the apple cart.

Perhaps her brother's rebelliousness had been partially to blame for propelling her into her role as the "good" one. Or perhaps wanting to please, to do what was expected of her, was simply part and parcel of her nature, she couldn't tell. The problem was, the older she got, the more those expectations seemed to be increasing. And whereas at one time she lived for the approval her obedience garnered, now she felt suffocated by it.

In other words, she didn't want to play anymore.

"The World Relief Fund conference in the States," Princess Ivana said. "That's next week, isn't it?"

They approached the drawing room where the guests were no doubt waiting. A pair of servants opened the carved double doors; one announced their presence:

"Their Highnesses, Princess Ivana and Princess Sophie."

Dread coiled in the pit of Sophie's stomach like a nasty, filthy beastie as she waited out the wave of helpless irony that washed over her, through her. That other little girls would wish to be princesses had always seemed so alien to the plain little princess who, even at the height of her approval-seeking mode, only ever wanted to be as ordinary as she looked, to have at least some say over her life. Her heart. How many times throughout her life had she been compelled to sacrifice her own desires for her position?

"Yes, Grandmother. Next week. And did I tell you—I'm on the short list for Director when Manuela de Santiago retires next month?"

And how many times would she be compelled to in the future?

"Oh? And…is this something you want to do?"

Sophie plastered a smile to her face as both the Italian ambassador and Jason swept across the room toward her like a pair of trout after the same fly.

"Yes, Baba," she whispered. "I truly think I would. Certainly a bloody sight more than I want to be here right now."

"Now, child," her grandmother whispered back, "as the Americans would say, *make nice.*"

And the beastie shouted, *Run!*

Of course, she didn't. Not then, at least. Being her stolid, staunch little self, Princess Sophie would no more have shirked her responsibilities than she would have danced naked in the palace fountain. In February. Except that, over the next several days, the beastie inside grew larger and nastier and hairier until she finally realized, two days into the conference in Detroit, that if she didn't take some sort of drastic action to get her head screwed on straight again, said head was likely to explode.

So now, seated in the taxi with her bodyguard Gyula, on their way to the airport for the return trip to Carpathia, Sophie pressed one hand to her roiling stomach as she craned her neck to glower at the equally roiling clouds visible through the taxi's smeared windows. Oh, she'd come up with a plan, all right. Now all she had to do was pull it off. Without throwing up. Sane people simply did not do things like she was about to do.

Which is precisely what everyone would say: Whatever had possessed that quiet, dependable young women to do something so...so...*impulsive?* And even now, as her heart jack-hammered underneath her serviceable taupe raincoat, she'd left little to chance. Except, perhaps, for opportunity, which not even she could control.

Her heartrate kicked up another notch as she lifted a leather-gloved hand and yanked down the end of the muted paisley silk scarf she'd turbaned around her head. Should anyone ask, she hadn't had time to wash her hair. Thus far, no one had.

"You are well, Your Highness?"

Though spoken softly, the words ripped through the taxi's muggy interior, prickling the skin at the back of Sophie's neck.

"Yes, yes, Gyula—I'm fine," she said in their native language over the whine and thunk of the taxi's windshield wipers. Although her bodyguard spoke English, after a fashion, she could tell the effort strained him. "The rain is making me irritable, that's all."

Gyula nodded toward the large Macy's bag at her feet. "You did some shopping this time, I see."

"I couldn't very well come to the States and not pick up a few things, now could I?"

She thought she saw a trace of bewilderment flutter across the bodyguard's features. Not that it was any of his business if she chose to go on a shopping spree. It was just that she never had before. In fact, it was almost a joke among the other European royals not only how much the Carpathian princess loathed to shop, but how hopelessly unfashionable she was. Not that it was likely, considering her recent purchases, *that* opinion would change.

They reached the airport a few minutes later, after which Sophie stood huddled underneath her raincoat while Gyula paid the driver and checked through their minimal luggage, wishing like bloody hell her stomach would stop its incessant torquing. The bodyguard then reached for both the shopping bag and her oversize canvas tote.

She clutched them to her, almost too late remembering not to let her eyes widen behind her glasses. "No, no—I've got them." Then, silently, she and Gyula trooped through a sea of damp, harried bodies to the gate, only to discover their flight had been temporarily grounded due to the weather.

And if that wasn't fate giving her the nod, she didn't know what was.

"Shall I hold your coat, Miss?" Gyula asked after they wriggled through a horde of passengers to the waiting area. "We may be here for a while—"

"No!" She swallowed. Smiled. "No, thank you, Gyula. I'm fine, really. Except..." She scanned the waiting area, her stomach taking another tumble when her gaze lit on the international ladies' room symbol across the way.

Blood whooshed in her ears. "I just need to..." She nodded in the direction of the rest rooms.

Gyula nodded in reply.

Sophie's legs shook so badly as she crossed the crowded floor she could barely feel her feet. Once inside the ladies', she ducked into a far stall, sending up a silent prayer of thanks that there were at least twenty other women in the rest room, which lessened the likelihood of any one of them noticing that the woman who'd gone into the stall wasn't the same person who'd be coming out.

Her breath coming in short, fevered pants, she peeled off two layers of clothes to uncover a cropped, beaded sweater and a pair of scandalously tight Capri pants. From the depths of the tote bag, she retrieved a pair of black platform wedgies which would add a good five inches to her five-foot-four, a small makeup bag, and another tote, larger than the first and a different color, folded into quarters, into which she transferred...everything. Somehow.

Dodging a boisterous toddler streaking away from his mother, Sophie tottered across the rest room to a sink where she shakily managed to put in a pair of dark blue contact lenses, then applied the makeup she'd practiced putting on for two hours last night. Nothing remarkable about any of it, she told herself as she spritzed styling gel into what was left of her hair, willing it into spikes. Just an ordinary airline passenger freshening up after her journey.

Then the contacts settled in enough for her to get a really good look at herself.

Oh, my.

She'd seen Mardi Gras floats less gaudy than this. Her startled gaze darted from the daffodil-yellow sweater that seemed to be taking inordinate delight in clinging to her breasts, to her sparkling, ruby nails, her crimson mouth, her smoky-teal eyelids, her…hair. Only the truly desperate—or the truly mad—would have butchered it like that. And then bleach the remnants Barbie blond.

Unfortunately, now she looked like great-uncle Heinrich in drag.

She twisted slightly to get a look at her profile in the tight pants and let out a soft gasp at the rather pert little backside winking back at her.

Goodness—where had *that* come from?

Well, never mind. While it may have seemed more sensible to become as inconspicuous as possible, in this case she had thought it far more prudent to divert attention away from her angular, and possibly familiar, face to other, not quite as well known, parts of her anatomy. So men would leer and women would roll their eyes and point out how tacky she looked to their daughters, but what was a little indignity compared with losing one's grip?

Ferris-wheel size earrings, sunglasses, perfume—she told herself it was strictly coincidence that the women on either side of her simultaneously left the rest room—a stick of chewing gum…and she was ready.

Stomach quivering, legs quavering, Princess Sophie Elzbieta Vlastos of Carpathia—aka Lisa Stone, Bimbette Extraordinaire—made her unsteady way out of the rest room and right past Gyula, who was alternately frowning at the rest room and his watch. Oh, but it was everything she could do not to break into a run—except she would have surely done herself a mischief in these shoes!—but she knew her only chance in pulling this off lay in her ability to feign nonchalance. And so, chomping her gum and feigning her little heart out, she strolled through the terminal, stopping at a newsstand just long enough to collect several paperbacks and at least one leer, and out to the taxi queue.

She sucked in the damp, heavy air like a newly freed prisoner.

Oh, she'd undoubtedly be tracked down, eventually—any first-year detective could follow her Visa card's glowing trail—but it would still take a while to find her. Undoubtedly, the palace would assume she'd gone much farther than a Michigan township barely sixty miles away.

If she ever got there, that is, since none of the first half dozen or so drivers she queried had the slightest notion where Spruce Lake was. As the minutes ticked by, the nerves she'd managed to quell long enough to get to this point renewed their assault, blasting her nonchalance—timorous to begin with—to smithereens. Her mouth dry as dust, she darted a furtive glance over her shoulder as she approached the next taxi. By now, surely Gyula would realize she'd gone missing—

"Excuse me?" She bent over to speak to the driver, swiping a collapsed spike of hair out of her eyes. "Do you know how to get to Spruce Lake?"

The driver, the human equivalent of a bulldog, eyed her for a moment, obviously taking in her lack of luggage, her jitters, her getup. Her accent, which, due to a number of factors, was more English than Prince Charles's.

"You from Australia or somethin'?"

"Or something. Well?"

"Yeah, I know Spruce Lake," the driver said. "Had a cousin lived out that way some years ago." He adjusted his ample form in the seat, scratched his chin. "Takes close to an hour to get out there, though. And then there's my time gettin' back…I dunno…"

"Name your price."

He squinted at her. "A hundred bucks."

"Done." She yanked open the door and scrambled into the

back. Even Sophie knew a gouge when she heard one, but haggling could wait until the other end of the journey.

Where she'd be free.

Steve Koleski could feel the music teacher's worried gaze through the back of his denim shirt. "It's okay, Mr. L.," he said, frowning himself at the tangle of wires that had vomited forth the instant he'd removed the plastic cover from the outlet behind the refrigerator. Whoever had done this job—he used the term loosely—should be shot. "It looks worse than it is."

"I may be old, Steffan, but I am not blind. That is too many wires for such a small area, yes?"

"Shoot, Mr. L.—this is too many wires for *Detroit.* Damn good thing that outlet sparked on you when it did." Steve pulled out the mass, which reminded him uncomfortably of his brain that morning, began untangling it. "Coulda been a lot worse." A shaft of sunlight sliced across the all-white room, warming a shoulder stiff from far too much yard work the day before, as low music with a lot of violins trickled in from the living room. At his feet, one of a trio of fat, black cocker spaniels whined for attention.

Mr. L. snapped his fingers. "Susie, come over here and stop bothering the man." Then to Steve, "Could I get you a cup of tea while you work? It's a good forty-five minutes before my next student."

Steve stopped the grimace just in time. "Yeah. Sure. That'd be great."

As the old man shuffled to the other side of the kitchen, Steve pulled his wire cutters from his belt, then set to work sorting out the mess as his thoughts drifted, for the hundredth time that morning, to the near blowup he'd had with his housekeeper before he'd left. No matter how many times he explained that things in aquariums go hand in hand with fourteen-year-old boys, Mac's latest acquisition had nearly sent Mrs. Hadley off the deep end. Nor did he suppose Rosie's penchant for falling asleep in strange places was sitting any too well, either. The poor woman nearly had apoplexy when she'd turned on the basement light and seen the three-year-old curled up at the foot of the stairs, fast asleep. Of course, she'd assumed she'd taken a tumble and that it would be all her fault and she just couldn't take that kind of pressure at her age....

So why'd you take the job? Steve had wanted to ask the pinch-faced woman. But he didn't dare. He needed Mrs. Hadley, even if he—or the kids—didn't exactly get all warm and fluttery thinking about her. She was the fourth housekeeper they'd had in eight months at a time when the kids desperately needed stability. Something was going to have to give, and soon.

Steve frowned at the wire cutters in his hand. Trying to make everybody happy was a real bitch, you know?

He swiped his forearm across his eyes to sop up a bead of sweat: the instant the rain had stopped, the temperature had begun to climb. "You want a regular two-gang outlet, or four?"

"Four, I think," he heard over the sound of water thrumming into a teakettle. "A kitchen can't have too many places to plug things in." The pipes groaned when Mr. L. turned off the water. "Plumbing's next, I suppose," he said on a sigh. The old man's boiled wool slippers scuffed across worn linoleum; the kettle clanked onto the old gas stove. Then he made a sound that was a cross between a chuckle and a wheeze. "This house and I, we're a lot alike, you know? Keep patching things up, get another couple years out of us. Speaking of which...after you finish in here, would you mind taking a look at the ceiling fixture in the guest bedroom? I think it's coming loose." The kettle's shrill whistle was cut off nearly before it began. "You like sugar?"

"No. Thanks," Steve said, taking the mug of steaming tea from the prim little man in his gray slacks, white shirt and brightly patterned bow tie quivering at the base of a chicken-skin chin. "The guest room, huh?" He took a sip of the tea, just to be polite. "You got a taker?"

The old man laughed. For fun, he'd registered his spare room with the local bed and breakfast association last year, although, since tourism wasn't exactly Spruce Lake's claim to fame, he rarely had guests. Every once in a while, though, somebody's cousin needed a place to stay while in town for a wedding, or some family would find his listing on the association's Web site on the Internet and spend a night in town on the way from somewhere to somewhere else. "Yes, Steffan, I got a 'taker,' as you put it. A nice young woman who called yesterday, said she needed someplace quiet for a few days, maybe longer."

A mild tremor of curiosity moseyed on through but didn't stop. "It will be nice," the old man continued, "having a little company, especially at night. During the day, I have my students, I can go out…but at night…" He shook his head. "The nights are hard."

Refusing to believe that sharp right hook to his midsection was some sort of agreement—it wasn't as if he was ever alone at night—Steve looked down to discover he'd finished off his tea. So he walked over and rinsed out his mug.

"This young lady," Mr. L. went on. "She sounded maybe…a little lonely?"

Steve shook his head, swallowing down a weary laugh. Honest to Pete—one drawback to living in a small town was that everyone knew your business. Ever since the divorce, no less than a half-dozen people had tried to steer him in the direction of assorted cousins, unmarried daughters, and best friends' sisters. A half grin tugging at his mouth, he turned around, wiping his hands on a dish towel. "Mr. L.? Just for the record? If things get so bad I'm reduced to being fixed up with a total stranger, just shoot me, okay?" Over the old man's chuckle, he added, "And how the devil does someone sound lonely?"

A pair of exuberantly bushy brows lifted over the tops of Mr. L.'s glasses. "Just listen to yourself, Steffan. Then you'd know."

Steve went rigid for a moment there, then traipsed back across the kitchen to the nest of wires jeering at him from the wall, yanked out a pair to tape them off, crammed them back in, then slapped the outlet plate into place and screwed that sucker back on so hard, he cracked the plastic and had to go get a new one from his truck.

"Something the matter, Steffan?" Mr. L. asked when Steve returned.

"Not a blessed thing," Steve grumbled, screwing on the new plate. Then, scowling, he gathered his toolbox and headed up the stairs, fighting off a herd of wriggling cocker spaniels...and even the slightest suggestion that the old man was right.

Like he didn't have enough stress in his life, what with worrying about the kids, trying to figure out how to balance a million and one obligations. The last thing he needed was some woman who wanted him to make her happy, too. And no, he didn't feel this way just because love had dragged him into a back alley and left him for dead. He was over Francine. Had been for some time. It was just...well, he just didn't have time for *lonely*.

Let alone the aggravation that invariably accompanied the opposite.

"Steffan?" wafted up the stairwell a few minutes later, "I need to run to the store. I should be back in plenty of time for my student, but if I'm not, would you mind letting her in?"

"No problem," Steve called back, watching out the window a minute later as, like an overfed hamster, the old brown Datsun stuttered out of Mr. Liebowicz's driveway and crept down the street.

He'd just finished changing out the fixture when the doorbell's chime made him jump. Before he could move, though, it rang again, accompanied by a faint, frantic, "Hello? Mr. Liebowicz? It's Lisa Stone!" followed by the bell being leaned on until Steve thought his head would explode.

He barreled down the stairs and jerked open the door, only to be nearly knocked over by a streak of overly perfumed blonde shrieking "Bathroom!" on her way past.

"Straight back, first door to the—"

"Found it!"

The bathroom door slammed hard enough to shake the whole house.

Chapter 2

Steve and the dogs stood in the open door, staring down the hall, waiting until the aftershocks died down. The blonde wasn't the only thing that had to go. So did that perfume. Whew.

"Hey!"

Distracted, Steve finally noticed the taxi waiting at the curb, the mastifflike driver glowering at him from his window. In what could only be called a daze, Steve wandered out onto the porch, allowing an oblique, disinterested glance at the stuffed shopping bag and canvas tote lolling against one of Mr. Leibowicz's Kennedy rockers. "You payin' the fare?" the driver asked.

But before he could answer, the blonde whooshed back past him and down the porch steps, trailing the scent of about a million flowers in her wake. Shoot, Steve didn't know a woman *could* use the bathroom that fast.

"Of course he's not paying the fare! Keep your shirt on!"

For some reason, Steve became transfixed with the way her short hair, like feathers, shifted and twisted in the breeze as she sailed past. The way the soft, sparkly sweater and black pants molded to her figure without strangling it.

The way she was about to fall off her shoes.

She glanced over her shoulder at Steve, then blinked a pair of the deepest blue eyes he'd ever seen on a human being, the color of the evening sky just before it swallows the sunset...

"Miss?"

"What?" Her head jerked back to the waiting driver. "Oh, right." She shifted, clumsily, to balance the tote on her knee—when had she picked it up?—in which slender hands, tipped in ruby red fingernails, rummaged for several seconds before extracting a wallet.

Hel-lo...major ephinany time: long red nails made him hot.

He felt his brows do that knotting thing again.

For crying out loud, she wasn't even pretty, not in any conventional sense—deeply set eyes with thick, natural brows, a high forehead, squarish jaw with a dimpled chin, a wide mouth. But what Steve saw—underneath several strata of makeup—were the unapologetically strong lines of good, solid peasant stock, a handsomeness he'd seen innumerable times in the faces of the women with whom he shared a common ancestry. He told himself the hitch of interest in his midsection stemmed purely from aesthetic considerations, a desire to photograph her, to catch the light playing across those compelling features.

She yanked out a wad of bills, then crammed the purse between her arm and her ribs. "Now...how much did you say?"

The driver glanced at Steve, then the blonde, knuckling up the bill of his ball cap. He cleared his throat, then mumbled something. Unfortunately, the man hadn't counted on Steven having hearing like a hound dog.

"A *hundred?*" Steve was down the stairs in two seconds flat, in full macho protective mode. "Where'd you pick her up? Cincinnati?"

"It doesn't really mat—" whatever-her-name-was began, but the suddenly obsequious driver stepped in with, "Ya know, come to think of it…it wasn't as hard to find the place as I thought. Whaddya say we make it—''

"Fifty," Steve supplied, just for the hell of it. For all he knew, maybe the man had picked her up in Cincinnati. Judging from the driver's reaction, however, he'd apparently called the man's bluff. There were, at times, definite advantages to having been a linebacker in a previous life.

A bunch of folds rearranged themselves into something like a smile. "*Just* what I was gonna say. How 'bout that?"

The woman looked from one to the other, her mouth open. When it finally snapped shut, Steve noticed her narrowed gaze had come to rest on him.

Huh?

Her mouth twisted, she peeled off five tens and handed them to the driver, who, with a wave and a impressive squeal of the tires, left.

Steve turned to introduce himself, extending his hand. "Hi, I'm—"

"Excuse me, but do I strike you as being a complete airhead?"

Somehow, Steve figured pointing out that she wasn't exactly dressed like the CEO of a Fortune 500 company wouldn't go over so good. "Hey—that guy was about to take advantage of you!"

"And you don't think I knew that?" One hand swiped back a feather. Underneath five-pound eyelashes, heat smoldered. And what was with that accent? "I knew what the taxi should cost."

"Then why—?"

Oh, he'd seen that look before. His mother was a master at it.

"Look, Mr. Liebowicz—"

Steve shook his head. "Koleski. Steve Koleski. Mr. L. had to go to the store. I was doing some electrical work for him."

A flicker of what Steve could only assume was relief passed over her features before she wagged one hand, dismissing his unwanted explanation. "Look, Mr. *Koleski,* it was no easy feat finding a taxi willing to come all the way out here, so when

I finally got this one, I would have bloody well promised the man my firstborn child if it meant getting me where I wanted to go. But I'm not stupid, believe it or not. The plan was, I'd pretend to agree with this man's ridiculous fee, wait until I was here, *then* tell him he was full of it.''

The laugh fairly burst from his lungs. "Full of it?''

She glared at him for a millisecond before twirling around, unsteadily, then taking off toward the house, feathers bobbing, fanny twitching.

"Hey!'' Steve bounded after her and up the porch steps just as she made a grab for the listing shopping bag, inertia propelling him into her as she attempted to shoulder her way inside. Bodies and bags tangled for a sizzling two or three seconds, during which Steve found himself seriously reconsidering his earlier position on women and loneliness and aggravation.

"Do you *mind?*'' she said, wrenching herself, and the bags, inside.

"I was only trying to help, for the love of Mike! Why on earth are you so fired up about this?''

The woman's gaze glanced off his, as fleeting as an electric spark, before she twisted around and noticed the dogs. With a soft *oh!,* she dropped the bags and fell to her knees in one motion, burying herself in unbridled canine euphoria.

Steve, on the other hand, was doing well to simply catch his breath.

"Oh! Aren't you the most wonderful things!'' she said to the panting, licking creatures, laughing as each one in turn tried to crawl into her lap. After a moment, she hauled herself back up, wiping dog spit off her face with the heel of her hand as she took in the high-ceilinged entryway, the sunlight-drenched living room off to the left. She wasn't exactly smiling as much as she simply seemed...pleased.

"So—Mr. Liebowicz isn't here?'' she suddenly said, not looking at him.

"Uh...no.'' At some point, he was going to have to figure out why watching this overly cosmeticized, perfume-marinated, smart-mouthed stranger wallowing in dog slobber was doing all the wrong things to his libido. "He had to go to the store. He didn't expect you until later."

She shrugged, but there seemed to be something oddly nervous about the gesture. "I wasn't sure, when I talked with him, what my...schedule would be like." She hesitated, as if about to say something else, then turned, picked up the bags again. "Do you know where my room is?"

Eyes locked. Bad move.

Bad, *bad* move.

"Uh, yeah," Steve said at last. "Upstairs."

She nodded, then clomped up the stairs, chattering to the dogs. Steve followed, frowning at the sea of undulating dog butts in front of him. "First door to your left," he said when she paused at the landing. "What did you say your name was?"

"Lisa Stone," she said after a beat or two, then disappeared inside the room, followed by her entourage. "Oh...were you working in here?"

"Oh, right." Steve hustled inside the room and squatted to gather up his things, clanking them into the metal toolbox. "I'd just finished up when you knocked on the door. Since it sounded urgent—" he glanced up at her, fighting the urge to grin, not fighting the urge to tease "—I figured cleaning up could wait."

A blush swept up her neck. Then that generous mouth stretched into a breath-stealing smile that was completely at odds with the globbed-on makeup and the awful perfume and the hideous shoes. And something snapped between them. What, he didn't know, didn't *want* to know, but damned if the tension didn't just evaporate.

"I, um, didn't realize I had to go until I got into the taxi."

One kind of tension, anyway. Another kind—more insidious and five times more deadly—mushroomed between them so fast he nearly choked.

Ordering everything to back off, cool down, and generally get a grip, he stood, letting the grin win out. "Bet that was the longest ride of your life, huh?"

Something like startled delight lit up her eyes before she

laughed, and if he thought the smile knocked him for a loop, the laugh just about sent him into another realm entirely.

Psst. And she likes dogs, too.

Right. And maybe he should check his *head* for faulty wiring. For one thing, he had no idea who this woman was, where she was from, why she was here, or when she was leaving. For all he knew she was married. Or had a boyfriend. Or was on the lam.

And the perfume was making him dizzy.

And—*and*—for another thing, his life was more crowded than a Tokyo subway. He had kids to raise. Crises to avert. Gardens to tend and chickens to feed and about a million photos to develop and wounds to help heal.

If his heart were a neon sign, it would be flashing NO VACANCY.

Lisa was holding out her hand. "I do apologize for my earlier behavior. I get cranky when I'm overtired." And Steve, not wanting to be rude, heaven knows, took her hand into his, grateful that—their brief, earlier tango notwithstanding—electricity didn't shoot up his arm from her touch. That only happened in those books his sister used to hide in her sweater drawer, anyway. But it had been a long time since he'd held a woman's hand in his, and he had to admit, it felt pretty damn good. Warm and soft and all that nice stuff.

And, boy, did he like that smile.

And, *boy,* did he have to get the hell out of there.

"I thought I heard voices!" Panting a little, Mr. L. came into the room, extending a knotted hand. "Miss Stone, yes?"

Lisa nodded, the feathers wafting around her face. One of those non-hairdos, like whatsername wore in *You've Got Mail.* "Thank you for taking me on such short notice," she said.

"It was my pleasure. The room will be suitable, I hope?"

"Oh…" She looked around the sunny, airy room, nodding enthusiastically. "It will be perfect."

"And you won't mind my music students?"

"Oh, no! Not at all! I adore music, almost any kind, really…"

Well, all this was just too copasetic for words, but Steve

had other things to do with his life than just stand around and watch Lisa Stone grin.

He picked up his toolbox, muttering, "I'll just be going, then," while backing out of the room, only to startle the bejesus out of himself when he banged the box on the doorjamb. Chagrined, he steadied the box, then turned to leave before he gave any further demonstration of his poise and grace.

"Mr. Koleski?" he heard behind him. Now, he knew damn well what would be there, when he turned around, waiting to trap him…yup. There it was. That smile. And a wistfulness—that's what it was, he realized—that prevented the smile from fully reaching her eyes. She speared her hand through her hair, then said softly, "Thank you for playing the White Knight earlier."

He cocked his head. "Even though you didn't need it."

An eyebrow lifted. "But that wasn't the point, was it?"

Oh, hell. No, that wasn't the point. Nor did he have any intention of trying to figure out too hard about what the point was, because he doubted he was going to like what he came up with.

"Hope you enjoy your stay," he muttered, then left before she had a chance to toss another one of those smiles his way.

She'd shooed the sweet old man out of her room shortly after Steve's exit, citing the need to unpack and rest. And shower, rid her skin of that horrendous perfume that had seemed innocuous enough in the department store. Instead, her thoughts spinning, she simply sat on the edge of the double bed, fingers skimming the hobnailed bedspread, and stared out the second-story window at the profusion of flowering fruit trees in Mr. Liebowicz's tiny backyard. It had been spring then, as well, she remembered, when she'd last visited the Detroit area with her parents, more than twenty years ago—

On a moan, she cupped her face in her hands. Never, ever before had she done something so…so illogical. Crazy. Rash.

Her hands dropped to her lap.

Exhilarating.

Not that her sense of responsibility had completely deserted her. Once safely away from the airport, she'd made the driver stop somewhere so she could call and leave a message on her grandmother's private voice mail—Carpathia might be small, but technology-wise, it was cutting edge—telling her she was safe and not to blame Gyula, who had been undoubtedly tearing apart the airport by that point, and that if Baba needed her, to contact her via e-mail.

She spotted the phone jack on the opposite wall where she could plug in her modem. So she could check her e-mail anytime she liked....

Sophie blew out a sigh. She truly loved her country, as well as the power for good her position gave her. It wasn't that she wanted to give up what she had. She didn't. It was just...just that, somewhere along the way, she'd lost herself in the process. And then had come Jason Broadhurst's proposal, which had muddled everything even more.

Not that there was anything wrong with Jason. Quite the contrary. In fact, he and Sophie served on the boards of several charities together, so she knew his sympathies even lay in the same direction as hers. And she truly ached for the loss of his wife so soon after their son's birth two years ago.

And, frankly, Jason's offer was by far the best she'd ever had. Oh, to be sure, there'd been suitors aplenty, from the time she was sixteen. But she wasn't a fool: her mirror told her, quite bluntly, that most men were only enamored of her position or money, or both. At least she and Jason got on together well enough. And she had to respect his honesty in proposing the alliance.

But it still came down to the same thing, didn't it? Men had pursued her because she was royal, because she was wealthy, or because she was convenient, but not one man had ever pursued her because he loved her.

Her future loomed in front of her, both a yawning void and a mountain of "musts"—her appointment as Director of the World Relief Fund was all but assured, a responsibility she both anticipated and dreaded—and she blinked back tears of what she realized were stark terror. She would do what she had to do, she knew that. Her sense of responsibility was far too ingrained for her to do otherwise. But what if this didn't work, this stealing of a few weeks for herself? What if, at the end, she was still as conflicted as she was right now? What if she couldn't reconcile *her* needs with those of the people who depended on her?

Shoving aside whatever this anxiety was, Sophie forced herself to stand and begin to put away her few new belongings in the paper-lined chest of drawers that smelled faintly of lavender sachet, her gaze flitting around the simply furnished room. She'd be anonymous here. And what could be safer than staying with an elderly gentleman?

An elderly gentlemen who hired handsome, protective, all-American male electricians?

Ah. She'd wondered how long she'd be able to stave that one off.

My goodness, she'd had quite a reaction to Steve Koleski, hadn't she? But why? Why now? And, for heaven's sake, why *him?* It wasn't as if she'd been locked in a convent her entire life.

Exactly.

Well…what did she see in him?

Green eyes flecked with gold and mischief, that's what, his short-cropped hair the innocent blond of a child's, a startling contrast to tanned skin stretched taut over lean, sharp features that were anything but childlike. An expressive mouth that a woman—well, this woman, at least—ached to touch, just to see if it was as soft and smooth as it looked. To see if it was real. A mouth that twitched, she noticed, just before it burst into a rather endearingly slanted smile.

She saw—*felt*—kindness. Protectiveness. Trustworthiness.

All nicely packaged in enough muscles to make one's mouth go dry.

Twirling a hunk of her butchered hair around her finger, she stared outside at the little flower garden below, her brows tightly drawn. What was it about the man that produced that tingling sensation in the odd body part whenever he grinned at her? Lust? Perhaps. After all, she didn't suppose she was immune to the things like that, strange and unfamiliar though they might be. But it was more than that. It was…she bit her lip in concentration, then let out a sigh. It was more like…excitement. Anticipation. The sudden, euphoric feeling a child gets when she sees a bicycle in a shop window and realizes she wants it more than anything in the world.

Except it was like wanting the plain, sturdy, reliable three-speed model instead of the flashy ten-speed.

Oh. Oh…dear.

She grabbed the tote, unloading the paperbacks onto the nightstand, her eyes burning.

Popular opinion to the contrary, being a princess didn't mean she could do whatever she wanted, even in disguise. In fact, just the opposite was true. She couldn't even take that nice, reliable three-speed out of the window, could she? Not even for an innocent—yes, innocent—little test drive?

No. She didn't think so.

She heaved another sigh, stacked the books on the nightstand, then dropped onto the bed, looked up at the light fixture Steve Koleski had just fixed.

There went the tingling again.

She sat up again to yank off the blasted shoes, tossing them across the room. Rubbing one aching instep, she fought—with remarkably little success—the memory of how Steve had smelled when they'd tangled in the doorway, all spicy-musky and just plain good, and how she'd let her ego out of its cage just long enough to let herself think that, just maybe, he was flirting with her. But in a slightly panicked kind of way, as though he wanted to but thought he shouldn't, for whatever reason.

But then…even if he was attracted to *her,* he wasn't attracted to her, but to the blowsy blond product of a weary princess's brush with hysteria. In two weeks, perhaps less, Lisa Stone would vanish into the same nothingness whence she'd been spawned.

And Princess Sophie would resume her tidy, orderly, dull life, one which held no place for ingenuous, handsome, protective American electricians.

She flopped onto her side, her head propped in the palm of

her hand, just as the sun shifted enough to glance off something shiny peeking out from underneath the dresser. Curiosity
lured her off the bed, then across the floor to pick up what
turned out to be a screwdriver. Steven Koleski's screwdriver
no doubt.

For the briefest of moments, she was tempted to stab herself
with it.

Fortunately, things seemed remarkably more clear the next
morning. Plainly, her reaction to Steven the day before had
been due to nothing more than an adrenaline overload, a sense
of danger heightening her sensory awareness. What she'd felt
hadn't been attraction—on any level—but simply *reaction*.
Stimulus/response, nothing more.

However, in all the excitement of actually carrying out her
harebrained plan, she'd forgotten a fundamental fact of life in
a small town: strangers' appearances begat curiosity. So it be-
hooved her to offer some sort of explanation in order to prevent inevitable, and tiresome, speculation.

At least, as far as the people in her "real" life were concerned, she was accounted for. Perhaps few of them understood, much less approved of, her actions, but nobody was
worrying about her well-being. Her physical well-being, at
least. Her mental state was something else again.

As far as those in her temporary hideaway went, however,
best to tell just as much of the truth to satisfy inquiring minds
and hopefully bore the nosy into forgetting all about her. And
she figured she might as well start with her host, who, in his
position as the town's music teacher, undoubtedly had a direct
feed into the main gossip artery.

Sophie found Mr. Liebowicz deadheading early roses in his
sun-speckled, lushly planted back garden, laughably quaint in
bright red plastic clogs and a big-brimmed straw hat secured
with a cord underneath his flabby chins.

"Oh! Good morning, my dear," the old man said with a
short wave. "Are you ready for breakfast?"

"No, no…no hurry." She tucked her thumbs in the pockets
of her white cotton Capri pants, inhaled the perfumed, early

morning air. "I'm rarely hungry this early. Besides—" she grinned "—you weren't supposed to feed me last night."

"I was doing the roast anyway, it was no trouble." He took his clippers to a climbing rose spanning a latticework archway. "But whenever you're ready, just let me know."

Still not sure how best to broach her subject, Sophie reached out to cup an exquisite rosebud the color of fresh butter. "You coax life from the ground every bit as well as you coax music from your violin."

That merited her a bright, surprised grin from underneath the enormous hat. "You are very kind, my dear," Mr. Liebowicz said. "But how did you know it was I who was playing?"

She shrugged. "You had several students yesterday. It wasn't difficult to tell when the teacher was demonstrating for the student."

The old man sighed, eyeing his liver-spotted hands. "These poor old things aren't very reliable these days, I'm afraid. But I suppose they still have their moments."

Sophie laughed, then bent to smell another rose, this one fully open, an intense, deep pink tinged with coral. "I'm sure you must be dying to know why I landed on your doorstep yesterday," she said quietly.

A finch warbled overhead. Then: "As someone forced from my own home in Poland fifty years ago by a certain German dictator's policies, I understand that people often have valid reasons for keeping secrets. But I will admit wondering about your accent…?"

Smiling, she straightened, then folded her arms across a light blue cotton sweater, watching Mr. Liebowicz clip and prune and coddle his precious flowers. "I was raised in Europe," she said, remembering her vow to herself to lie as little as possible. "But my father was English. As was my schooling."

"I see." He turned to her, his expression partially muted by the hat's shadow. "But—" his thin lips twitched into a kindly smile "—nobody comes to Spruce Lake without a reason, Miss Stone. We have no tourist attractions, no views to speak of, nothing to lure someone seeking excitement, or even diversion. Nothing except…sanctuary, perhaps?''

All she could do was stare at him.

''You came with little luggage, and the clothes you have are obviously new. You are in hiding, Miss Stone. If that is indeed your name.'' The old man shrugged, then returned to his task. ''Are you running from the law?''

Her laugh was startled. ''No.''

''Then it is of no concern of mine why you are here.'' He moved on to the next bush, squinting at a bud, from which he removed a layer of aphids. ''Although you may find me a good listener…?''

She hesitated, then said, ''It's nothing, really. I just suddenly realized I desperately needed to take some time for myself. To relax. To perhaps think through a few things.''

''Ah. One of those, what do they call them? Workaholics?''

''I suppose, yes.''

He tilted his head, resembling a flower himself in the silly hat. ''Too busy to take time to smell the roses?''

She laughed again, then, hugging herself, made her way over to a small wooden shed tucked away in one corner, the stupid shoes clumping on the brick path. ''Except,'' she tossed over her shoulder, ''I find I really don't know *how* to relax. I've already gone through two novels, just since yesterday.'' Like a small child, she peered inside the darkened shed which smelled of damp wood and earth and other vague, gardeny things. ''I do need the time away, but—''

''What you need is a change, then. Not a rest.''

She turned then, one hand on the door frame. ''Yes. Yes, I suppose that's it.'' On a sigh, she added, ''I find idleness doesn't suit me very much.''

The old man waved his clippers at her in agreement, and she chuckled. Then her gaze lit on the bicycle, leaning against the shed's back wall. ''Oh! Does the bicycle work?'' she called out to him, already halfway inside.

''It was my daughter's,'' Mr. Liebowicz said, closing in on her. ''It's been years since anyone's ridden it. Here—'' He motioned for her to bring it out. ''Let's have a look.''

So she did, divesting the poor thing of its cobweb shroud. The tires were flat, but otherwise it looked in decent condition. "Would you mind if I borrowed it while I was here? After I got it fixed up, of course."

"No, not at all. There's a bicycle shop not six blocks away, in town, that can fix those tires for you. I'll be happy to pay for getting it in shape—"

"Nonsense. If I'm going to use it, the least I can do is foot the repair bill."

"Well, then—take it, with my blessings. The countryside is beautiful, this time of year. And a half hour in that direction—" he pointed west "—takes you to a stretch of woods and farmland that may remind you of home."

She blinked at him, questions fluttering like moths in her brain.

"Your accent may be English, my dear," Mr. Liebowicz said with a smile, "but your features are pure central Europe."

After a moment, she hugged the dear old man, clearly startling him, then knelt by the bike, checking the chain. "Perhaps a few nice, long bike rides will clear out the old brain, you know?"

Mr. Liebowicz stroked the dulled silver handlebars, then nodded. "Perhaps so, my dear. Perhaps so."

Chapter 3

"Mrs. Hadley—please." Steve did some fancy shuffling through several half-dressed kids and a dog in order to plant himself in front of the bulldozer of a woman headed for his front door. "If you could just stay until—"

"*Mis*ter Koleski." A pair of frigid blue eyes smacked into his. "I only took this job because the agency said you were desperate, so you knew from the beginning I was only here on a trial basis. Well, the trial's over!" A pudgy hand swept him out of the way as the woman tromped through the old farmhouse's uncarpeted living room, tugging her pale blue blouse down over hips that conjured up images of large, scary beasts.

Steve's peripheral vision caught the six-year-old standing by the doorway, his eyes wide with confusion and fear. "For crying out loud, Mrs. Hadley—it wasn't like Dylan meant to do it!"

The housekeeper spun around. "No six-year-old should still be wettin' himself, Mr. Koleski!"

Dylan ran from the room, sobbing; frustration flared into a fury. Steve felt no compunction about turning on the woman standing in front of him with her chin jutted out to Wisconsin. Thank God Mac was out feeding the chickens. The fourteen-year-old was fiercely protective of his younger siblings, and he tended to fly off the handle if he even suspected that someone was hurting one of them. At the moment, Steve understood all too well how the teenager felt. "It's only been eight months. And Dylan's only six, in case you missed it. *Six.* He can't help it if he still has nightmares."

Now he noticed the twins, both still in their nightgowns, Bree with rollers in her short hair, sidling out to see what all the commotion was about. Mrs. Hadley turned again to leave; Steve caught her by the arm. "Just wait one blessed minute, all right?" he said in a low voice, then turned to the girls. "Guys, I know you hate to do this, but I really, really need you to get Dylan cleaned up and dressed this morning."

Courtney, her long, dark hair a tangled mass around her slender face, groaned first. But Steve cut off her protest with a pointed glare he'd learned from his mother, and the two of them trudged dejectedly down the hall, calling for their little brother, while George—the brown-and-white half hound, half whatever mutt that had come with the house—trotted along happily beside them.

He turned back to Mrs. Hadley. "If you leave me in the lurch like this," he said softly, "don't expect me to give you any recommendations."

Mrs. Hadley's jaw dropped, closed, then flew open again. "I did my job, Mr. Koleski, you know darn well I did! You're spoiling these kids, is what. Just because they went through a rough patch don't mean they don't need discipline and limits! They got you so tied up around their little fingers, it's a wonder they haven't set the place on fire!"

Her word choice couldn't have been more deliberately cruel. Steve jerked one hand up to halt the tirade, then jumped slightly when he felt a tug on his jeans leg. Without even looking, he swept three-year-old Rosie and her lovey—the heart-patterned, and very ratty, crib quilt she always carried around with her—up onto his hip, swallowing hard when she tucked her head into his collarbone and poked her thumb in her mouth, conveying a trust both implicit and explicit that this big man would protect her almost as much as her lovey did.

A trust Steve took extremely seriously.

Bug-eyed and now dressed in nearly identical bell-bottomed jeans and scoop-necked tees, the twins, with a cleaned and dressed Dylan in tow, crept back into the living room, Bree with her arms locked around her ribs, Courtney twisting a lock of hair around her finger. Three sets of dark brown eyes all fixed on the scene, three already mangled hearts subjected to yet more stress.

"And that one's far too big to be sucking her thumb, too," the dour-faced woman in front of him said, and Steve lost it. Calmly, but he lost it.

"Mrs. Hadley?" he asked, smoothing a tangle of dark brown hair away from the baby's face as she nestled more closely against him.

"What?"

"Why on *earth* do you hire out to care for children when you obviously dislike them so much?"

Thin lips pressed together until they nearly disappeared. Then the woman whirled around, banging back the screen door on her way out. Everybody including the dog wandered out onto the porch to watch her leave, which she did in a spectacular fashion, tromping down the drive to that old blue bomb of hers. She hurtled her impressive body inside and slammed the door, then gunned the car down the rutted dirt driveway in a cloud of dust, as if petrified the kids were going to turn into ten-foot monsters and eat her alive.

As her car sped toward the end of the driveway, though, Steve caught movement out of the corner of his eye—a cyclist coming down the road from the main highway. The road curved a bit, right before it got to the foot of his drive, the entry partially obscured by a forest of volunteer elms he'd been meaning to take out ever since he bought the place. His heart bolted into his throat when he realized the cyclist and Mrs. Hadley, who clearly wasn't even thinking about slowing down, might not see each other in time—

"Hey!" he shouted, taking off down the steps and out toward the road, Rosie laughing and bouncing in his arms, the other kids hot on his heels, George barking his damn fool head off. "*Hey!* Slow down! *Slow down!*"

But of course, the older woman couldn't possibly hear him. And he doubted she was looking at her rearview mirror—

Oh, *hell!* Steve ground to a halt, his heart hammering painfully at the base of his throat while the twins and Dylan jumped up and down beside him, shrieking and waving. And now he saw Mac streaking toward them from the back, making more noise than any of them. Steve silently swore at himself for letting them out, because if anything happened, if they saw—

His stomach heaved as Mrs. Hadley took the turn at full throttle, spinning out onto the road at the same moment the cyclist rounded the curve. The kids screamed even louder as car and bicycle swerved to avoid each other, the car quickly straightening out and rocketing down the road. The bicycle, however, wobbled for a second or two, then toppled over into the brush.

The word that rang out a moment later from the bushes was one he regularly gave Mac hell for using.

Sophie was reasonably sure she'd live. Whether she wanted to was something else again.

The ground seemed to vibrate beneath her battered body—pounding footsteps, she realized, intermixed with a dog's frantic barking. A second later, she found herself surrounded by a herd of short people, all with brown hair and eyes, all shouting, "Are you all right?" and looking both extremely worried and extremely relieved to find her conscious. The dog, a large, rather smelly mongrel, got to her first, whimpering in her face as if to ask where he—at this level, his gender was not in question—should kiss first to make it all better.

"For the love of Pete...! George, kids—get out of the way!"

Oh, dear God in heaven. Tell her it wasn't...

After judiciously determining her arm wouldn't fall off if

she moved it, Sophie shielded her eyes from the early morning sun and looked up into a pair of familiar gold-flecked green eyes set above a shocked grimace.

It was.

"Judas Priest, lady!" Steven carefully untangled limbs from bicycle, letting it fall with a loud clatter off to the side before squatting beside her. "What the Sam Hill are you doing way out here at this time of the morning?"

She thought, briefly, of sitting up, decided against it. "Are you always this solicitous when people land in a heap in your bushes?" She tried moving the other arm, peered up at him. "Or aren't these your bushes?"

"These aren't anybody's bushes. They're squatters. Lie *still*, for godssake."

Sophie suddenly realized Steven's brusqueness stemmed from concern, not rudeness. He'd transferred the youngest child, an adorable little thing with long dark hair and bangs that practically fell into her equally dark eyes, to a taller, more slender girl on the cusp of adolescence, then set about gently feeling for broken bones. Or so she assumed.

All four children, she realized, looked remarkably like each other. And absolutely nothing like Steven.

"These your children?" she asked.

His glance was nearly as brief as his answer. "For all intents and purposes."

She angled her neck to watch his deft progress down one leg, determined not to react. Right. The sexiest man she'd ever met with the strongest, gentlest, most efficient hands she'd ever felt was taking his time skimming those hands over her flesh and she wasn't going to react? A bit worse for wear, she might have been, but she wasn't dead, and the parts that weren't shrieking in agony were very aware that this man in a white, tight T-shirt was something definitely worth waking up the hormones for. Just to look, unfortunately, but it had been a looooong time since her eyes had been anywhere near such a feast.

Perhaps focusing on his face would distract her from his hands.

Oh, all right—so it had been a long shot.

His expression was earnest and focused, she was reasonably sure, solely on her skeletal structure. So she followed suit. Cheeks. Jaw. High, broad forehead. His brows and lashes were as pale as his hair, which for some reason she'd always found off-putting before this.

"I suppose—" She swallowed, tried to reestablish saliva flow. "I suppose you know what you're doing?"

"Well enough." Apparently satisfied, he started in on the other leg.

"The lady gots lots of boo-boos," the littlest one pronounced in a voice that, in twenty years or so, was going to rival Greta Garbo's.

"She sure does, honey," Steven said, never taking his eyes off Sophie's leg.

"C'n I give her some of my bandy-aids?"

"Sure thing…what?" This last was directed at Sophie, who'd feebly raised one hand.

"I realize I might regret dispensing this tidbit of information, but I didn't land on my, um, legs."

His hands stilled as he slowly twisted to face her, allowing her to see that, judging from his terrible attempt at keeping his expression blank, he understood. "I see." And then the smile blossomed, wicked and sweet and just this side of cocky. And if she hadn't already had the wind knocked out of her, the smile would have done it for sure. "And I don't suppose I need to check *that* out for broken bones, huh?"

Oh, dear, but that grin was deadly.

And just like that, her imagination conjured up a very brunette woman with remarkably dominant genes who'd undoubtedly helped create all these children.

"A very astute observation," Sophie said, deciding the time had come to haul herself upright and be on her way.

"Wow, lady—" This from an older child she hadn't noticed before, a youngish teenager with close-cropped, nearly black hair. Which meant there were *five* children. And also meant that Steven had gotten a very early start in the reproductive phase of his life, since the kid looked at least fourteen or so, and Steven, she surmised, couldn't be more than in his mid-thirties. The kid was inspecting her bicycle, which she could tell, even from this angle, wasn't going to be transporting anyone, anywhere, anytime too soon. "You like totally demolished this."

She silently swore, then began the arduous task of gathering together assorted body parts and convincing them to work together just long enough to get upright. She'd tackle actual movement at a later date.

"What are you doing?"

Clutching the splintery post-and-rail fence for support, Sophie shot Steven a glance, then decided, no, she needed every scrap of effort she possessed to accomplish this one task. "Standing up, if everything will cooperate long enough to accomplish my objective."

The initial excitement over, the children had begun to drift back toward the house. Steven crossed his arms over his chest, clearly waiting.

"Hold on, hold on," she said, feebly swatting in his direction. "I'm working on it." She tried not to let him see her grit her teeth as she forced Leg One in front of Leg Two. Oh, for heaven's sake—she wasn't seriously injured. So why did it hurt so bloody much?

"Got any idea when you might be planning on taking a second step, here?"

She fought down the urge to laugh, if for no other reason that she was sure that would hurt, too. "Oh, you are just a paragon of patience, aren't you?"

"Got me a bumper sticker that says just that," he said without missing a beat, then announced, "Let me carry you to the house—"

"Like bloody hell!"

"Lady, if this is part of your I-gotta-be-me routine, I don't have time, okay? I've got four kids to get to school, my housekeeper just drove away in her huff—"

She swatted a hank of hair out of her face. "That was your housekeeper who nearly did me in?"

"Up until ten minutes ago, yeah. Number four in a series.

Which means now I'm going to have to sweet-talk my mother into baby-sitting for the little one so I can go to work. So, right now, I'm not in the best mood, okay?''

"Baby-sitting?" Sophie blinked, confused, then said, "Oooh…your wife works, too, then?"

A frown pleated his brow for a moment, as if he was wondering how she'd made such a bizarre leap in the conversation. "Wife?" Then his expression cleared. "Oh. Because of the kids. I get it." Then he shook his head. "Nope. No wife. Now let's go."

He took a step toward her; her hand shot up even as her brain tried to force this latest information into a slot marked *Of No Consequence.* "Mr. Koleski, it's not that I don't appreciate your situation, really. It's just that—" She bit her lip. "It's going to hurt."

His expression softened, as did his voice. "It's going to hurt just as much to walk. At least this way will be quicker. And I'll try to be as careful as I can, okay?" He came around to her side, held out his arms.

"Why don't you go on ahead and I'll catch up later?"

"Why don't you just grit your teeth and let me help you?" he said, squatting slightly, then scooping her up into his arms. She sucked in a sharp breath as tears stung her eyes.

"Damn, I'm sorry," he said against her temple. "You okay?"

No, she was definitely not okay. But not because she hurt, which she did, but because the last thing she needed was to have some man who looked like this and smelled like this and smiled like this carrying her around like this.

"Just…don't dawdle," she said under her breath, and he chuckled.

He carried her in silence for a couple of seconds, his athletic shoes crunching against the dirt driveway as they approached the tree-shaded, two-story house that seemed to be growing with much the same abandon as the out-of-control lilac lunging halfway across the front steps. Not to mention the herd of profusely blooming rose bushes in a drunken tangle off to one side of the house. But the lawn had been recently mowed, and even though the house could use a new coat of white paint, the deep green shutters were all perfectly aligned, the screens in the windows obviously new. A frenzied squawking erupted from the back of the house, only to just as immediately subside. A second later, the dog came trotting out from behind the house, tongue lolling, looking inordinately pleased with himself. A giggle of pure delight bubbled up from Sophie's chest.

"You have chickens?"

"Not to mention several rabbits, God-knows-how-many cats and a pygmy goat. So tell me something."

She carefully twisted her neck to look up at him, only to realize how close their faces were. He'd just shaved, obviously, his skin the smoothest it would be all day, still tingling a bit, no doubt, from his aftershave...

"W-what?" she managed, clicking back to the right channel.

"Where'd you get that accent?"

"From my father," she said simply, tightening her hands a little more around his neck, breathing in his scent a little more than she had any right to. "Where'd you get those children?"

They'd nearly reached the porch by now; the scrapes and bruises groused a little when he shifted her weight to carry her up the few steps, giving the lilac a wide berth. "I'm their guardian," he said, his soft words conveying the weight of all that word implied. "Think you can make it into the house on your own?"

"What? Oh, yes, I'm sure I can."

He gently let her down, bracing one hand on the screen door handle a moment before opening it. "Ted MacIntyre, their father, was my best friend all through school." He shook his head, his breath escaping in a slow sigh as he looked out over her head for a moment, then back to her. "Sometimes, you just do what you gotta do, you know—?"

The door pushed open, knocking Steven out of the way. The littlest one stood there—still in her nightgown, Sophie now noticed—holding out a small, colorful box. "I found 'em, Unca Teev. My bandy-aids. For the lady."

Touched more than she could say, Sophie reached out and took the box from the child. "Oh, my goodness—" She clutched the box to her midsection, smiling for the little girl. "Are these your very special bandy-aids that nobody else can use?" The baby nodded. Sophie hesitated, then touched the silken hair. "Thank you, love. Thank you very, very much."

The little girl gave her a shy smile, then ran back inside the house. "What's her name?" Sophie asked, then looked up to find Steven's gaze riveted to hers, his expression unreadable, but intense all the same.

A second passed before he answered. "Rosie. Well, Rosita, actually. The children's mother was Honduran," he added with a hint of a smile as he finally led her inside, the screen door slamming shut behind them. From the depths of the house, she heard what sounded like a small battle. Seemingly oblivious, Steven led her through a very cluttered, minimally furnished living room to a hallway off to one side. "I've got a first-aid kit in the bathroom down here," he said, only to halt when he realized Sophie wasn't exactly zipping along behind him. "Sorry—"

"No, no." She made herself smile, only to flinch when the wall shook underneath her hand. "It's all right, really. Do you need to—?" She carefully nodded in the direction of the fracas.

"I've probably got another thirty, forty seconds before things get seriously out of hand," he said. But still, she caught the tension hardening his features, as he showed her into the bathroom, turned on the light, then stepped inside only long enough to pull a first-aid kit out of a cupboard over the toilet. She managed not to gasp when she caught sight of her reflection in the mirror over the sink; between her still not having the hang of how to use the hair gel and the events of the morning, she looked like the Bride of Frankenstein. And did she have a comb on her person? She did not.

"If you can just get started," Steven began, apology swimming in his eyes.

Sophie laughed over her wince as she first lowered the toilet lid, then herself down onto it. "I doubt whether there's anything here that requires triage. Go ahead.'' She shooed him out with one hand, already surveying the contents of the well-stocked kit. With five kids, she didn't wonder. ''I'll be fine....''

When she glanced up again, he was gone.

Twenty minutes later, he'd somehow gotten the right sandwiches, drinks and fruit—Bree only ate Gala apples, Courtney golden delicious, Dylan bananas—into the right bags, all shoes located and on the correct feet, all permission slips signed and trip money dispensed, and all the kids out the door in time to catch the school bus. With a weary sigh, George flopped down on the worn linoleum at Steve's feet.

''Yeah, that was a rough few minutes, wasn't it, boy?''

George managed, barely, to thump his tail in agreement.

And the murk cleared from Steve's brain long enough for him to remember he had an accident victim in his bathroom. He strode down the hall, knocked on the closed door. ''How you doing in there? Need any help?''

''Not at all,'' came the chipper reply. ''Only three more wounds to go. But I'm afraid I've put a severe dent in your iodine supply.''

''Don't worry about it.'' He thought a moment, then said, ''I've got a couple of calls to make, then I can drive you back into town on my way into work. That okay?''

''Yes, that would be lovely.''

He wandered back out toward the living room, hand on back of neck.

Yes, that would be lovely?

Nope. Something was way off, here. The clothes and makeup did not jibe with that accent. Or her manner. Even in black bicycle shorts and a tank top, even made up like Elvira's sister—and what *was* with that hair?—she was classier than any woman he'd ever known.

And maybe when he had a spare couple of minutes—ten, twenty years from now—he'd try to figure it out. Now, however, he had about a million phone calls to make, and so was extremely grateful that Rosie, still in her nightgown, he realized, had plopped herself down in the middle of the debris-strewn living room floor, giggling at Mr. Noodle's antics on *Sesame Street.*

Sighing, he glanced around the room. The house was a lot like the dog: sorta this, sorta that. Somebody'd decided to add a few rooms to the original two-story structure, probably ten years before Steve's birth. The result was not what one would call aesthetically pleasing. Or particularly well built. Floors slanted, door didn't always shut tight, that kind of thing. But he could afford the payments, it was out in the country, and it had six bedrooms.

The house was furnished, if you could call it that, with whatever anyone had seen fit to foist off on him. On *them,* now. All donations were welcome, as long as they didn't smell like someone's basement or weren't too pukey a color. It wasn't as if he didn't like places that were all fixed up and nice-looking, as much as he simply didn't have the energy to be bothered. If someone wanted to give him their cast-off sofa, and it was still in reasonable condition, well, that saved him from having to go to some furniture store and pick one out, didn't it?

Not to mention having to buy one. Ted and Gloria had both had life insurance policies, but those had gone into a trust fund for the kids' education. And Steve had quickly discovered just how fast five kids could eat up the cash. Still, between his working for his father and his steadily increasing income from his photography, they did okay.

Ignoring yet another twist to the old gut, Steve walked back to the kitchen and called his folks, both to ask his mother to baby-sit and to tell his father he'd be late. Then, leaning with his back against his tornado-stricken kitchen counter so he wouldn't have to look at it, he picked up the phone to call—yet again—the employment agency. He'd just gotten through to the director when he saw Lisa make her way slowly down the hall, her legs and arms pockmarked with assorted bandages and Pokemon "bandy-aids," but otherwise moving fairly well for someone who'd just done a forward vault off a moving bicycle.

He lifted a hand in acknowledgment, then pointed to the phone. With a little smile, she nodded, then lurched off toward the living room. In sensible little white sneakers, he noticed.

Just as he noticed that the bicycle shorts left little to the imagination—

"Mrs. Anderson! Hi!" He tore his gaze away from things he had no right to be gazing at and concentrated on the subject at hand. "It's Steve Koleski..."

The conversation went straight down from there. Five minutes and a great many sighs later, all he had was a half-assed apology for Mrs. Hadley's behavior and the possibility of a *wonderful* woman (an adjective Mrs. Anderson used with great frequency and with scant regard to reality) in her mid-fifties whose employer's youngest child was graduating from high school and thus would be seeking a new position in about two weeks. Other than that, though, Mrs. Anderson was sorry to say, she had no one. No, she insisted, *no one.*

Steve hung up and groaned loudly enough to make George lift his head. Two weeks? How the hell was he supposed to work full-time and manage five kids on his own for two weeks? Granted, the older kids still had a month of school, so at least they were otherwise occupied most of the day, but he couldn't impose on his mother to sit for Rosie that long. Not that she minded, but Rosie wasn't his parents' responsibility. She, and her siblings, were his. A responsibility he'd willingly accepted when he'd told Ted and Gloria he'd be thrilled to be the children's godfather, even though, like most people, he never dreamed—

"Excuse me?"

Lisa's perky accent jarred him out of his musings. She stood at the kitchen doorway, holding Rosie's hand, a pair of creases nestled between her heavy brows. "Are you all right?"

Between the gentle, obviously genuine concern in Lisa's voice and the way she and Rosie had clearly bonded in such a short period of time, it was everything Steve could do to keep himself together. But he did. He had to. "More or less," he said with a shrug. "It's just been a doozy of a morning, that's all."

Lisa quirked her bright red mouth. "And having a cycling casualty to tend didn't help matters any, I'm sure."

"That wasn't your fault," he said softly, and the quirk twitched into a smile.

"No, I don't suppose it was. Well, except for being foolish enough to not think anyone else might be on the road, at least. Anyway," she said on an exhaled breath, "if you tell me where sweetie's clothes are, I can get her dressed for you."

Steve was around the counter in three strides, shaking his head. "Forget it. You...sit somewhere. I'll get her dressed—"

A tiny glower met his attempt to pick Rosie up. "No."

Now down to his last milligram of patience, Steve squatted in front of her, matching her glower for glower. "Lisa's not feeling very well, honey," he tried, except, naturally, Lisa pulled the rug right out from under him by announcing in that prim little way she had that she was feeling just fine, thank you, and if he'd simply tell her where the child's clothes were, they could get on with it.

"See?" Rosie said, and Steve gave up.

"Fine, fine." He got to his feet. "She and the twins share a room, upstairs. Her clothes are in the small, white dresser under the window. Her shoes, however, could be in Alaska for all I know—"

"No, silly!" the child said, yanking her sandals up to her shoulders. "They're right here!" Then she strutted out of the room, shaking her head.

They both followed the baby out into the hall, standing at the foot of the stairs and watching her ascent for a moment before Steve heard himself say, "Their parents were killed in a fire, last August." He felt Lisa's gaze zip to his face, heard the soft "oh" of surprise and sympathy fall from her lips. "I got this call, two-something in the morning. Mac, in hysterics, calling from the hospital."

For the rest of his life, he'd remember that night. That call. The devastating feeling of utter helplessness that swept through him when he tore into the ER to find a scared, filthy, thirteen-year-old boy trying to keep it together for the sake of his younger brothers and sisters, a kid refusing to let the social worker the police had quickly gotten on the case take them away, insisting his Uncle Steve would be there, his Uncle Steve would take care of them....

"Steven?"

He glanced over, nodded. Continued. "They'd just bought this old house, over in another township. We knew the wiring was bad..." He paused, collected himself. "I was supposed to go up there the next weekend, start working on it. The fire started in the wall between the kitchen and Dylan's bedroom, in the middle of the night. Ted and Mac—he's the oldest boy—woke up first, got the twins and the baby out, then realized Gloria had apparently gone in to Dylan sometime during the night and fallen asleep on his bed. Ted tried to get to them, but a wall collapsed, trapping him."

He stopped, tried unsuccessfully to quell the nausea that swamped him everytime he had to explain. "He never had a chance. But before the fire department got there, Mac...Mac went back in. He managed to get Dylan out through a window, but his mother..." He shook his head. "That ratty old quilt Rosie drags around? That's about all that was left, only because she took it with her when Ted grabbed her from her crib."

"Oh, God," Lisa whispered. When he dared to look at her, he saw something in her expression that soared far beyond compassion. Light from the living room windows slashed across features he could only liken to the stark, pure beauty of a desert landscape as emotion, naked and raw, writhed in her enormous blue eyes. "How horrible for them. For you."

And in that moment, even though he didn't know who the hell this woman was, he was sorely tempted to believe he could trust her with his life.

A temptation that scared the hell out of him.

Deliberately looking away, Steve leaned against the wall at the foot of the stairs and let out a sigh. "It's been...hard, to say the least. Hell, my life has been about as uneventful as a human's can be, I suppose. Oh, there've been the usual disappointments and heartaches, but nothing like..."

He lifted his hand, let it fall with a slap to his thigh. "Criminy, Lisa, I'm in so far over my head with this, it isn't even funny. Dylan nearly died, too, from smoke inhalation. And even though he won't talk about it much, I know Mac blames himself for not being able to save his mother. Each kid reacted, is still reacting, differently. Some days seem fairly normal, you know? And I think, okay, maybe we're moving on, maybe the worst is over. And then, bam! We're right back where we started and all I know is if there was any way in God's earth I could take away their pain, I would. But I just don't know how. And why the hell am I telling you all this?''

She'd been standing apart from him, just listening, her arms folded underneath her breasts. Now those breasts rose with the force of her sigh as she shook her head. "Because you needed to," she said, just as a very indignant little girl appeared at the head of the stairs, demanding to know where ''lady'' was.

For at least a full minute, Sophie barely heard Rosie's chatter.

Her work brought her into constant contact with human trials. Yet, for all the horror stories she'd heard, the aftermaths she'd witnessed, none had pierced her heart more than this. But why? Certainly, as tragic as this situation was, the plight of these particular children was no more poignant than the thousands of others she'd been privy to over the years.

But it was, she realized, much more personal, somehow. And rekindled memories she'd thought long since faded and worn and harmless.

Not to mention stirred all sorts of highly inappropriate feelings for the man who'd taken all this on, feelings she had no business entertaining, even for a few minutes. Still, when was the last time she'd met a man strong enough to admit he didn't have all the answers?

And who would have guessed that masculine vulnerability could be so appealing?

Seated on Rosie's toddler bed—which was so close to the girls' bunk beds, there was barely any room to move—Sophie took in the heaps of scattered clothes, the open, jumbled closet, the pop star posters covering most of the wall space, the PC set up on somebody's desk. Her *closet* was twice the size of this room, she thought in amazement as she helped the toddler into a pair of patterned shorts and a bright blue T-shirt. She imagined the cramped quarters bred a fair number of fights, whether the girls had chosen to live like oysters in a tin or not. But she also imagined, despite everything the girls had gone through, there was a lot of giggling in here at night when they were supposed to be asleep, a lot of secrets shared and promises made. A sense of normalcy Sophie had always craved but never known.

And never would. Not really.

Tenderness stirred languidly through Sophie as Rosie showed off an obviously new collection of stuffed animals, snapping into something no less tender but far sharper when she remembered the fierceness of Steven's gaze when he spoke of the children, the haunted, hungry shadows in his eyes whenever he looked at her. Oh, she doubted he had any idea of the shadows' existence, that anyone else could see them, but they were there all the same.

It was, however, not her place to even begin to identify those shadows, let alone attempt to dispel them. Because if she let herself get close enough to do either, they would surely suck her in.

So she smiled instead for her new little friend, tentatively touching her sleek, dark hair even though she knew just how dangerous it was to allow herself that simple luxury of touching, of making a connection which would, inevitably, have to be broken. "Shall we go find Steven?" she said, and Rosie nodded, spinning around to grab the drab, precious little quilt off the bed.

Chapter 4

The little girl's resumed chatter as they returned downstairs momentarily obscured the fact that Steven was in the middle of a very heated argument with someone on the phone.

"Look, Ms. Jefferson, I appreciate Family Services's position." His voice at once soft and feral—Papa wolf protecting his pups, Sophie realized—Steven shifted to haul Rosie up into his arms, cradling the phone between his jaw and shoulder. "But consistency, they've got. *I'm* the constant in their lives, okay? Maybe I can't help it that the Fairy Godmother hasn't been doing so hot when it comes to doling out housekeepers who have a clue how to handle a batch of kids, but nobody— *nobody*—is going to take them away from this place. From *me*."

Brittle silence followed, during which Sophie was afraid to breathe.

After a moment, Steven said, "I've been warned, in other words…yeah, I understand. Two days." He came within a breath of slamming down the phone, then jerked to attention when he realized Sophie was standing there.

"You ever feel like the world's pulling you in seventeen different directions?"

Her heart knocked in recognition. "Often," she said, earning her a curious glance. But before that curiosity had a chance to form a question, she formed one of her own. "And which direction is yelling the loudest?"

He shifted the baby in his arms. "Guess."

The phone rang; he snatched it up, leaving her to survey the living room.

Despite the messiness, she liked it. She liked it very much. It was a crazy house, she'd decided, the rooms rather stuck onto each other as need, not any sense of design, dictated. The floors creaked, and the wind probably seeped through like water through a sieve in the winter, but who cared? The furniture was basic and well-worn, the kind that invited you to go ahead and eat in the living room if you wanted to, it didn't mind. A person—a woman—could feel very much at home here.

Not that she could be that woman, but still.

She brushed back her hair from her face as a breeze, soft as a toddler's kiss and scented with roses and new-mown grass, floated in through the open, curtainless windows. A thousand watts of sunlight flooded in as well, bouncing off unevenly-plastered walls the color of vanilla custard.

It was then that she noticed the photographs, mostly black-and-white and framed in simple white mats and dull silver frames, lining the far wall of the room. Portraits, mostly. But not just of people. Of life. Family life. She recognized Steve's brood in several of them, although most were of people she didn't know. In one, a pretty blonde laughed at a man with a ponytail and earring as he tossed a little girl in the air. In another, water droplets sparkled like frozen diamonds across the shot as a family with two tall teens and a pair of toddlers splashed each other in a swimming pool.

But the one that most caught her attention, at which she simply stared for a full minute, was one in which a man, his dark hair mussed like a bad wig, sat slouched in a restaurant booth with his chin in his hand, the light from the window slashing across his handsome face as he watched a woman and a little girl "talking" to each other a few feet away, their hands flying so fast, part of the picture was a blur. The pair were signing to each other, she realized. But the love shining from the man's eyes, the adoration tilting his lips into a gentle smile as he watched who Sophie assumed were his wife and daughter so leapt from the photo, she almost felt like a voyeur.

She could feel Steven watching her.

Sophie turned, her eyes stinging, to see him buttoning up a blue-and-green plaid cotton shirt over the white T-shirt. "These are incredible," she said softly. "Anybody can take pictures, but these..." She gestured toward the photos, shaking her head. "It must be very difficult to capture the emotion behind a photo."

His fingers stilled on the buttons, his gaze bouncing off hers before it floated over to the photos as if he'd forgotten they were there. "It always amazes me, what the camera sees. How incredible the everyday stuff can seem, you know?"

She smiled. "Did you study with someone?"

"I minored in photography in college." He finished up the buttons, then tucked the shirt into his pants, Frowning. As if there was more he wanted to say.

"Minored? So it's a hobby, then?"

The colors in the shirt, the wash of sunlight trembling in the air, turned his eyes into a pair of glittering tourmalines when he looked at her. "No. It's a passion," he said quietly, and she wondered if she imagined the frustration vibrating beneath his words. "Come on," he said then. "We can go, if you're ready." Before she could even nod, he'd called Rosie, who came skipping to him, the dog nearly knocking her over in his determination not to be left out.

"Yeah, you mangy mutt, I guess you can go, too," Steven said, striding to the front door and swinging open the wooden-framed screen. Minutes later, all of them piled into his extended cab pickup truck—a minivan sat on the other side of the driveway, she assumed for family outings—Rosie and the dog in the back seat, the bike in the truck's bed, Sophie carefully strapped in on the passenger side. Which, as luck would have it, put her far too close to both Steven's scent, which wasn't even identifiable enough to put into words, and his mood, which she had no trouble identifying at all: rotten.

True, she barely knew Steven Koleski, but she'd never met anyone she'd felt deserved a leg up more than this man did. Not that she thought money was that much of an issue—poverty was easily identifiable by the sense of hopelessness in its victims' eyes—but this was clearly a man with far too many plates up in the air. Thus far, she guessed, he'd been able to keep them from crashing—through sheer bullheadedness, if nothing else—but for how long?

And, typically, she found herself desperately wanting to help.

But how? As Princess Sophie, she had any number of resources at her command. For one thing, she could easily procure a housekeeper for him, even if it meant "borrowing" one of the palace staff for a few weeks. She could even, with her connections, have his photographs placed in a London or Paris or New York gallery like *that*. But revealing her identity might cause more problems than it would solve. For one thing, she'd lay odds that Steven Koleski had more pride than blood running through his veins. While she doubted he'd be adverse to any avenue of help that would enable him to keep these children, somehow she suspected he'd eat worms before he'd accept anything he could even remotely construe as charity.

Especially from a princess.

But, as Lisa Stone, what did she have to offer?

Sophie dared to sneak a glance at the set features of the man sitting barely two feet away, an ordinary man with the extraordinary power to capture some part of her that no man ever had before. He made her feel…connected, somehow, to the rest of the human race. She frowned down at her bloodred fingernails, then shifted her gaze out the window.

When she'd come up with this crazy idea, she hadn't really thought about whatever personal benefits she might enjoy as a "regular" person. She hadn't known how much fun it could be to be treated as an equal, to have someone tease her, even laugh at her, as if she were "one of the guys." That felt good. Extraordinarily good. And she'd be kidding herself if she didn't admit that she had no desire to jeopardize these stolen moments of anonymity by revealing a truth which might cause more harm than good.

But her yearning to help this man, these children, stemmed from something far deeper. For all her dedication to children's issues, her involvement thus far had always been peripheral, if not downright theoretical. Yes, she'd helped set up the Children's Home, and she'd done the usual hospital visits, the de rigueur tours of refugee camps, but she'd never been actually *involved*. Suddenly, here she was, faced with the first real opportunity she'd ever had to personally make a difference in five children's lives, even if only for a couple of weeks. And she didn't exactly find the prospect of perhaps being able to help ease the stress lines in Steven Koleski's handsome face wholly unpleasant, either.

She was taking a tremendous risk, letting herself get close enough to care. But this was an opportunity that might never come her way again.

He'd known Lisa Stone for, like, five seconds, and already he knew to be leery when she got too quiet.

Of course, he wasn't being exactly loquacious, either. Steve wasn't sure which of them itched to asked questions more, although he was sure neither of them had a clue how to go about it. And it rattled him the way this complete stranger could sear through his defenses with a pointed question, an astute observation, a simple smile.

No woman, he realized with a little jolt, had ever looked at him like that before. Not so's he'd remember, anyway. As if she saw...him. Not who she imagined she could eventually turn him into, but who he was.

And as if she genuinely liked what she saw.

Take the business about his photography. It was nuts to think she really had any idea what it meant to him, but something in her eyes sure made him think she did.

But how could she? Nobody did. Nobody knew how often he'd shoved his ambition behind him in the name of family loyalty, practicality, logic. Duty, in other words. Nobody was a free agent in this world. Not really. Everybody's lives and ambitions were inevitably and inextricably intertwined with everyone else's in their circle; peace was rarely achieved without compromise.

And he done more than his fair share of compromising over the past few years.

So when Lisa had asked about the photography, he'd been shocked to discover just how poorly he'd handled his disappointment over having to, once again, put his own ambition on hold. To discover a seed of selfishness at his core he'd thought long since eradicated.

But not nearly as much as he'd been to realize how desperately he wanted to confide in her. How desperately, despite all the hard evidence accumulated over the past little while that proved his desire not just foolish, but futile as well, he wanted to be able to trust a woman. *Any* woman.

This woman.

And the sheer force—not to mention the idiocy—of that desire was making it very difficult to breathe. He could only believe—could only accept, for his sanity's sake—that he felt so impelled to spill his guts to Lisa because she *was* a stranger, someone who'd only be around for a short time.

At least, that had better damn sight be the reason.

"What did you say the dog's name was?" she suddenly asked, when the mutt stuck his pointed snout over the back of the seat to slurp her face.

He glanced over, not in the least liking his reaction to her low, throaty chuckles as she squirmed—but not really—away from the dog. "George. At least for the last couple of years. If he had a name before I got him, I wouldn't know."

"George," she said, ruffling his fur, then gently shoving him back. She remained twisted around, her brow pinched in concentration. She'd chewed most of her lipstick off, leaving her expressive mouth a soft rose color. "What, exactly, is he?"

"*Caninus Godonlyknowsis,*" Steve said. She laughed, and Steve felt the fist of tension in the pit of his stomach unfurl, just a little. As if, just for this moment, maybe life didn't suck.

That maybe, somehow, things were going to work out. "Day I closed on the house," he said, "I came up here with the keys, and there he was. Lying on the porch like he was waiting for me to come home and let him in."

He could sense, more than see, her grin. "And you did."

"I didn't seem to have much choice. He's dumber than dirt, but he worships me unconditionally." Steve tossed a glance her way, then back to the road. "There's a lot to be said for that."

For some reason, he wasn't the least bit surprised when she pretended to be offended for the dog's sake. Out of the corner of his eye, he saw her twist around to the panting dog. "Did you hear that? You're not dumb at all, are you?" George barked. Which wasn't surprising, either. One thing you could say about old George, he was real good at keeping up his end of the conversation. "No, I didn't think so." She turned back around, her arms crossed. "Rather cheeky thing to say, don't you think, considering that unconditional worship business?"

Steve considered this for a minute, then said, "The chickens might have something to say about that."

"Excuse me?"

"He chases chickens. Cats, no. A cat could come up to him and blow raspberries in his face—nada. But chickens drive him nuts." He turned to her. "Like I said. Dumb."

The breeze coming in the truck's windows was blowing her feathery hair every which way. Which was very sexy, he realized with a light but firm kick to the gut. She didn't seem to give a damn, either, which was even sexier, for some reason. "On the contrary," she said, her eyes sparkling like sapphires. "He's just smart enough to pick on a species with a lower IQ than his."

A chuckle spread out from the center of his chest as that fist uncurled just a little bit more. "Huh. Never thought of it like that."

Looking inordinately smug, Lisa pivoted back around to face front, which is when Steve realized that the cautious, prickly young woman he'd met two days before seemed to have taken a hike, as well. Despite her assorted wounds, her less-than-pulled-together appearance, she seemed to be completely enjoying herself.

And damned if Steve's woebegone ego didn't decide to take at least some of the credit for that.

A minute or so passed in comfortable silence, interrupted by Lisa's occasional question about something they passed. Then, obviously content in the back seat, Rosie started singing softly to herself behind them.

"What are you going to do?" Lisa asked quietly. "About the children?"

His moment of quasi-serenity popped like a bubble. "At the moment, I haven't the slightest idea."

"I take it there's some question about your being able to keep them?"

"According to Family Services, yeah." He turned to her, his heart hitching at the concern in her eyes. "Not according to me."

She nodded, then looked out the windshield, frowning as she braced one hand through her hair to keep it out of her face. "But…if you're the legal guardian, how *could* they take the children away from you?"

"Because I haven't been granted full custody. Not yet."

"I don't understand."

"Ted and Gloria didn't have a will, see. So even though it was always understood that I'd take care of the kids if anything happened to them—both their folks have been gone for some time—there was nothing in writing."

"I see. And there was no other relative?"

"There's one cousin on Gloria's side. She seemed nice enough, the one time I met her at their wedding fifteen years ago, but she's got four kids of her own. There was no way she could take on another five. So the choices were, split up the kids into separate foster homes, since, again, not many families could take on five at once, or grant me temporary custody, even though I'm not married. And they only did that because I promised to have a full-time housekeeper, at least until Rosie started school."

"Only…you keep losing housekeepers?"

"Bingo." He turned onto the maple-lined street where his parents had lived for close to thirty years. "My folks live up there. You mind if I drop Rosie off first, then take you to Mr. L.'s, since it's on the way to the shop?"

"No, not at all."

They pulled up in front of the immaculate little brick-faced ranch house, the walkway lined with just-planted marigolds; when he asked if she wanted to come in, she shook her head. "Uh, no…I think I'll just sit out here and discuss chicken-chasing with George, if you don't mind."

Mind? Relief positively flooded through him.

Except—as Steve should have known—a strange woman sitting in her son's truck was not something Bev Koleski was likely to ignore.

"Come here, sweetheart," his mother crooned to Rosie, simultaneously removing the quilt-toting baby out of Steve's arms and twitching back the living room sheers.

"I really, really appreciate this, Ma—"

Bev dismissed her son's efforts to suck up with a swat of her hand. She let go of the curtains long enough to adjust her trifocals. "Who's that?"

"Lisa Stone." Steve dumped a baby bag with two changes of clothes onto a blue-and-white striped club chair. "She's staying with Mr. L. for a few days."

"What's with the hair? She looks like a goosed haystack."

Considering his mother's helped-along brunette waves had been frozen in place since the Reagan administration, this was not an unexpected reaction. "I have no idea, Ma."

Now, over the little one's head, a pair of curious amber-colored eyes met his. "And how come she's in your truck at this hour of the morning?"

He sighed. "It's a long story."

"I got time."

"Yeah, well, I don't. Pop's going to have a cow as it is. Hey, munchkin—" He held out his arms. "I've gotta go, okay? Give me a hug?"

With a grin and a nod, Rosie lunged out of his mother's

grasp and into his, wrapping her soft, plump arms around his neck. He closed his eyes, absorbing the sweet, innocent show of affection, wondering how, or if, he could ever feel more for his own flesh-and-blood than he did for these guys. Maybe his head felt permanently muddled these days about a lot of things, but this wasn't one of them. God knows, he hadn't looked for, or expected, instant fatherhood. And God knows, nothing was as terrifying as trying to figure out how to handle a six-year-old's night terrors or a fourteen-year-old's misplaced guilt or a set of twelve-year-old twin girls' anxieties about their changing bodies, but not a day passed that Steve wasn't grateful for one thing:

That, even though he didn't have all the answers—okay, most of the answers—at least he'd been there to catch the ball when it had come sailing into his court.

He finally let a now-squirming Rosie down, then turned to find his mother still in position, arms folded across a sleeveless print blouse nearly as old as the hairstyle. "She looks very nice."

Steve just laughed. "The woman's thirty feet away. In a truck. What makes you think she's *anything?*"

"She's talking to the dog."

"That makes her crazy. Not nice."

"The *hair* makes her crazy. Talking to George makes her nice."

Shaking his head, he opened the door and was halfway down the walk when his mother called after him, "That Francine—she never talked to dogs, did she?"

Oh, brother.

"My mother thinks you're nice," he said, starting up the truck, figuring the comment would probably make Lisa laugh. What it did, was make her choke.

"And how, pray tell, did she arrive at that conclusion?"

"Easy. You were talking to Fleabag back there."

This time, she did laugh. And yes, he liked hearing her laugh, even if he didn't like what hearing her laugh did to him. Which, no, didn't make a lick of sense, but then, life arely did these days. He'd given up on logic ever coming to roost anywhere near his existence some time ago. Except, while he was busy musing about all this, he noticed she'd gone quiet.

Again.

"What's up?"

"I, um…have an idea. About the children?"

They turned onto Mr. L.'s street. "Oh?"

"*I'll* do it."

He frowned. "You'll do what?"

"Fill in until you get a permanent housekeeper."

When Steven's gawking at her stretched to the point of involving safety issues, she gently redirected his attention to the road. It was another several seconds, however, before he apparently found his voice.

"Why on earth would you want to do that?"

A reasonable enough question. "Because you're in dire straits, for one thing. And I adore children."

Silence crackled between them for another block or so until Mr. Liebowicz's house came into view. Sophie cleared her throat. "So, um…what do you think—?"

"I think you're completely off your nut. Which is what I'd be to hire someone I don't even know."

The sounds of a tortured violin spilled out from the open front window when they pulled up into the driveway. Arms crossed, Sophie settled back against the seat. "I suppose that's not an unreasonable reaction."

"Damn straight. How the heck am I supposed to explain you to Family Services? Besides, you're supposed to be on vacation, aren't you?"

Sophie squinted in his direction, wondering if he was fully aware he hadn't actually said "no" yet. Wondering even more if she'd realized, right up until this very moment, how much she wanted him to say "yes."

She tightened her folded arms over her middle, twisted her mouth into a grimace. "I don't suppose you have to 'explain' me at all. Just tell them you found someone. As for my being on vacation. It's more along the lines of…of…" Biting her lip, she desperately scratched around in her brain for a satisfactory answer. "That I'm on temporary hiatus from my life." She stole a peek at his profile, immediately deduced that, as satisfactory answers went, this wasn't.

"I don't suppose," he said, "you'd care to expound on that topic for a moment or two?"

She'd been afraid of that.

One of the bandages was coming loose; she pressed it back down, muttering, "I know this is going to sound completely daft, considering what I just volunteered to do…but I can't, really."

She could feel his glare on the side of her face, just for an instant. Then he said with a lethal softness that sent a shiver up her spine, "I have a major problem with secrets, Lisa. I don't ask much from people, except that they be honest with me. Now, if you hadn't just made the offer you did, I wouldn't give two hoots who you were, or what you were hiding from. While I'll admit to being as curious as the next person when a stranger shows up in town, I also figure that some things are none of my business. When it involves the kids, though, then it *becomes* my business. Big time. So, I guess what I'm saying is…I appreciate your offer, but no thanks. If it's money you need, I hear Galen Farentino who runs the Italian restaurant in town is looking for a waitress—"

"I don't need the money," she said, too quickly, then realized how that might sound. "I mean, I've got…enough to tide me over, to pay my expenses while I'm here. I didn't come here looking for a job."

"Then why—?"

"Haven't you ever, even once in your life, felt compelled to do something, simply because it seemed *right?*" She turned to him, then, forcing herself to met his gaze, forcing him to meet hers. "Because you saw a need and realized—" she pressed one hand to her chest "—here's something I can do! Here's a way for me to maybe make a difference!"

"How very altruistic of you."

"Last time I checked," she shot back, "that wasn't exactly a character fault."

After an excruciatingly long moment, Steven shifted his gaze out the window, his left hand knotted on top of the steering wheel. "These aren't 'ordinary' kids, Lisa. They've been through hell—"

"I know that."

He shifted, squinted at her. "We're talking post-traumatic stress syndrome for a couple of them. Wet beds, nightmares, temper tantrums—"

"I *know* that."

Their eyes locked for several seconds, and she saw the war in his, desperation battling it out with caution, his need to care for the children fighting with his need for someone to help care for the children. And something more, she thought. Some personal war, perhaps?

He nodded in her direction. "Your injuries—"

"Aren't life threatening, Steven. I may hobble for a day or two, but I'm hardly incapacitated."

One palm scrubbed across his face. "I don't suppose you have any references?"

She shook her head even as her heart rocketed into her throat.

"Can you cook?"

"Not really, no."

"Drive?"

"As in, an automobile?" At his sigh, she pointed out, "At least I'm being honest."

The sound that came out of his mouth sounded too pained to be called a laugh. Then he said, "Look...I really appreciate your offer. But I do need more than a body, here."

Several nice, taut seconds of silence stretched out between them after that.

"You know what I mean," he said quietly, not looking at her, his neck a tad more scarlet than she remembered it being ten seconds before. The twin hot spots in her cheeks probably matched, quite nicely.

"Of course," she said, staring at her hands.

She hopped when Steven banged his hand against the steering wheel, then knotted it again in obvious frustration. "You can't, or won't, tell me who you are. Or even where you're from. You can't cook or drive. You have no references. So give me one good reason why on earth—"

"I've spent the past ten years working for and with children who've been severely traumatized. And my parents were both killed in a plane crash when I was ten." At his startled, questioning look, she added, "Yes. That much is true." Then she leaned forward, again locking their gazes, again coming appallingly close to breaching a gap she knew bloody well she dared not breach entirely. "I know exactly what those children are going through, Steven," she said softly. "I know what it feels like to have your world ripped apart, to feel helpless and frightened, even when there are people there to take care of you. I know what it feels like to know that nothing will ever be the same again, and not have a clue what to do with that feeling. I know what it feels like to wonder if the hurt will ever, ever go away. And I know that, for the most part, it does."

Then she did the very thing she promised herself she wouldn't do: she touched him. "I can't offer you forever. In two weeks, I have to go back to my life, honor my commitments and responsibilities. But maybe, just maybe, in those two weeks, I can be of some use."

The wrestling continued in those gold-flecked eyes for several moments more before, at last, she said quietly, "Is it so impossible to believe that someone just wants to *help?* Or do you think you've got the market cornered on unselfishness?"

That flush swept up his neck again. "Let's just say… experience has taught me to be careful."

"Which is as it should be," she said gently, earning her a sharp look. "And I know I'm asking you to go against all your instincts—"

Then she stopped. Stopped trying to justify herself, stopped trying to sell herself, stopped trying to convince the man to do something he didn't want to do. Or, at least, thought he shouldn't do…

"Okay," Steven said on a rush of air.

Her face jerked to his. "Okay?"

"Okay. You're hired. You're right—I'm up against a wall. And at the moment I suppose it's more important to have someone around who gives a damn about the kids than it is someone who can cook and drive."

A strange, wonderful, frightening feeling swarmed through her: the giddiness of accomplishment. After all, this was the first time she'd ever applied for a job, the first time she'd had to pass muster before being allowed to do something. There was a major difference between being expected to take on a task and having to fight for the opportunity to do it. Quite a heady feeling, that. Still, even though she knew she was pushing it, she had to know...

"But what finally convinced you to take me up on my offer?"

He was out of the truck and had her door opened before he spoke. And when he did, his forehead was crumpled into such a frown, his pale brows nearly met over the bridge of his nose. "I'm not entirely sure," he finally said after she extricated herself from the truck. "When I figure it out, maybe I'll let you know."

And that was the God's honest truth, Steve thought as he left Mr. L.'s, after promising to pick Lisa up later. He really wasn't sure what, exactly, had convinced him to finally accept her offer. Oh, sure, the bit about her understanding what the kids had been through was a damn compelling argument. But the woman was, by her own admission, living a lie. So why should he believe that part of her story when she'd made it perfectly clear everything else about her personal life was off-limits?

Well, he didn't know why he believed her, but he did. Call it instinct, call it naiveté, call it a basic need to trust his fellow humans that would probably be his undoing, eventually, but he just didn't think a regular person could fake emotion like that. The way she'd looked him in the eye...either she was telling the truth or she was one helluva good liar.

But there was something else, something he couldn't have identified five minutes ago, something he wasn't all that sure he could pin down now. Whatever it was she was running from, he knew it was serious. Maybe not life-threatening—she didn't seem frightened as much as pressured, he didn't think—and she clearly planned to return and deal with whatever it was that had made her take off to begin with. And any woman willing to take on housekeeping for five kids—five kids with some heavy-duty emotional junk cluttering up their psyches—was no wimp.

Maybe that's what it was, he realized as he pulled into Koleski's Electrical's tiny parking lot. Underneath the makeup, the strange hair, the borderline sleazy outfit—all of which he was sure was a sham, anyway—the lady had guts.

And that, he thought as he and George got out of the truck, headed toward the office, was enough to get her a job as his housekeeper, despite the million and one things he didn't know about her—and which she clearly had no intention of revealing.

But it was those million and one things that would keep him from falling into the same trap twice.

Chapter 5

"I will certainly miss your delightful company," Mr. Liebowicz said, rearranging the music on the piano. "But I think this is a wonderful thing you are doing for the children. For Steffan, as well. He has not had an easy time of it."

Towel-drying her hair after a shower, Sophie stood in the doorway to the old man's studio. "Well, yes, with the children—"

"I am not just talking about the children." The old man settled himself at the piano, his hands on his knees. "He was married, did you know?" She shook her head, draping the towel around her neck. "Yes. For three or four years, I think. I didn't know his wife, although I gather Mala—that's Steffan's sister, her children have just started taking lessons— didn't think very much of her. After what happened, I can certainly understand her reservations. You see, Mala told me that, before Steffan married Francine, he made it quite clear that if anything happened to his friends, he had promised to take care of their children. Not that anyone expected…well, you understand. In any case, Francine told him it didn't matter, she understood." Mr. Liebowicz sighed. "Except, when the unthinkable happened, she demanded he put the children in foster care. When he refused, she left.''

Sophie felt all the blood drain from her face.

I don't ask much of people, Lisa, except that they be honest with me.

"My God," she whispered. "He must have felt completely betrayed.''

"At the very least. So for you to volunteer to do this, even temporarily, is bound to make an impression on a man who not only has his hands full, but one who is probably hurting almost as badly as his charges?''

The old man's words hovered in the air for several seconds before settling into her brain. Then she got out of there before her knees gave way. Sophie collapsed against the wall outside the studio, her knuckles pressed against her temples. Having his wife walk out on him, on top of everything else.... Dear God—no wonder the man looked haunted!

But that didn't mean—

She squeezed shut her eyes, forced herself to think rationally. Clearly. True, there'd been the odd buzz or two between her and Steven, but that was nothing more than the normal...stuff that went on between ordinary, healthy people who were, for all intents and purposes, unattached. The friction caused by a few stray hormones being randomly released into their respective atmospheres, that's all. When she and Steven got too close to each other, the hormones occasionally collided. And Steven's not knowing who she was certainly went a long way toward eradicating the intimidation factor that usually squelched, quite handily, any temptation toward buzzing and the like between a commoner and a princess.

So. There really was no reason to let her imagination run amok, now was there?

She told herself sternly, hying her little buzzing self up to her room to collect her things.

But what if—

Quiet!

But what if—the little beastie, unfortunately, had no qualms in the least about running amok—the buzzing was actually an indication of something potentially more serious? What then? By all accounts, her parents had fallen for each other within three days of their initial meeting. And her grandparents on her father's side, a week.

Sophie jerked open the top drawer to the dresser, snatched her clothes out of it, crammed them into the shopping bag, came to a dead halt.

Offering whatever comfort she could to the children was one thing. Offering anything more to Steven Koleski than temporary friendship was…

Was…

Out of the question.

Impossible.

Extremely impossible.

And bloody fascinating to contemplate.

Out came the tote bag, in went her makeup, her undies, the computer—she'd already e-mailed her grandmother, vaguely told her about her plans—the books. Now that she thought about it—and wouldn't it have been nice if she'd thought about any of this two hours ago, before the damn beastie pushed her over yet another cliff?—just how *did* she think she was going to share living quarters with the man for two weeks, to listen to that laugh and watch him cuddle the baby and smell him fresh from the shower every morning (even her fancy red fingernails tingled at that one) and come out at the other end intact?

Because she'd made a promise, and she wasn't going to back out now.

So she would simply have to remind herself, every day—if not every hour—of the irrevocable temporariness of the situation. Of the stupidity, not to mention the futility, of entertaining anything even remotely resembling a romantic/sexual thought about Steven Koleski. Besides, with any luck, she would be far too busy, and far too tired, to even think about buzzing.

She hoped.

She was still working on that hoping business an hour later
when Steven and George picked Sophie up to take her back
out to the farm.

"Where's Rosie?"

"I'll pick her up from my mother's later," he said, chuck-
ing her bags, such as they were, into the bed of the pickup.
Not looking at her.

Ah.

"You know," she said, standing on the sidewalk with her
arms crossed, "if you want to back out, I'll understand."

His gaze lanced through the heavy, humid air between them.
"Do *you?* Want to back out?"

She shook her head.

"Fine. Then we don't have a problem. So get in," he said,
opening the truck door. When she didn't move, he let out a
sigh. "Please."

She got in, shut the door, fastened her seat belt. Steven did
the same.

"And you *don't* understand," he added, starting the engine.
But when she looked up at him for further explanation, it was
obvious none was forthcoming.

Once out on the road, he asked her if it was okay if he put
on the radio. She said she didn't mind, except he didn't bother
asking what kind of music she liked, which she thought
seemed a trifle out of character for someone who otherwise
seemed generally mindful of his manners. So, as some old
James Taylor song blasted out of the radio's speaker—which,
to tell the truth, was perfectly all right—she decided that somebody had slipped into a world of his own. One in which conversation was optional.

Just as well, she supposed, settling in to watch the scenery
zip past as she idly scratched George's head. With any luck,
he'd remain this distant for the next two weeks.

Since the high school let out earlier than the lower grades,
Mac—whose given name was Evan, Steven had loosened up
enough to reveal, although the boy had gone by the nickname
since he was six—was already at the house when they got
there. He was taller than she by a couple of inches, she now

noticed, his frame gangly underneath in a wrinkled, unbuttoned shirt over a plain blue T-shirt and droopy jeans. To Sophie's surprise, the boy was apparently making snacks for the other children for when they returned. And his shock at seeing Sophie with his guardian was so obvious, it was almost laughable.

"What's she doin' here?"

Steven lowered Sophie's bags to the floor. "Lisa's going to help out for a couple weeks, until we can get someone else."

The boy darted a glance in her direction that was so brief, it was as if the deep brown eyes hurt to look at her. "What do we need her for? Me and you, we can take care of the kids just fine—"

"We've been over this, Mac," Steven said, patience pulling the words taut. "I work. You're fourteen. Family Services doesn't think—"

"Family Services is stupid." The boy slammed a knife onto the butcher block counter. He picked up a peanut butter jar lid, slapped it onto the jar. "Family Services don't know their ass from—"

"Mac!" Steven's voice rose, just a bit. Just enough. Face red, Mac clamped shut his mouth, anger vibrating from him in waves, before he spun on his rubber-soled heel and stormed from the room.

Steven kneaded the back of his neck, the air spilling from his lungs in a long *whoosh*. "Sorry."

This might be the point at which a sane person would admit she'd made a mistake. But then, Sophie had left her sanity in a stall in the ladies' room in Detroit Metro airport three days ago and her new supply hadn't yet come in. So, mustering up her bravado, she walked over to the counter, noticing the precision with which the kid had cut up apples and celery, spread peanut butter on them, the way he'd arranged them in spokes on a large plate.

"For what?" She looked back. "For Mac's blowing up because we sprung my arrival on him?"

"No. For not having the guts to tell you I figured that's what his reaction would be."

She tilted her head. "For not being completely honest with me?"

Steven's mouth thinned, just before he pushed out a contrite, "Yeah."

"For allowing circumstances to dictate just how much of the truth to reveal—?"

"All right!" he bellowed, his hands flying into the air. "You made your point!"

Ooooh, she thought, she could make more points than that. But she wasn't that insane. And there were more important things to be dealing with at the moment.

"Steven," she said softly. "If you expect me to be either appalled or shocked by the way Mac's acting, don't bother. My brother acted much the same, after my parents died. He used to hurl chunks of his grief at anyone who came within twenty feet of him. Even me, who was grieving just as much as he was. It took me a long time—well after we'd all got over the major hurdles—to realize there's some sort of unwritten code among you male types, that's it's okay to be angry, but not to show how much you're hurting."

Steven probably thought his features revealed nothing, probably didn't even feel his brows lift slightly in surprise, was completely unaware that his jaw tightened, just for a moment, before he spoke.

"So...his rudeness doesn't bother you?"

"Well, of course it bothers me. The boy's in pain. But if you're wondering if his behavior is going to throw me..." She shook her head, thinking of all the children in pain she'd seen in the past few years, victims of the sudden devastation of war and natural disaster, of the slower, but no less devastating effects of grinding, relentless poverty. Her heart always broke. It always would. But that didn't mean she'd shy away from it. "No. It won't."

Steven scrubbed a palm over his chin, his shoulders visibly relaxing for a second, only to tense again. "There's more." Steven glanced down the hall, back to her. "Before the fire, he was heavily into sports and art. Since then, however, he refuses to get involved with anything. All he wants to do is stay here…"

"Where he can be close to the other children."

One brow lifted. "Yeah."

"My brother and I were inseparable for some time after our parents' deaths, as well." Steven nodded. "Is he in counseling?"

"We tried. But Mac refused to go after a few sessions. He said all he wanted to do was forget how much it hurt, and all the counselor kept doing was poking at it, making it hurt more. I finally gave up forcing him to go." A glimmer of wary hope lit his eyes, just for a second. "Comments?"

She smiled. "Only that I understand how he feels. And it's early yet, for these children. Very early."

From down the hall, a stereo blasted on.

"If that bothers you—" Steven began.

"No. It doesn't."

Steven nodded, again. George gulped water noisily from a metal bowl beside the refrigerator, then collapsed onto the kitchen floor with a groan. Outside, birds twittered, breezes blew, life went on. Inside, awkwardness vibrated between them until Sophie thought she'd scream. And yet…

And yet.

There was awkwardness, and there was awkwardness. This wasn't the typical uneasiness that almost always wedged itself between people whom society and custom had decreed to be from radically different stations in life. Instead, whatever this was that suddenly made it difficult for her to look directly at Steven, that sucked the air from her lungs and the moisture from her mouth, had nothing to do with rank or privilege, but with something far more primitive. Far more basic.

Far more dangerous.

For the first time that she could remember, she was acutely aware of herself as a woman, *only* a woman and nothing *but* a woman.

A woman, she realized with a jolt, who was making the man standing five feet in front of her as awkward and unsure as she.

But she rose to the occasion. "I assume I have a room?"

"What? Oh, yeah…let me show you…"

And Steven catapulted out of the kitchen as if flung from a slingshot. Still stiff—and getting stiffer by the minute—from her earlier fall, Sophie minced along behind.

"It must've been a mother-in-law quarters or something," Steven said, pushing open the door to the darkened bedroom jutting out from the back of the house. "It's an add-on, but not too badly constructed, considering."

He crossed the floor, carpeted in a gold-and-brown tessellated pattern that had probably been someone's idea of chic, twenty years ago, to another door, which he swung open as well—"Bathroom"—then to another—"Closet"—then yet to a sliding glass door, hidden behind a set of mustard-colored draperies which he quickly yanked open, flooding the room with late afternoon sunshine. "Your very own private patio," he said, his expression neutral. "I hope it's okay."

Hands on hips, she twisted around, taking in the solid, massive cherry furniture, the floral comforter on the bed, the well-worn, but obviously comfortable armchair in one corner, slip-covered in enormous burgundy-and-tan roses with mossy leaves. She looked at him. Smiled. "It will do quite nicely."

He looked relieved. And oddly irked that her opinion mattered to begin with. "The furniture was my grandparents', from the forties."

"It's charming," she said, and meant it.

"Well." He backed toward the doorway. "I need to get to that appointment—"

"Oh, please—" She shooed him with her hands. "Go on. I'll be fine."

"The other kids will be home soon, but I imagine Mac will go down to meet the bus. And…there's clean linens in the closet at the head of the stairs. For your…bed. And things. And I suppose…we'll figure out dinner when I get back? Around six-thirty?"

"Oh. All right," she said, trying to look bright and cheerful and on top of things when, in fact, her stomach had gone to Jell-O.

A minute later, she heard Steven's truck start up, back out of the driveway. She thought, for about a half second, of knocking on Mac's door and doing the olive branch bit, decided instead to take the moment to gather what few wits she had left and figure out exactly what she was going to do.

George was only too willing to help her unpack, which took all of a minute. She was up to two pairs of shoes, now—the clunkers and the pair of white Keds she'd found in a little shop in town, which she now wore. Her "real" clothes were relegated to the depths of the closet, along with her laptop; the other things she plopped in a couple drawers in the bureau, and that was about it. Then, sucking in a sharp breath, she drifted back out to the living room of the house for which she was now, more or less, responsible. For the next two weeks, at least.

Which really was a wreck, wasn't it?

She thought of all the servants in the palace whose unobtrusive work she'd taken for granted, for so long—the maids who kept the seventy-room palace sparkling, the cooks who prepared meals every bit as lavish as one could find in any five star Parisian restaurant, the nannies who'd cared for Alek and her as children. A veritable army of hired help, all to take care of a handful of people.

For some reason, she'd never thought of herself as spoilt or pampered, really, perhaps because she was not by nature a slob and thus didn't drip clothes and assorted paraphernalia all over the palace for other people to pick up after her. But neither could she deny she'd never cleaned a toilet or made a bed or cooked a meal for herself, other than a quick sandwich in the palace kitchen after the servants had gone to bed.

And now here she was, expected to cook and clean and care for a family of six, all by her precious little self.

Hands parked on slightly bruised hips, she thought about that for a few seconds, then gave her head a single, sharp nod. Every project that had ever landed in her lap, she'd always tackled with every ounce of determination she had in her. No test was worth taking unless she could achieve the highest scores; no fund-raiser was worth the bother unless she could beat the goal by at least fifty percent. So. If she was going to be a "regular" person for the next two weeks, she was going to be a "regular" person with everything she had in her.

Or die trying.

With a sigh, she began sorting through an avalanche of magazines and newspapers drowning the coffee table, letting out a soft "oh" when she found one with recipes in it.

Really—how hard could this be?

Princess Ivana nearly jumped out of her skin when her grandson waltzed into the palace's library, his collarless silk shirt open at the neck, his designer sports jacket slung casually over one shoulder, and simply plopped himself down in the Louis Quinze armchair across from her desk as if he'd just come in from a jaunt into the village—not suddenly appeared for the first time in months.

Alek stretched out his long legs, toeing off one Italian leather loafer, then cocked his far-too-handsome head at her. As usual, a comma of reddish-brown hair—much like his mother's had been—swagged over his forehead, making him look far younger than his thirty-six years. As did his lazy, insouciant smile. A smile that could—and had, she gathered—charm a woman into doing just about anything.

A charm to which Ivana herself had fallen prey far too many times.

The smile broadened, accentuating the slight dimple in his right cheek. "Surprised to see me, Grandmother?" Before she could answer, he leaned forward to call the dogs, a pair of white Alsatians she'd had for nearly twelve years now. "And how are my girls doing?" He smacked his denim-covered thigh, inviting Sasha to put her enormous paws up on his leg, then looked at his grandmother, scratching both dogs at once.

Ivana leaned back in her desk chair, her fingers laced in front of her. "Little you do surprises me anymore, Alek."

"Good. Then I take it I can announce my homecoming without risk to your heart." At her obviously stunned expression, he laughed softy, weariness, she thought, more than indulgence, tarnishing his silver eyes. "Shocked?"

"Enough to make me take back what I said earlier. What on earth—"

"—brought this on?" He shrugged. "Age, perhaps. That inevitable process called growing up. I know you thought it would never happen—God knows, I didn't—but damned if it hasn't."

She eyed him warily. "You're home?"

He lifted his hands. "The prodigal has returned."

"You're...giving up the racing?"

"Except for a small, private race outside Nice in a couple weeks, yes. Jeff Henderson's coming over, for the first time in what, five years?" He grinned. "We have a small...wager. So...where's Soph?"

Alek's sudden reappearance had momentarily displaced her concern about her other grandchild. The one who, up until three days ago, she'd been able to count on. "We don't know, actually."

Alek's hand stilled in Sasha's fur as his gaze shot to hers. "What?"

"She went to a World Relief Fund conference in the States, gave Gyula the slip in the Detroit airport. She's been in contact via e-mail, but refuses to tell me where she is. And now she tells me she'll be tied up for another two weeks."

At that, Alek's dark brows rose over the famed Vlastos nose. Then, suddenly, a smile burst across his face. "The devil you say! She gave old Gyula *the slip?*"

"You could at least sound concerned, Alek. As I said, we have no idea where the child is."

Chuckling, Alek leaned back in the chair, his corded forearms folded across his chest. "The child is twenty-nine, grandmother." His expression clouded. "Do you have any idea what brought this on? I mean, she always seemed content with her life, her charity work—"

"She hasn't been *content* for some time," Ivana said, more sharply than she intended. "And then Jason proposed to her—"

"Jason?" Alek leaned forward in his chair. "Jason *Broad-*

hurst?'' Ivana nodded as Alek slouched back, frowning. "I didn't know they were even dating."

"They weren't. He proposed the alliance for convenience' sake, I gathered."

She watched as her grandson's eyes darkened to slate, as all traces of humor vanished from his expression. "And I suppose you were encouraging her to accept?"

Warmth flooded Ivana's face. "Jason's a good man. And it's not as if—"

"—men were exactly beating a path to her door?" he finished softly, his hand fisted on his knee. "Bloody hell, grandmother—and you wonder why she's run away?" After a moment, he stood and crossed to Ivana's desk, his hands in his pockets, the stern set to his mouth belying the casual stance. "She still have the same e-mail address?"

Ivana nodded.

"Good. I'll write to her later, tell her I'm home." He started out, then turned back, his expression more earnest, more thoughtful, than Ivana ever remembered seeing it. "She deserves more than that, you know. If anyone in the world deserves true love, it's Sophie."

Then he left the room, the dogs trailing him, leaving Ivana quite incapable of coherent thought.

Chapter 6

George was the first thing to greet Steve when he set foot inside the door that evening.

The acrid smell of charred meat was the second.

Which was, in turn, quickly followed by the panicked expressions of four kids. Well, three, anyway. Mac's face positively radiated disgust, overlaid with an I-told-you-we-didn't-need-her smugness that would have brought a sigh to Steve's lips, if he'd had a chance.

Rosie was trying to use George—who didn't mind, really—as a stepping stool to get up into Steve's arms. Steve scooped her up before she reached the dog's head. "How bad is it?" he whispered to Bree.

"Bad. She's been at it since four."

"And you should *see* dessert," Courtney piped in.

"There's dessert?" Steve asked.

"That's what she said it was."

"Oh!" Lisa popped into view, looking inordinately tickled with herself. Not to mention perky as all get out. She'd redone her hair so that it stood out around her head in a series of...hooks, was all he could think to call them, and she'd apparently "dressed" for dinner in a black miniskirt and tights and those god-awful shoes, topped with a little white blouse that managed to convey innocence and *hot*-damn sexy at the same time. "You're home! Good! We can sit down to eat anytime you're ready."

Four sets of eyes zinged to his, imploring.

"I thought I said we'd, um—" Steve scratched his head "—discuss dinner when I got here?"

Her shoulders hitched underneath the blouse. "It seemed silly to wait when you had so much food in the house."

"But I thought you said—?"

"That I didn't know how to cook?" She laughed. "Well, for heaven's sake, primitive man didn't exactly go to Cordon Bleu before he cooked for the first time, did he? Well, come on, everyone, before everything gets cold." Then she spun around and clumped back into the kitchen, humming a little as she went.

Steve had to admit, he found her enthusiasm touching. Even if his stomach was circling like a wary mongrel. And speaking of wary mongrels, it did not escape Steve's attention that George, to whom "kitchen" and "heaven" were synonymous, had parked himself in a corner of the living room as far away from the kitchen as he could get and not be outside.

Oh, boy.

"Kids? C'mere."

They did, but not because they wanted to. One eye on the kitchen door, Steve whispered, "Look, we're gonna have to eat whatever Lisa cooked—"

"No way!" Mac said. "Steve, you haven't seen it. It's—"

"Really gross," Bree supplied.

"Totally," Courtney said.

"Guys…" Steve took in a breath. "There are times in life when one has to make certain sacrifices in order not to hurt someone's feelings—"

That got the eye-rolling routine.

"—I mean it. Whatever she's done, it won't kill you. Hold your breath, swallow it whole, I don't care, but you have *got* to get through this one meal."

"And what then?" Mac asked. "If she thinks we like it, that's only going to encourage her to continue."

Kid had a point. "How's about we just get through tonight, and let me worry about what comes later, okay? And for God's sake, quit looking like you've just been condemned to the guillotine."

"Unca Steve?" This from Dylan, who was tugging at his sleeve. "What's a gee-o-teen?"

"It's what we're gonna wish happened to us after we eat this meal," Mac muttered under his breath.

Steve's heart lurched when he saw all the trouble Lisa had gone to. Although they usually ate at the large pine table in the kitchen, Lisa had opted to use the dining room, digging out the linen placemats from the mahogany sideboard—which, along with the china cabinet and the matching table, had also belonged to his grandparents—and fixing it up like she was expecting Queen Elizabeth to join them. Even the cheapo Wal-Mart glasses seemed to sparkle in the candlelight given off by the half-dozen emergency jobbers he kept on hand for when the electricity inevitably went during a thunderstorm.

"Sit, sit!" she said, grabbing Rosie and planting her on her booster seat. "Everybody help themselves off from whatever's closest to them, then pass the food around to your right."

Steve took his place at the head of the table, realizing the platter of meat—hamburgers? Salisbury steak?—sat in front of him.

Candlelight notwithstanding, they were suspiciously dark. And, he realized after three attempts at piercing the surface of the one closest to him, amazingly resilient. But he persevered until he'd landed one of the suckers, dutifully passed the platter to Bree on his right, who looked at the meat, then at him, much as George looked at him when it was time for his annual shots.

And just think, Steve thought, staring down into the bowl that Mac had just passed *him*. She hasn't seen the broccoli yet.

Last time he checked, broccoli wasn't supposed to be gray, was it?

The rice was gummy, the biscuits a tad more golden than he thought Pillsbury had in mind, and the gravy—ah. So it was Salisbury steak—unusually…textured.

Dread churning in his stomach, no doubt in anticipation of what he was about to put in it, Steve looked up to see, sparkling at him from the other end of the table, Lisa's bright blue eyes, bursting with pride. And he instantly knew what it must be like to face an oncoming car's headlights.

He sawed off a hunk of the…meat, lifted it on his fork, as if in a toast. "This looks wonderful, Lisa," he said, absolutely refusing to look at any of the children, then stuffed the…meat into his mouth. On either side of him, four ominously quiet children did the same. And finally, once Mary Poppins down there was sure everyone else had begun, she, too, took her first bite.

Still chewing—he imagined he'd be working on this one for some time to come—Steve watched her.

And his heart broke.

He didn't think he'd ever seen horror eclipse a person's features so quickly. Or so thoroughly. He watched her jaw move up and down twice, three times, before she brought her napkin to her mouth, spit out the piece of meat into it. "Oh, dear," she said, so softly he could barely hear her. "I guess the meat's a bit tough, isn't it?"

Then she sampled the broccoli.

And the rice.

She didn't bother with the biscuits.

Even in the candlelight, he saw a flush spread over her cheeks, her breathing go ragged from trying to keep control. "I'm so…sorry," she whispered, then got up from the table so fast, she knocked her knife off her plate, which clattered to the floor as she took off out of the dining room. Five seconds later, he heard the door fo her bedroom slam shut.

Steve stood immediately, tucking his napkin under the rim of his plate. "I'll be right back," he told the kids.

"But what are we supposed to eat?" Courtney whined.

"Have I *ever* let you guys go hungry?"

He hadn't meant to bellow, but judging from the kids' wide

eyes, he apparently had. The younger ones all shook their heads, while Mac picked out the softish middle of a biscuit to give to Rosie, who wasn't the least bit perturbed or disturbed by the situation.

"Then I won't let you starve tonight, either. Just sit tight for a minute, okay? Actually…why don't you all clear the table, huh? And don't give anything to George—I don't want to be up all night cleaning up dog barf."

Steve stood outside Lisa's bedroom door for several seconds, trying to decide just how much his life was worth. Man, there was a lot of cursing going on in there.

And a lot of crying, from what he could tell.

Oh, what the hell—it was only a life, right?

He rapped softly. "Lisa?"

The cursing came to an abrupt halt. Then: "Go 'way."

"It's okay, honey—"

"Hey, Steve," Mac called from down the hall. "Bree wants to know whether we should throw the food in the garbage or down the disposal?"

On the other side of the door, something slammed against something else.

Steve lunged down the hall toward the kitchen. "Thanks a lot, guys," he hissed. "What are you trying to do—traumatize the woman for life?"

Mac seemed to brighten up. "You think maybe she'll go away?"

Irritation prickled every nerve ending Steve had. And a few he didn't. "Watch it, buddy," he said in a low voice, taking some satisfaction in seeing the teen's smirk fade. "And I'd opt for the garbage. Those burgers or whatever they are are liable to clog up the disposal."

Then he sprinted back around to Lisa's bedroom.

Yep. Still crying.

He knocked on the door again. "I'm coming in."

"No!"

Too late. He was in. She stood with her back to the patio doors, her face a soggy maze of black streaks. Underneath a forest of wilting hooks, mortification blazed from those im-possibly blue eyes. And her lower lip was quivering.

Helluva time to discover he was also a sucker for quivering lower lips. Even if they were set in a face that looked like something from *The Rocky Horror Picture Show.*

Steve plastered himself against the door, arms crossed, which still put only the width of a not overly large room be-tween them.

"So, tell me one thing."

She sniffled, swiped at her nose with her hand. "W-what?"

"What's for dessert?"

The corners of her mouth twitched…and she dissolved into tears.

Ah, hell.

Steve glanced around, espied a tissue box on the bureau which he snatched and handed to her. Which meant he had to get close enough to touch her, if he'd been so inclined. Which he was. Oh, he was so inclined to touch her, he was about to pop.

Except, he knew that touching her was a really, really bad idea, because something about this woman had gotten about a million feelings roaring around inside him that he'd not only thought were dead and buried, but which he'd planned on remaining dead and buried until he was. And even if he had thought that maybe, someday, he might resurrect the little bug-gers, what was happening now was too damn fast and way too damn intense for him to even have a clue as to what they even were, let alone what to do about them.

And if touching, as an act of comfort for another human being in pain, wasn't such a natural thing for him to do, the whole issue would be moot.

So, since the alternative was not touching at all, what he did, after she plucked out a tissue, blew her nose and said, "Thank you," was to pat her shoulder and making the sort of soothing noises he made when one of the kids fell off of some-thing. Very safe. Very proper. Very nonsexual.

Oh, yeah. He'd been wondering how long it would take for

that word, or one of its derivatives, to wriggle into his thoughts.

Then Lisa sniffled and said, in a tiny voice, "I just wanted to surprise you."

A whole new slew of feelings surged through him as he realized—*kaboom!*—he really liked this nutcase.

He couldn't help the smile. "Mission accomplished."

She did not, however, smile back. Man, he couldn't remember the last time he'd seen someone look that miserable.

Man, he wanted to hold her.

No, you don't, Koleski.

"I can't go back out there," she said, sniffling and scrubbing her hand across her cheek.

Her eyes widened when Steve reached out to take her hand in his. Shaking his head, he turned it over so she could see the black smudges that had transferred from face to palm. "Not until you wash your face, at least. You'll scare Rosie half to death."

With a little horrified yelp, she twisted away and scampered into the bathroom. The sink sat directly across from the door, which she didn't close. She grabbed a washcloth, squirted some liquid soap onto it, then attacked her face like Lady MacBeth trying to scrub her husband's blood from her hands. A good five, ten seconds passed before Steve realized just how much he was admiring her miniskirted bottom.

And her legs.

The shoes, though...uh, no.

He jerked up his head.

"You know," he said as he watched her exfoliate at least the first couple layers of skin, "not that I'm an expert or anything, but I hear they make that stuff you put on your eyes waterproof now."

She glared at him in the mirror. Scrubbed harder.

"It wasn't that bad, Lisa. Dinner, I mean. I mean, for a first attempt—"

"Oh, sod off, Steven. If you don't mind, I could do without the patronization."

He swallowed the grin that wanted so badly to erupt at that.

Still, there was something almost vulnerable about her defiance, as if standing up for herself was something stiff and unused, like a new pair of shoes. And that simply mowed down his defenses, sending his hormones cartwheeling and a good eighty, ninety percent of his blood on a leisurely, but hell-bent, trickle southward.

What the hell—?

"I didn't mean it that way," he said gently. She tossed him a "yeah, right" glance in the mirror. "Besides, everybody has to screw up at least once in their life, right? So now you've gotten your screwup out of the way, you can take it easy. The rest of the journey should be a piece of cake."

She actually smiled. Well, if you knew what to look for, you could see one corner of her mouth tweak up.

And Steven felt like a god or something, getting her to smile.

Why, why, *why* did this strange—in more ways than one—woman appeal to him so damn much? It made no sense. Come on—even if he had been free to pursue things, he really hated those shoes. Not to mention the bizarre hair. The hair could draw blood, if a guy wasn't careful.

Her face cleaned up, she rummaged in a small bag on the sink and began to repair her makeup, clearly stalling for time. The row of lights over the mirror showed off all those planes and angles in her face to perfection. Which, he had to admit, kinda worked with the hair. Then he frowned, as something niggled at the back of his brain, like a dream you can't quite recall. It was almost as if…nah.

She misjudged the wand-to-lash ratio, smeared mascara over her just cleaned cheek. Muttering something he didn't quite catch, she wiped it off, repeated the process, then flashed those deep blue eyes at him in the mirror again. "You can leave now. I can pretty much guarantee I won't hang myself with the drapery cord."

"Good. Because then you'd miss out on Galen Farentino's pizza."

She took great care in screwing her mascara top back on, still watching his reflection. "Pizza?"

He shrugged. "It's that or cold cereal. And I made a pledge to myself that the kids would have a hot supper every night, one way or the other. And no comment from you," he added when she opened her mouth to say whatever it was she was about to say, he wasn't about to find out.

"Oh," was all she did say before, with a hand probably far less steady than she'd like it to be, she did the lipstick thing. Vamp red. Dewy. An incredible contrast with the ivory skin, the zonk-blue eyes. And you know, the hair, now that he thought about it, was actually kinda sexy, all messed up like that. Like she'd just gotten out of bed or something.

More blood shifted.

"If you don't like pizza," he said, quickly, to distract himself from all this wayward blood, "they've got terrific subs. And salads. All kinds of salads. Or you can probably get something fancier from Galen's regular restaurant, next door."

After a beat or two, she shrugged. The short, boxy top she wore just skimmed her collarbones.

God, she had great collarbones.

"I love pizza," she said softly, then jammed the lipstick cap back on and stuffed it in her pocket.

But she wouldn't turn around.

Against his better judgment, Steve closed the gap between them, until he stood in the bathroom doorway, until he was close enough to smell…her. Not that hideous perfume she'd been wearing the other day, not anything in particular, but just a soft, sweet woman smell he hadn't realized he'd missed until that very moment.

"You have to let go of the sink sometime, honey," he said, and a short laugh popped out of her mouth before she finally faced him.

"Hey—" He reached out, grabbed her hand again. Only this time, he wasn't letting go. Not even when he felt every muscle in her body tighten. Not to mention a few crucial muscles in his. "I know the kids probably don't see things this way, but they're only kids, what do they know? But even if the results weren't exactly—"

"Edible?"

"—what you expected," he said firmly, his thumb—of its own accord, he swore—tracing small, warm circles in the palm of her hand, "this is one of those cases where it really is the thought that counts. In eight months, Lisa, not one of the women the agency sent went to the kind of trouble you did for those kids. Yes, they cooked, but they did it because it was part of their job description. You did it—even though you didn't know how—because you really wanted to do something nice for them. Someday, I hope they understand that."

Her lips parted to let a soft "oh!" pass as tears welled again in her eyes, as her pulse began a rapid tap-tapping in the hollow of her throat. She looked so stunned, so...delighted by the simple compliment, Steve's own pulse picked up quite nicely, too.

Brain to fingers...go ahead. Touch her cheek. You know you want to—

The bedroom door popped open. With a breathy little cry, Lisa snatched back her hand so fast she bumped into the counter.

"We're *starving*," Dylan announced, stomping into the room, dragging Rosie along with him.

Casually, as if his brain cells weren't combusting like crazy, Steve turned around to smile into two sets of dark brown, puppy dog eyes. "Oh, you are, huh? How's pizza sound?"

A huge grin exploded across the little boy's face. "All right!" he yelled, then spun around and hauled his sister back out of the room, singing, "We're going for piz-za, we're going for piz-za..."

Chuckling, Steve faced Lisa again, who flashed him a look that set that weird little half memory nipping at his brain again. Maybe it was the way she thrust out that strong chin, so at odds with the apprehension still etching a crease between her brows. Or perhaps it was something about the determined set to her mouth, he couldn't say. But all he knew was, something like an electric jolt zipped through him as he suddenly got a clear image of another face, so much like this one it was uncanny, silently regarding him the way she did, just for a moment, before she clunked out of the bedroom on those dumb shoes.

She shook all the way into town, a fine trembling that she doubted anyone else would notice, unless she tried to speak. Why she was shaking, she wasn't sure. Obviously, her culinary disaster had a lot to do with it. Even though none of the kids said anything, she knew that meal would be permanently etched in their memories. She could just imagine them, years from now, screeching in laughter as they remembered the night when, oh, whatsername, you remember, the one with the funny accent, tried to cook for us?

The meal, they'd remember forever. Her name, she doubted they'd remember this time next year.

And would Steven remember her name—or, at least, the one she'd told him—this time next year?

And that thought got everything shaking all over again.

Except for Alek, who'd always been a prince in the truest sense of the world to her, no man had ever been as kind and thoughtful as Steven Koleski had been to her just now. Oh, men had been variously polite, respectful, pleasant, obsequious, but not…this. Not caring. Compassionate.

He wasn't perfect—who was?—but he was good.

Good.

That simple, ordinary word would never seem simple or ordinary again.

"Okay, gang," Steven called out as they slid into an angled parking space, "all's ashore that's going ashore!"

Amid much chatter and unsnapping of seat belts, the kids clamored out of the van—all except Mac, who'd declined to join them, declaring he had homework which Sophie could tell from Steven's expression he sincerely doubted—and into the brightly lit, amazingly crowded pizzeria. Steven spotted a table large enough to accommodate them all, nudged Sophie over to it. Then, over the din of laughter and kids' yelling and chairs scraping against the tile floor, Steven explained that Galen Farentino—who was actually half Irish, half Slovak, but who had a habit of marrying Italian men—had originally bought the long-in-the-tooth diner next door about a year and half before and converted it into a wonderful Italian restaurant. However, shortly after her marriage to Del Farentino—a local contractor with whom Steven had worked many times and who had overseen the restaurant's remodel—this second building had become available, too.

"So it just seemed to make sense—Dylan! Rosie! Get back over here, guys!—to expand, making this 'wing' more casual, you know, so…"

"Uncle Steve," Courtney broke in, "c'n we each get two pieces? And salad?"

He shooed them toward the buffet. "Go. Live. Anyway, as I was saying—"

"I gots to pee." This from Rosie, standing in front of them with her fingers curled over the table edge so that all they could see were eyes and bangs. Steven sighed, started to call one of the girls back.

"Oh! No, don't call them." Sophie snagged his wrist, ignoring the flush that warmed her cheeks. "I'll take her."

Steven looked so relieved, she nearly laughed. "I'll get your food, then. What do you like?"

"Everything!" she said over her shoulder as a very determined little girl yanked her back toward a rest room she'd obviously visited many times before.

A tall, slender redhead in black slacks and a simple white cotton sweater was standing at the sink, drying her hands. "Hey, Rosie," she said, her turquoise eyes lighting up underneath her coppery bangs. She tossed her wadded up paper towel into the trash. "Who's your friend?"

Frowning, Rosie twisted her head up to Sophie.

"Lisa Stone," Sophie replied with a smile, recognizing the woman from the photo she'd so admired earlier.

With a smile of her own, the redhead stuck out her hand, the gesture strong, almost masculine in its directness. "Galen Farentino. Nice to meet you."

"Oh—as in *Galen's?*"

"As in." They briefly shook hands, then Galen said, "I

thought I saw Steve and the gang come in a couple minutes ago.''

Rosie's tug on the hem of Sophie's blouse reminded her why they were there to begin with. "Oh, right." Holding up one finger, she said to Galen, "Little bladders wait for no one," then ushered her little charge into a stall.

"Tell me about it," she heard Galen say on a chuckle. "I've got a six-year-old stepdaughter. I know where every toilet is within a fifty-mile radius. But then, big bladders aren't always the epitome of patience, either. Especially these days," she said on a weighty sigh. "So—I take it you're the new housekeeper?"

Sophie finished tending to the little girl, then steered her out to the sink, straddling the tiny girl from behind and turning on the water. "You want soap?" she asked Rosie, who nodded enthusiastically. Sophie squirted a dollop of pink soap from the dispenser over the sink onto her own hands, then briskly squished it through Rosie's tiny fingers, much to the child's delight. "How did you know I was the new housekeeper?"

"It's a small town, hon," Galen said over Rosie's giggles. "The grapevine around here is on warp speed. In fact, a body can't sneeze around here without a half-dozen people telling you to take care because there's a nasty cold going around."

"Then," Sophie said, shutting off the water, "I suppose you know I'm only filling in."

"Now that, I didn't hear."

"So the grapevine is fast but selective," Sophie said good-naturedly, and Galen laughed. Sophie hauled Rosie up onto the edge of the counter so she could dry her hands. "But, yes. I'm just here for a couple weeks."

"Oh." After what Sophie could only describe as a speculative pause, Galen said, "Let me guess. You're not from around these parts."

"True." Sophie lowered the child to the floor, checked her makeup in the mirror. Honestly—she'd surveyed her reflection more in the past few days than she had in her entire life up to that point. "My father was English," she said, yet again, then noticed, in the mirror, that Galen had gone extremely pale, her light freckles suddenly far too prominent against her white skin.

Sophie whipped around. "Are you all right?"

Galen held up one hand, the other braced on the wall, as if waiting for something to pass. After a moment, she nodded, sucked in a deep breath. "I've just been having these little woozy spells the past few days. Overwork, I guess."

Woozy spells. That comment about her overactive bladder. Hmm…

"Perhaps," Sophie said, as diplomatically as possible, "you should see your doctor?"

"Oh, I'm sure it's…" Then the turquoise eyes flashed to hers, wide with shock. "Oh, dear God," Galen whispered. "It can't be…could it? Oh…*oh!*" Her gaze shot to the mirror, her hands to her tummy. Then, on a little cry, she ran from the room.

"What's wrong with Galen?" Rosie asked.

Sophie smiled, gave the child a little kiss on the top of her silky, dark hair. "I'm not sure, love. But I think it's something very, very good."

In the few minutes they'd been gone, three more bodies had landed at their table—a pair of ginger-headed children around Dylan's age, and a pretty, round-faced brunette with a bright, dimpled smile.

A *very* pretty brunette. A very pretty brunette with, from what little Sophie could see, what men referred to as a lush figure. A very pretty, lush-figured brunette who obviously knew Steven extremely well, judging from the way her hand kept landing with unabashed familiarity on Steven's arm as they talked.

"Auntie Mala!" Rosie shrieked, snaking her way through the crowd to throw herself into the woman's arms.

Just like that, the little green-eyed monster jumped up and blew raspberries in Sophie's face.

And wasn't that ridiculous?

"There you are!" she realized Steven was saying, grinning

at her and waving her over. "Lisa, this is my sister, Mala, and her two kids, Carrie and Lucas."

Oh. Of course. Auntie Mala. How silly.

Sending the stupid little monster packing, Sophie sat where Steven indicated her pizza awaited her—which happened to be right beside him—then offered her hand to the very pretty brunette across the table who was no longer an issue, even though she never *was* an issue because there *were* no issues and if Sophie didn't find some way to staunch her hemorrhaging thoughts *this instant,* she'd be a complete basket case before the week was up.

"I could not face my kitchen tonight," Mala shouted over the noise of six kids all talking at once. She poured herself a glass of soda from the large pitcher in front of her, then smiled, showing off the twin dimples. Her eyes, Sophie noticed, were more golden than Steven's, shimmering like peridot underneath her straight, shoulder-length dark hair, which she wore tucked behind her ears. "After an entire day sorting through Fred Hinkle's books—"

"Mala's an accountant with her own business," Steven interjected, one hand flying out to stop his nephew's arm from sending a slice of pepperoni, like a miniature Frisbee, sailing across the table.

"Oh?" Sophie said politely around her first bite of the best pizza she'd ever had, all the while trying desperately not to laugh at the bespectacled, buzz-cut-headed little boy's thwarted expression.

"Oh, yeah." Mala picked off an olive and shoved it into her mouth, only to jab one clear-polished nail at her son's plate. The pepperoni having been deep-sixed, he'd moved on to black olives. "Lucas. Drop it. Now." She grimaced. "Hooligans. I'm raising a pair of hooligans. Anyway, I was far too brain-dead to cook, so here we are." She leaned forward, cupping the hand between her and her children around her mouth. "And they'll eat things on pizza they'd die before eating at home," she whispered, and Sophie laughed, only to jump when a glass of soda spilled, sending a torrent of cold, sticky liquid streaming into her lap.

She heard Steven swear under his breath as they both grabbed napkins at the same time and began mopping up, while kids looked on and Mala scolded a tearful Carrie—Sophie looked up at that, insisted it was no big deal, please don't worry about it—and she realized that nothing more than a soggy napkin and a thin layer of cotton separated Steven's strong, competent, masculine hand from areas of her body where no strong, competent, masculine hand had gone before.

She froze. Then, somehow, got out, "Why...don't you concentrate on the table, and, um, leave this part to me?"

Their eyes met. Realization dawned in his.

My goodness, but the man was cute when he blushed.

Sophie was still busy mopping and sopping when she looked up to see an enormous man with dark, shaggy hair and a blond wisp of a little girl come through the restaurant door...and make a beeline behind the serving counter for Galen. In response to her obvious staring, Mala twisted around. And let out a sigh befitting the most lovestruck adolescent.

"Del Farentino, Galen's husband. And their daughter, Wendy." Another sigh. "Now there's a man to give the rest of us poor slobs hope, let me tell you."

"Hey!" Steven interjected. Mala swatted at him.

"You're my brother. You don't count."

Then Dylan and Lucas both announced *they* had to pee, and Mala and Sophie cheerfully decided Steven could do the honors.

Sophie, however, found herself transfixed with watching Galen and Del, especially after what had just happened in the ladies' room. And, without even realizing she'd just grabbed the grapevine, she blurted out, "I think Galen's pregnant."

Mala said "What?" with such vehemence, Sophie finally tore her gaze from the obviously besotted couple across the restaurant to look at her.

"What on earth makes you say that?" the brunette asked, as if Sophie had just said something truly bizarre.

So she told her about the conversation, and Galen's reaction.

"Oh, wow," Mala said, dropping back against her chair. Then she leaned forward, her voice hushed. "Okay, this is like in the strictest confidence, but Galen had a tubal ligation, years ago, when she was married to her first husband—both she and Del were widowed, did you know that?'' Sophie shook her head. ''Yeah, which is one reason why everybody in town was so thrilled when they found each other, you know. Anyway, apparently Galen kept having all these miscarriages, and then she had a ectopic pregnancy which I gather nearly killed her. So…''

Mala swiped a hank of her hair behind her ear, frowning. ''See, she told me, after she and Del got married, she wanted to try to reverse the sterilization, even though she only has one tube, but Del said, no way, he wasn't about to let her take that kind of risk, not with her medical history. So like what are the odds, that she really is pregnant? A thousand to one, maybe? And even so—'' A stream of air pushed through her lips as she sat back again, picking off the mushrooms from Lucas's mangled pizza beside her. ''Man…talk about your curveballs.''

Just then, Steven and the two little boys returned, and Mala gave a little shake of her head to indicate the conversation was over, that this was a secret between them.

It was silly, really, but Sophie felt just the tiniest thrill of pleasure at having a secret to share with someone. Of being accepted. Of feeling a part of something…real.

And then Steven's thigh brushed against hers when he sat back down at the crowded table and a thrill of an entirely different nature chased after the first.

Brother and sister launched into a conversation about the kids or whatever, Sophie wasn't entirely sure, as she suddenly settled quite firmly into a spate of bittersweet melancholia the like of which she'd never experienced before.

She might almost call the feeling homesickness, except that the longing was for something she'd never had, not something she missed. It wasn't that she'd never felt loved, she quickly reminded herself. But…although her parents had loved her, her mother's position and her father's work as a physicist had often pushed them to the periphery of her experience, even before their deaths; although her grandmother loved her, Princess Ivana's duties when Sophie was growing up had been hard on normal family ties as well; although her brother Alek loved her, being six years older and suffering from chronic wanderlust, he'd not been a part of her day-to-day life for some time.

In other words, one could feel loved and still feel disconnected.

Not that she expected anyone to feel sorry for her. She didn't feel sorry for herself, for heaven's sake. She'd led a life of privilege and comfort that most people would envy, after all, and to complain about it would seem the height of pettiness.

So why did she feel so...so...petty?

A light touch on her wrist made her start. Shaking herself out of what was on the verge of becoming a major broodfest, Sophie turned to run smack into Steven's considerate gaze. "You okay?" he said so only she could hear.

An ordinary, polite inquiry. Nothing more. Yet intimacy suddenly crackled between them with enough force to make her breath catch in her throat.

Out of nowhere, a sudden desire to lean against that strong, solid chest, to feel his arms holding her close, protecting her from demons that only existed in her own head, tore through her with white-hot, blinding ferocity. *Need,* she thought, swallowing hard. That's what this strange, frightening feeling was. A need for contact on its most basic level. A need to touch and be touched, to be connected to another human being in some way, any way, all ways.

To feel what it meant to be truly alive.

Afraid to speak, afraid that, somehow, he'd see through her and know what a silly little thing she was being, she only smiled, and nodded, and quickly looked away.

Except, when she caught Mala's gaze in hers, the other woman's brows lifted, just slightly, as what Sophie feared was a knowing smile slowly spread across her face.

Chapter 7

The problem with being the protective type, Steve mused as he got Dylan out of the tub later that evening, is that the urge to take care of people didn't come with an on/off switch. Ever since he was a kid, whenever he saw someone unhappy, no matter what the personal cost, he wanted to make them feel better. A serious character flaw that had gotten him in plenty of hot water before, and would no doubt get him in hot water again, and again and again, over the course of the next fifty or sixty years.

Like now.

Hell. He'd promised he wouldn't pry, but it was killing him to watch Lisa go all quiet and, he thought, sad on him like that and not know what to do or say.

Just as it was killing him that, as if he didn't have enough sadness to dispel in this house already, he'd taken on even more.

And it was really killing him that this crazy drive of his to make everybody in his life happy was, in this case, getting seriously tangled up with another kind of drive that was totally

out of place and inappropriate and was the last thing he needed
to be dealing with right now.

Maybe ever.

So, while one part of his brain was engaged in carrying on
a conversation with the ever-chattering Dylan as they got teeth
brushed and jammies on, another part of his brain was ramming home, in no particular order, the following, painfully
self-evident truths: that Steve didn't know who this woman
really was; that whoever she was wasn't going to be around
after two weeks and he didn't do flings; that there wasn't a
shred of space left in his life, let alone his bedraggled brain,
to fit in one more responsibility or worry; that frankly, after
Francine, if he never had to deal with another woman's whims
and foibles, it would be too soon.

There was, after all, a big difference between having survived the battle and being dumb enough to throw yourself
right smack into another one.

Okay? Okay. Now that *that* was settled…

He scooped the giggling little boy in his arms and loped off
down the short hallway to the boys' bedroom to find Lisa
standing just inside the room, a plate of foil-wrapped pizza in
her hands, while Rosie, already in her nightie, played with
some trucks on the floor. Steve would have suggested the
doggy bag anyway, had Lisa not beat him to the punch.

"And let me give it to him," she'd said.

At which point, Steve pointed out she might be setting herself up for rejection. "It would hardly be the first time," she'd
said, and he'd let it go.

After a fashion.

Now, standing here, watching the boy's expression harden
as he regarded Lisa from the top bunk, Steve's heart twisted,
both for the bitterness that had set up what seemed to be permanent camp in what used to be a pretty happy-go-lucky kid,
as well as the pain that kid was about to cause a woman who
didn't have the good sense to know when to back off.

"I'm not hungry," the boy muttered, flopping over on the
bed, pretending to be absorbed in a comic book. Correction:
graphic novel.

Still, just as he was about to call Mac on his rudeness, Lisa said softly, "Perhaps you're not." Steve wondered if she realized her hands were shaking. "But it is customary," she went on, "to say 'thank you' when someone does something for you, even though you may have precious little use for their efforts."

Mac's head snapped up, his eyes nearly black underneath plunged brows.

Okay, time to head this one off at the pass.

"Lisa—"

A smile of sheer determination sliced the word off at the knees. "Didn't you say something earlier," she said, still softly, "about reading to the younger ones before you put them down for the night?"

As in, *I don't need to be rescued, buddy, so take a hike.*

Steve hitched Dylan higher on his hip, snagging Lisa's eyes in his. Despite the irritation brewing in his gut, he was not about to let it show in front of the children. Still, his only thought was stopping this, now, getting her out of here before things got messy. "Rosie won't sit still to let me read unless she has her lovey. And I can't find it."

Underneath the drooped spikes, one eyebrow lifted. "It's on the arm of the sofa. Where you put it when we got back."

He couldn't have said why her stubbornness steamed him so much. Her willingness to take on Mr. Bad Attitude should have thrilled him. But for all her bravado, and genuine compassion, she had no idea what she was getting herself into. None.

And what was the point anyway? Whatever gains she might make with Mac—if any of them were that lucky—would be washed away like a sand castle in the tide as soon as she left.

"Lisa," he tried again, which got a pointed glare and an exasperated sigh.

"We'll see you *later,* Steven."

After which they stared at each other for several interminable seconds while three sets of underage eyeballs pinged from one to the other and something far too close to sexual energy for his peace of mind pinged between him and Lisa.

Getting the hell out of here was definitely the wisest choice. For a whole boatload of reasons.

"Count on it," he said curtly, then grabbed a pair of Dylan's pajamas off the child's bed and called Rosie. "Come on, honey—time to read."

Just before he ushered the little ones from the room, however, he caught Lisa's gaze. She didn't say a word, but her eyes said "Thank you" all the same.

Honestly. Damn woman was crazier than a loon.

Honestly. Sophie didn't think she'd ever get Steven out of the room. And she imagined he was going to have plenty to say when they next met. But she couldn't think about that now, not with this child glowering at her like this.

Why she was so determined to break down Mac's barriers— or at least, begin to, since she hardly expected to work miracles in two weeks—she had no idea. Nor had that been her intention when she'd volunteered for battle. Exactly. Still, when she thought of all the children she met in the course of her duties for whom she could little more than offer a minute of two of compassion, perhaps she simply couldn't resist the challenge of being able to do a little more.

If a certain somebody would let her, that is.

She set the pizza down on a desk in the room and crossed her arms, fully prepared for whatever Mac was about to dish out. And judging from the scowl that swallowed up his features, he was about to dish out plenty. She knew Steven wouldn't understand why it was important to her that he leave her to deal with this on her own, but it was. All her life, she'd let other people run interference for her, press secretaries and personal secretaries and bodyguards shielding her from whatever she might find onerous or unpleasant. While she understood their motives, the result was, once again, that she'd been left not only feeling disconnected, but ill prepared to deal with real life.

Something which the scowling teenager in front of her had been dealt in spades.

Sophie took in the various snazzy car posters on the walls—

another race car fanatic, she thought on a sigh—then at the cages and glass tanks set on a dozen surfaces of the room. Hamsters, gerbils, lizards, fish…and, she realized with a start, a not-exactly-small snake hugging a broken off tree limb. She bent down to the securely-lidded tank and cocked her head. "A boa?" she asked.

"Yeah," Mac said after a moment. "He eats mice. Live ones."

"Oh, I know. My brother used to let me feed his."

She smiled to herself at the resulting silence.

"What is it with you, anyway?" Mac suddenly said behind her. She twisted around to see the boy sitting upright, his still-slender chest heaving inside a faded blue T-shirt underneath an open plaid shirt. "We're like total strangers. You're not even gonna be around very long, right? So why do you give a damn about us?"

"Evan MacIntyre," she said quietly, "what would your mother say, hearing you swear like that?"

Shock streaked, just for a second, across his face before he once again schooled his features, narrowed his eyes. "Nothing, since she's *dead*."

"So is mine," Sophie shot back. "But at least I respected mine enough to think how my behavior might reflect on her."

Breathing hard, the kid jerked away. But the expected retort didn't materialize.

Foolishly encouraged, she took a step closer to the bed, arms still crossed, stomach quaking, realizing this was the best she could do. "My parents were killed in a plane crash when I was ten," she said, adding, before her comment had a chance to fully register, "so I know what you're feeling—"

The comic book flew across the room where it smacked into the opposite wall. "Just cut it out!" Mac yelled, his voice strained. "I swear, if one more person tells me they know what I'm feeling, I'm gonna puke!" He smacked his chest with his fist, clearly hiding his sorrow behind an impressive display of rage that reminded her so much of Alek twenty years ago, her eyes burned. "You're not in my head, okay? I mean, I'm sorry you lost your folks, but it's not the same thing." He shook his head, drawing his knees up to his chest, a child drowning in adult emotions he had no idea how to handle. "It's not."

"Because of the way they died, you mean?" she pushed, probably stupidly, but that's what came to her to say, so she said it.

"Yes. No." He hugged his knees more tightly, speared shaking fingers through his nearly black, close-cropped hair. "I don't know, okay? I'm not some stupid shrink. I can't explain what I feel, I just feel it. And I just know…" One hand lifted, only to slap helplessly back to the bed. She watched as he so desperately battled for control and thought how much boys were alike all over the world, no matter what their background. Then he startled her by saying, "You didn't watch your mother die, I bet."

She swallowed down a cry for his pain, still so new, so sharp, so incomprehensible. "No," she said softly. "I never even got to see them after… No," she repeated.

She saw the struggle in the boy's features, his good-heartedness—she knew that much about the child, just from what Steven had told her in the car coming home—warring with his need to stay angry, to keep the grief at bay.

"Then you don't know how I feel," Mac said flatly to some point beyond the foot of his bed.

Several seconds passed before Sophie finally realized that was as far as this conversation was going to get. And, quite likely, as far as this relationship would get, as well. The kid was right—she was only going to be here for a short time. She couldn't afford to get involved, after all, to let herself get all tangled up with the children's emotional needs.

Or to let her own needs tendril with theirs.

So she gestured to the dog, who'd been greedily eyeing the pizza for the past half hour. "Come on, George. Do you like pepperoni—?"

"Wait."

She'd already gotten to the door. "Yes?"

"Thank you…" Mac said, then cleared his throat. "Thank you for bringing me the pizza, okay? But I'm really not hungry. I fixed myself a big sandwich while you all were gone."

Her heart swelled before she had a chance to stop it. "Well, that's all right, then. Suppose I just wrap it up for later, when you *are* hungry?"

"Whatever," the kid said with a shrug, then picked up another comic book and started leafing through it.

Well, Rome wasn't built in a bloody day, either, Sophie thought with a smile as she softly shut the door behind her.

"You don't have to do that."

Clearly startled, Lisa jerked around, a dripping plate in her hand, only to jerk back when the water dripped onto her bare foot. She'd changed somewhere along the way into a pair of those pants that stopped several inches above the ankle and a soft, baggy sweater that wasn't all that baggy when it curved around her bottom.

Which, see, was precisely why this wasn't going to work. At all. Being constantly distracted by your housekeeper's bottom was definitely not a good thing.

Since it was a school night, the kids were all asleep. The little ones had insisted she help tuck them in, which meant when Steve went to hug them, they both smelled of her. And he'd caught the twins dispensing shy "good nights" to her, clearly ready to accept her, to bond with her. And then, maybe a hour ago, he'd not only noticed Mac slipping into the kitchen to spirit away the cold, leftover pizza, but Lisa's soft, wistful expression when she ran into him in the hallway and realized what he was doing.

Not to mention her smile of triumph when she walked away.

And then there was, oh, a bunch of stuff. Like the business in the pizza place with the water in her lap. The way she and Mala clearly took to each other, right off the bat.

The fact that every time she looked at him, he realized what a lonely bastard he really was.

So, no. This wasn't working out.

Lisa set the rinsed plate in the drainer, reached into the plastic tub for the next. "But I thought washing dishes was part of my job description."

What? Oh. Right. "What I meant," Steve said, "was that

you don't have to wash them by hand. There's a dishwasher right there.''

Couple of beats passed right by on that one. ''But…I like washing dishes by hand,'' she said. ''It's very…soothing.''

Steve leaned against the door frame, his arms linked, fighting a smile. ''You've never used a dishwasher before, have you?''

She stilled, obviously not knowing how to answer. Steve let out a long, tortured sigh, pretty much hating himself at that moment. ''Don't take this the wrong way, honey…but I think this is a mistake.'' He paused. ''For many reasons.''

Lisa yanked down the faucet handle, pivoted to face him, that angular chin front and center. ''I can learn to operate the dishwasher, Steven. And probably learn to cook. I'm not stupid—''

''You're also not the type of woman who's ever *had* to cook, or use a dishwasher, are you?''

That wasn't fear, exactly, that flashed in those big, blue eyes, as much as…what? Defiance? ''And that's why my being here is a mistake?''

''No.'' *No.* And he didn't need to let himself get off track. He could tell that his blunt denial had knocked her off balance.

''Oh,'' she said, nodding. ''This is about Mac, isn't it? The way I wouldn't go scurrying out of the room when you wanted me to.''

Steve sucked in a quick breath, balanced on it for a second or two before letting it out. ''Partly, maybe. But not the whole reason.'' He looked down, scratched his arm, looked up again. ''The real reason.''

She yanked a dish towel from the holder on the cabinet door, began wiping her hands. Even from here, he could tell her polish was badly chipped. ''I don't suppose you'd care to expand on that a bit?''

''Well, let's put it this way…'' He crossed the room, slowly, meeting the questions flickering underneath her raised brows, giving her plenty of time to figure out what he was about to do. To run.

He should have known.

So, since she didn't run, once he reached her, he had no choice but to lift his hand, gently brush away a hank of that funny hair off her face. No choice but to let his knuckle find its way down her cheek, so soft, so soft...

She swallowed. Shuddered, just slightly.

Stood her ground.

So he had no choice but to lower his mouth to hers, because clearly she wasn't getting the point. And then, once their lips were firmly sealed, where else was his hand going to go but to the back of her neck, which meant that his thumb, naturally, found the sweet, frantic pulse at the base of her throat.

Her hands, however, remained firmly clamped on that dish towel, boy, even as her mouth opened and sighed and gave and took, and Steve grew dizzy and hard and came damn close to panicking over a stupid kiss. One *he'd* initiated, for the love of Mike.

And one that he was going to break, any second now...

Another two seconds, maybe three, and that was—

Okay, just as soon as she shifted, he'd let her go....

Somebody murmured, he wasn't sure who, and suddenly, there was air where only a moment before there'd been lips.

Slightly swollen lips, underneath the biggest damn eyes he'd ever seen on another human being. A breeze floated in from somewhere, fluttering her feathery hair, chilling his damp mouth. She didn't move. George suddenly heard a dog barking in a distant galaxy, barked in reply.

She still didn't move.

And neither did he.

Oh, man, this was weird.

"Lisa?"

She blinked. "Yes?"

"I just made a pass at you."

"Yes, I know."

"And that doesn't bother you?"

After a moment, a small smile twitched her lips. "Short term or long term?"

"Dammit, Lisa. Don't you get it? I'm attracted to you! Very

attracted. And that's not good. Not good at all. Because being attracted to you—or any woman—right now is a distraction I not only don't need, but don't want. So having you around all the time is a really rotten idea.''

And still she stood, staring at him with that damn Mona Lisa smile dancing over her mouth.

His hands jerked up to his sides and his mouth opened, but whatever he was going to say went galloping off into the sunset when she burst into laughter. And while he stood there like an idiot, she finally extricated her hands from the poor strangled towel, turned to hang it up.

"Then why," she asked in an irritatingly reasonable voice, "did you kiss me?"

"To scare you, obviously!"

"Oh," she said, clearly surprised. "I see." Her brows dipped thoughtfully, she grabbed a sponge and began wiping up the counter. She might be inept, but she was certainly big on cleanliness. The living room hadn't looked that good in forever. "Well, I'm sorry to disappoint you—" she tossed him a glance over her shoulder "—but you didn't."

No kidding.

"Lisa," he said, "this is strictly a sexual thing, see."

He saw her miss a beat in her mad cleaning, but she said, "Well, of course it is, Steven. After all, we've just met. What else could it be?"

The dizziness was returning. Steve knuckled the space between his brows, let out a sharp sigh. "It's just been a while, is all."

Another moment passed, during which she rinsed out the sponge, set it by the faucet to dry. "Since your divorce, you mean?"

Compassion cushioned her words. Genuine and freely offered and packing a wallop that nearly stole his breath…wait a minute. "How did you—?"

"Mr. Liebowicz," she said with a shrug, then turned around, hitting him with, "So what are you saying? That you're afraid you can't control yourself?"

Their gazes were locked now, boy, good and tight. Ten feet

and a smelly dog separated them, and still a host of those little greenish-blue electrical jobbers spazzed between them.

"You asked me this after what just happened?" he managed.

"Oh, Steven…you said yourself the kiss was just a scare tactic."

She had him there.

"So?" she said.

He sighed. "No. No, of course not."

"Well," she said lightly, "there you are. No problem."

And it wasn't as if, with all these kids around, the opportunity to lose *complete* control was likely to present itself, was it? But did he really need the distraction of having to call his hyper libido to heel every time he looked at her?

And if that's all this was, cold showers and avoidance maneuvers could, he supposed, get him through the next couple of weeks. But what he couldn't deal with, didn't want to deal with, was the suggestion that his attraction went deeper than hormones. Way deeper. All-the-way-to-China deeper.

Because, see, even discounting the obvious logistical problems of his having neither the energy nor desire for any sort of romantic thing right now, what was the one thing he absolutely demanded from any woman he might even theoretically consider letting into his life? Huh? Remember, Steve?

That's right. Honesty.

Francine had shown him, oh so clearly, how easy it was to say one thing and mean quite another, what amazingly little effort it took for a woman to look a man straight in the eye and smile and tell him exactly what she thought the man wanted to hear, only to turn tail and run when things didn't go like she'd figured they would. In other words, experience had taught him that trusting a woman came with a price.

And he was running just a tad low on funds right now.

So. Whatever this nutso feeling was, it could just go right back where it came from. And the most expedient way to accomplish that, far as he could tell, was to tell Lisa—or whoever the heck she was—to do the same.

Except she was saying, "Well, then, as long as you're not

in any danger of losing control—'' with that, she did this nonchalant shrugging thing, sending the overlarge neckline skudding a bit to the west ''—I don't see a problem.''

What?

Damn.

Steve crossed his arms, tried to scowl. ''You're not the one facing two weeks of cold showers.''

One eyebrow lifted, disappearing underneath the straggly bangs. ''Says who?''

He very nearly took a step back on that one. But then she sighed, and the sound was so…heartfelt, he couldn't have kept the scowl in place if his life had depended on it.

Okay, he was a softie. So sue him.

She tugged back a kitchen chair, sinking with another sigh onto the padded vinyl seat. ''Do you know why I'm here? No, of course you don't,'' she said, waving her hand. Then she screwed up that generous mouth—bare now, from the kiss— as if trying to figure out how much she should say. At last, toying with a hunk of her hair, a piece right by that long, slender neck, she said, ''You see, just before I came here, somebody asked me to marry him.''

Well, that sure shorted out the old brain for a moment or two.

Until he realized she didn't look exactly bowled over by the prospect.

He yanked back a chair of his own and joined her at the table, fighting the urge to take her hand in his, make it all better. ''Let me guess. The man doesn't exactly fire your rockets?''

She laughed, a little, at that, but her breezy attitude of moments before had flown the coop. ''He's a widower with a toddler son,'' she said quietly. ''And he's a good man.'' Another sigh. ''Excellent husband material, frankly.''

''But you don't love him?''

That's right, Steve, old boy. Just go ahead and dig yourself in deeper, why doncha?

Both elbows planted on the table top, she rammed her hands through her hair, holding it away from her face. ''We've known each other forever," she said, not looking at him. "It's not as if I don't *like* him—"

"That's not what I asked."

And deeper.

After a long moment, she shook her head.

"Does…?" *And deeper still.* "Does this guy love you?"

"No."

Her immediate response shot right out of her mouth, aimed, it seemed, straight for Steve's gut. And why in God's name had he asked, anyway? Was this any business of his? No.

No.

"His wife died," Lisa was saying, "two years ago, shortly after his son was born. He was hopelessly in love with her, I gather, and has quite made up his mind not to fall in love again." A tiny shrug. "He's been very honest with me, I'll give him that, that this is strictly a matter of convenience."

"And you're actually *considering* such a stupid thing?"

So much for tact. Which had never been his strong suit, God knew. But he'd even surprised himself with that one. However, whether or not he had any permanent use for this generous, crazy, subterfugeous—if that was a word—woman, surely *somebody* might. The idea of her hooking up with some bozo just because it seemed like a reasonable idea—to one of the parties involved, anyway—appalled him.

The idea of all those sweet, trusting kisses going to waste…

His breath caught somewhere south of his throat. Way south.

"Let's just say," Lisa said, "I haven't ruled it out. I don't want to hurt him, either. But…"

She shrugged again, and silence settled between them like a fog. Sensing that something was amiss, George squeezed his big old head onto Lisa's lap; wordlessly, she cradled his muzzle, scratched his ears, and Steve found himself musing about how George wasn't the kind of dog just everyone took to. Especially women, who, for whatever reason, seemed to prefer their dogs, like their men, to be more trendy. Not to mention trainable. George was just George, clumsy and oversize and a little on the smelly side when the wind blew the wrong way.

A what-you-sees-is-what-you-gets kind of dog. Oh, yeah…it took a damn special woman to love old George here. A woman without pretensions or expectations. A woman who…

…was looking at him with a very strange expression on her face.

Oh, hell. She must've started talking again and he'd tuned her out.

"So you see," she said, worry and resignation warring it out in her eyes, "neither of us is exactly in a position to let anything, um, get out of hand. And after all, we're both adults." She licked her lips then, which probably wasn't the smartest thing to do if she thought she was trying to diffuse the sexual tension. "Surely this isn't the first time you've been physically attracted to someone but knew you didn't dare act on it?"

No. But—

A familiar cry cut off whatever he was about to think. Let alone say.

Lisa was already on her feet, headed out of the kitchen. "Wasn't that Dylan?"

"Yeah. Probably means he's wet." Suddenly beat, Steve hauled himself upright—barely—and lumbered toward the cries. "I'll get it—"

"No," Lisa said. "Let me—"

"He's my responsibility, Lisa!"

"You really are a case, aren't you?" she said in a fierce whisper, already to the stairs. "You hired me to help, so let me help, for heaven's sake! Now where are the clean sheets?"

There she went, messing with his head again. Being *nice*.

"How's about," he said on a yawn, "you clean the kid, I'll change the bed."

"All right," she said after a beat, then headed up the stairs. And the two or three hormones that hadn't yet checked out for the night sighed at the glimpse of that cute little sweater-swathed derriere twitching in front of him as he dragged himself upstairs after her.

* * *

Dylan was sitting up in bed, in the dark, whimpering softly. "I'm sorry," he said, his voice still drugged with sleep and tears. "I didn't mean it...."

"Oh my goodness, little one..." Sophie quickly shuffled through all sorts of cars and things to reach the bed. "It's okay...it's okay." She reached out for the soggy child, carefully guiding him out of bed and down the hall to the bathroom, crossing Steven on his way to the bedroom, clean sheets propped on one arm, focused quite intently on what he was about to do.

As if that kiss had never happened. Let alone the conversation that had followed it.

A tremor raced through her body, heating her blood and her skin and everything else that happened to be in its way. And then he'd made that "cold shower" comment—

Her cheeks flamed even more. Six languages, she spoke, but right now she couldn't form a single coherent thought in any of them. How on earth had she managed to stay as cool as she had, as if she were just the most worldly wise woman around? As if men came on to her all the time.

Men like Steven. Men without agendas, hidden or otherwise.

She supposed if she was being her politically correct self, she should feel indignant, or at the very least annoyed, that the man had, um, a thing for her. But the truth was, well, it was all rather thrilling, actually, having a man attracted to her for no other reason than *he found her attractive*.

Oh, my—her heart was positively thundering. Not to mention other parts of her body. This was getting a bit more "real" than she'd intended, perhaps, she thought as she began peeling cold, soaked pajamas off the wavering child in front of her. Even if, ironically, Steven's interest in her wasn't in *her*, but in this blue-eyed blonde phantom she'd made up.

And why not? Lisa Stone could dress any way she wanted. Lisa Stone could talk back, and joke, and be irreverent. Lisa Stone could say whatever she felt and not worry about offending entire nations. Lisa Stone had spunk, whereas Princess Sophie, well, didn't.

Lisa Stone could even, she supposed, have an affair if she wanted to.

She froze. Just for a second. Then, on a sigh, she returned her attention to the yawning child in front of her. Speaking of *real*. Sophie doubted even the most devoted, besotted parent in the world could find this task pleasant. However, she surprised herself with her own efficiency, getting Dylan washed and dried and re-pajama'd, all the while trying to rein in all these pointless thoughts her brain seemed so determined on spewing out.

Feeling the child's soft cheek nestled against her shoulder when she carried him back to his room was something else again. "Did you have a bad dream?" she whispered, then felt a sleepy little nod.

"'Bout monsters. They wanted to eat me."

"Oooh…" She hiked him up higher on her shoulder, then clumsily lowered herself to a wooden chair at a desk in the room, rubbing the little boy's back while she watched Steven silently complete the bed change. Her senses were on overload from Steven's woodsy scent mingling with the child's soapy one, her awareness of Steven's broad, swift movements, Dylan's sweet heaviness against her, his soft breath fanning over her collarbone.

"I used to have dreams like that," she whispered, not wishing to awaken Mac in the bunk above Dylan's. "When I was little. And do you know what I did?"

Dylan shook his head against her chest.

"I remember, in my dreams, I used to go right up to those monsters and say, 'Fine, then—come eat me!' And every single time, I'd wake up."

"Yeah?"

"Mmm, hmm. And then, you know what?"

"What?" The word was suspended on a yawn. She stroked the little head, rocking a little.

"I learned to tell myself what I was going to dream about, every night. Good things. And rather soon after that, I stopped having the bad dreams."

A moment passed before she realized that Steven had completed his task and was standing, hands on hips, watching her. She lifted her gaze, met his.

Smiled.

"Bed's ready," Steven then said softly. In the darkness, he bent over to touch Dylan's head, his warm, rough fingers colliding with Sophie's. He jerked back, straightened. "Want me to fly you in, squirt?" he said with a tenderness that cramped her heart.

Dylan nodded "yes" and Steven scooped him out of Sophie's lap, *vrooming* him into his dry, clean bed before giving him a grunting hug and kiss. Then he faced her, his expression unreadable in the scant light coming in from the hallway. "Thanks," he murmured, almost as if it was a strain to get the word past his lips, then strode out.

More than a little puzzled—even from what little she knew of the man, she doubted he found gratitude a chore—Sophie stood as well, but hadn't quite reached the door when she heard a whispered, "Hey!"

Mac.

She turned, trying to see in the darkness. "I thought you were asleep—"

"You didn't mind cleaning up the kid? I mean, you didn't get mad or nothin'?"

"Why should I have? It's not as if he wets his bed on purpose."

After a long moment, Mac said, "Yeah, well, all those other women Steve got in to help? Either they made a real stink about it, or else they refused to change him, said Steve could do that."

"Oh. Well, I'm not those other women."

Even in the feeble light, she could feel his gaze, steady and accessing, before he flopped back down, punching his pillow underneath his head.

"Good night, Mac," she said, but he didn't reply.

Shaking her head, she tiptoed out, finding Steven in the living room a few moments later, seated on the sofa. He was leaning forward, his head in his hands, looking for all the world as if the simple act of breathing was more than he could handle at the moment.

"Steven, for goodness' sake—go to bed."

From behind his hands, she heard the tired chuckle. Then he looked up, his hands still clamped to his head, as if it might otherwise roll off his shoulders. "Can't. I've got two rolls of film to develop tonight. Besides—" he yawned "—we haven't settled our little problem yet."

She'd been afraid he'd say that. "About my staying, you mean?"

He let out a long breath, then leaned back against the sofa cushions, scratching the dog's head in his lap. "This is dangerous," he said quietly.

Again, that tremor raced through her. "Only if we let it be."

Again, he chuckled, a soft, warm sound that only heightened the tremor. "Oh, honey...I could promise on my grand-mother's grave not to touch you, and that wouldn't diminish the danger one iota." He tilted his head at her, his lips equally tilted in a smile too weary to straighten out. "You know that, don't you?"

Yes, she did. Heavens—he didn't have to touch her. That smile alone—the memory of his kiss—was enough to send luscious feelings she'd only, to that point, dreamt about, swirl-ing through her blood. Warm feelings. Arousing feelings. Feelings she needed to send packing as quickly as possible.

Who'd given her body permission to bypass her brain like this? It wasn't as if no man had ever smiled at her before, for goodness' sake. But this was the first man whose mouth seemed directly connected to her nipples.

Oh, dear. That hadn't come out quite right, had it?

But be that as it may. She tucked her arms against her ribs, suffocating the feelings as best she could, and said, "But you're not the type of man to act on an impulse, are you? Or to—what's the phrase?—make a play for a woman once she's made it clear she's off-limits."

Because she was off-limits. As was Steven, for her. Some-thing she'd have to remind herself even more forcefully than before, despite all the warm, nipple-tingling feelings his smile provoked, even if Jason weren't an issue—and, to be honest, she wasn't all that sure he really was. Because, the fact was, as real as this was, it wasn't *her* reality. And never would, or could, be.

He was watching her, not smiling, not frowning, just... watching. Finally he said, "No. At least, I never have before."

A shudder raced up her spine. And the little beastie made a return appearance long enough to say, *Maybe you should rethink this....*

Oh, splendid—*now* the bloody thing decides to be cautious?

"Steven, I realize this may be hard for you to understand, but for the first time in my life, I feel...needed. Useful. Don't..." She paused, hugged herself. "I will do whatever you think best, but I'd really appreciate it if you didn't take that away from me."

He pulled himself back upright, groaning all the way, then skimmed a hand across his short hair as he yawned, the other hand braced on his knee. "Lisa," he said to the air in front of him, "you have no idea how much I want you to stay." His gaze drifted to hers. "Or how much I want you to go."

"Well. I suppose it has to be one or the other, doesn't it?"

The dog scrambled out of his way as Steven rose to his feet. "Yep. Sure does."

"And?"

"And..." He shut his eyes, a rueful half chuckle rumbling up from his chest. "If you stay, it's on one condition."

"Oh? And what's that?"

"That we both stay out of each other's way as much as possible."

And without giving her even a chance to reply, he walked away.

Bloody cheek.

Chapter 8

Three days later, unannounced and bestowing kisses and grocery bags—to Rosie and Sophie, respectively—an imposing,
dark-haired woman who announced herself as Bev Koleski
sailed through the farmhouse's front door with the obvious
intention of taking her son's erstwhile housekeeper firmly in
hand.

The other kids were all at school, Steven at work, and
George—no fool he—had gone out to put the chickens
through their paces the minute Mrs. Koleski set foot in the
house. Which meant there was nothing to shield Sophie from
the woman's effusive enthusiasm save her wits.

What was left of them at this point. Now, even in her royal
role, Sophie's schedule was hardly what one would call leisurely. Most mornings, she was up before dawn to begin a
round of meetings, conferences, goodwill visits, often ending
with some state function or other that often lasted until the
wee hours of the morning. Still, that was nothing compared
with keeping up with a very energetic, very smart little girl
who, Sophie had discovered the hard way, could silently

wreak havoc on a room in the space of three-and-half minutes. In other words, she was about to keel over from exhaustion.

And only ten more days to go?

Insert hysterical laughter here.

As whacked as she was, however, she knew Steven was even more so, still trying to keep all those plates up in the air. In ten days, *she* was free to leave.

He wasn't.

And that bothered her—oh, all right, worried her—more than it should have, considering. And while Princess Sophie would never have dreamed of poking the famed Vlastos nose in where it didn't belong, Lisa Stone would have had no compunction whatsoever about giving him a jolly good *Now see here.* If she could have snagged him for longer than thirty seconds, that is, which, since his "we need to stay out of each other's way" declaration, was like trying to chase a rabbit with her feet tied together. And made her more tired than ever.

So it was in this bleary, not exactly chipper frame of mind that she faced Steven's mother, who was extracting packaged chicken parts and potatoes and things at lightning speed from assorted white plastic bags, thunking them up onto the counter which Sophie hadn't yet had a chance to clean since breakfast, a fact which the Bev the Indomitable no doubt noted.

"Now, look, hon," she began, a goddess of domesticity in coral polyester and a soft, powdery fragrance that was surprisingly quite pleasant, "nobody's born knowing how to cook, okay? It's no sin getting into your twenties and not knowing how—"

Sophie thought better of mentioning that, at that point, she was hanging on to her twenties only by the slimmest of threads.

"—as long as you learn by the time you need to." Mrs. Koleski dug deep, deep into her purse and yanked out what Sophie assumed was a cookbook, which she smacked up onto the counter. Considering the size of the woman, Sophie decided that anything dealing with smacking merited serious attention. "So. Now's a good a time as any, right?"

Sophie picked up the cookbook, dog-eared and splattered

with memories and a fair amount of grease, and began to leaf through it. Not that she wanted to rush things—after all, she'd just learned how to operate the dishwasher, as well as the washer and dryer—but she didn't suppose cooking would be such a bad thing to add to her repertoire. Of course, she'd have precious little use for it, once she left—she pushed the thought past the dull ping in her heart—but still. One never knew when the impulse to whip up a meat loaf might strike, after all.

And it would be nice to have something edible waiting for Steven when he came home. Something that didn't come in a microwaveable tray, that is.

She pushed past that ping, as well.

"I figure we can start with something even an idiot couldn't screw up, then move on from there," Steven's mother said, and Sophie laughed.

"What?" Mrs. Koleski asked, not unkindly.

Sophie couldn't exactly tell her that this was the first time anyone had implied she was an idiot. To her face, at least. So she said instead, "Oh, nothing. This is just all so…new."

That, needless to say, got a curious look. "So tell me—what on earth made you volunteer for this, anyway?"

At that moment, her purple overalls already smudged with dirt, Rosie came running in from outside and straight into Sophie's arms, flushed with excitement and prattling about a "bootiful" butterfly she'd just seen by the pumpkin patch.

Rosie comfortably ensconced on her hip, Sophie turned to Mrs. Koleski. "This is why," she said, tucking the baby's head underneath her chin.

The older woman's expression softened, even as she kept her gaze pinned to Sophie's. "Then why only for two weeks?"

"I have…obligations back home."

"And where is that, if you don't mind my asking?"

Sophie smiled, then walked over to deposit the amazingly heavy child onto a kitchen chair, offering to get her some juice. Rosie nodded; Sophie crossed to the refrigerator. "The last thing I wish to do is to be rude, Mrs. Koleski—"

"But you're not going to tell me."

She smiled. "No."

Sophie held her breath, hardly daring to believe, even for a moment, that Steven's mother would leave it there. But, surprisingly, she did, instead watching the little girl slurp down her drink. "We could hardly get her to talk, before you came. Did you know that?"

Startled, Sophie whipped around. "No. No, I didn't. Steven never said—"

"He told me, that first morning you were here—when that witch nearly ran you over with her car?—when he called to ask me to sit, how Rosie just took to you like she'd known you forever."

Sophie watched the child, who'd been the epitome of garrulousness since her arrival. "She really didn't talk?"

"Oh," Steven's mother said with a shrug, "a word here and there, maybe. But certainly nothing like what she did just now. And Steve tells me Mac's coming around, too?"

Sophie sighed. "We've reached the point where he talks to me without growling, I suppose. But Mac's a bit like a stray dog who wants the food but is afraid to get close enough to eat it."

The older woman seemed to study her for a moment, then glanced over at the empty coffeemaker, not yet rinsed out from breakfast. "You know how to make coffee?"

"What? No, sorry. No matter how early I set my alarm, Steven's always up before me, so he makes it."

"Well, the way I see it, making a decent pot of coffee ranks right up there with learning to tie your shoes. Get on over here," Mrs. Koleski said, tromping over to the counter. "And get the coffee out of the fridge on your way."

Sophie fought the urge to salute. There was, however, an odd sort of comfort in having all vestiges of self-determination whisked out from beneath one. A few minutes later, Rosie back outside with George, both ladies settled at the kitchen table with cups of coffee, Steven's mother began a circuitous conversation that would, Sophie imagined—hoped—eventually come to some sort of point.

"You know, I love my son, but he's got a stubborn streak in him a mile wide."

Sophie said, "Mmm," or something equally intelligent, then settled her mug—ordinary people, she'd quickly discovered, have little use for bone china—back onto the vinyl-covered, jelly-smeared table.

"He gets hold of an idea and that's it. Head like the Rock of Gibraltar, nothin' can get through. But after almost thirty-three years, I figure I know him better than he knows himself, probably." Bev took a sip of coffee, her brow furrowed. Sophie waited. "And part of that includes knowing how to read between the lines, if you get my drift."

She didn't, but she said "Mmm" again.

"Like the last few days. He calls me about something or other, and I say, 'So how's the new housekeeper workin' out?' and all he says is 'fine' and changes the subject. Oh, he talks about how well the kids are gettin' on, since you came, but he won't say diddly about *you.*" She leaned back then, an expression of definite significance glowing from her features.

"Mmm" wasn't going to cut it this time. "I'm sorry, Mrs. Koleski. I don't—"

"Every other woman he's had in here, he'd talk my ear off—about how unsympathetic they were with the kids or whatever. You come along, and he says next to nothin'. And I'm thinking, this means somethin', and that's a fact."

Sophie simply stared at her for several seconds. What was it with people in this town and their penchant for matchmaking? "I hope you don't think—"

That got a laugh, a warm, rich sound straight from the soul. "That you're the answer to his prayers? Not hardly, hon. After what he went through with that Francine...well, if I thought you *were* after him, I'd be pretty ticked off, let me tell you. But you're working wonders with the kids, you're nice, and you're cute. So it's only natural, that he gets a bit of a crush on you, right?"

The woman had fine-tuned left-handed compliments, Sophie decided, to an art form. Although she hadn't been cute since she was five years old, and that had only lasted about a day and a half. In any case, Sophie's already stretched-thin patience was just about used up.

"I'm sorry—is there a point to this?"

Another laugh. "Marty's always gettin' on my case, too, about how it always takes me so long to get down to brass tacks. Okay, hon, here's the deal…" Her bosoms settled on the tabletop when she leaned forward. "Since he doesn't listen to me—who listens to their mother, right?—I thought maybe, just maybe, he might listen to you. You know, since he obviously likes you and all."

Oh, well—*that* cleared things right up. "About?"

"About how he's got to make up his mind what he wants to do. See, all his life, Steve has had this thing about tryin' to make everybody happy." Then she sighed. "Which is admirable, don't get me wrong, but not so good if it means neglecting yourself. You know how some men are addicted to sports? With Steve, it's obligations. All those *musts* and *shoulds* and *haftas* that can kill a person, if you're not careful, you know?"

Yes, she knew. All too well. But she still had no idea what on earth any of this had to do with her.

"Take his photography. You know about that?"

"Only that he obviously loves it and he's extremely talented."

Mama Bird preened a little at that, then said, "But I bet you don't know that the only reason he hadn't gone into it full-time is because his father has his heart set on Steve's taking over the family business one day, just like he did from his father, that Steve is afraid he'll hurt him if he tries to walk away. So I thought maybe you could talk some sense into him."

In other words, Steven's mother wanted her to give him that jolly good *Now see here* which Sophie just this instant realized would be a major mistake, no matter who delivered the message.

"Oh, no, no, no…" The chair scraped against the floor as she stood, shaking her head. "This is none of my business—"

"You can't see that he's running himself into the ground, trying to be everything to everybody?"

"I didn't say that."

"And don't you think he should do what *he* wants to do?"

"Absolutely. But it's hardly my place to tell him that."

"Why not?"

Sophie couldn't help gawking at the woman, although she did manage not to let her jaw drop. "Because I'm a total stranger? Because you're basing your assumptions about my influence on a few phone calls during which you've admitted Steven doesn't even talk about me? This is family business, Mrs. Koleski. And after a few days, I'm not going to be part of this family. Besides—" She clamped shut her mouth, the words screeching to a halt in her throat.

"Besides what?"

Oh, why not? "Steven's a big boy, Mrs. Koleski. No, please—let me finish. Yes, I've seen how tired he is, how much he pushes himself. And that's hard to watch. I...know what it's like to try to make everyone happy, to get yourself so balled up with obligations you can't even find yourself anymore. But it wasn't until I was choking and sputtering on all my obligations that I realized what I was letting happen, that I had some mental housecleaning to do. How is it any different for Steven? Whatever conclusions he comes to, whatever decisions he makes, will have to be on his own terms, I'm sure."

She looked down at her hands, then back up into Steve's mother's unreadable expression. "What you're seeing isn't stubbornness, Mrs. Koleski. It's pride."

After a moment, the older woman started to laugh. "Too bad you aren't sticking around, y'know? I mean, yeah, the makeup could stand a bit of toning down, but you're one smart cookie, that's for damn sure." She got up from the table, still chuckling while Sophie stood there at a complete loss for words. But Mrs. Koleski had, apparently, moved on to more important subjects. "And speaking of cookies, there's sheets in the drawer underneath the stove," she said. "Grab a couple and I'll show you how to make peanut butter cookies."

But as Sophie struggled getting the recalcitrant sheets untangled from the pile of pots and pans with which they shared living space, she could have sworn she heard the front screen door swing shut.

With any luck, Steve thought as he took off in his truck, nobody'd even know he'd been there. He'd only come home for a minute to change his shirt, anyway, thanks to Mrs. Jackson's muddy-footed Great Dane's not yet having mastered the lesson on *down*. Might not even have bothered at that, had he not been close to the house, figured what the hell.

He'd forgotten his mother had said she'd drop by this morning, until he saw her Corsica in the driveway. Which would have been reason enough to steer clear of the kitchen. But, like the fool he was, he just had to see how the two ladies were getting on. *If* they were getting on. So, after he'd changed his shirt, he'd tiptoed to the door and, well, eavesdropped, a plan only possible to begin with because George was outside.

Just for a second, he'd told himself. Just to be sure Lisa wasn't in tears or anything. Except, when he realized he was the topic of conversation, he couldn't tear himself away.

Stubborn, huh? Well, he guessed there was some truth to that. He supposed he could be pretty muleheaded about some things, especially when it came to the kids. At least no one could call him wishy-washy, right?

Judging from what he did hear, he apparently had missed some crucial lead-ins. Just as well, though, he imagined, knowing his mother. But then Lisa had starting in telling his mother why she wouldn't do whatever it was she wanted Lisa to do, and he heard all that stuff about how she'd run from her obligations, and that, of course, churned up his curiosity even more.

Who the heck *was* she?

And why was she defending his right to dig his own holes so vehemently?

He frowned, punching on the radio as he drove. Wasn't what she'd said, as much as the way she'd said it, that had gotten to him. The passion shimmering just beneath her words. If he didn't know better, he'd swear what she'd said, about his needing to make his own decisions, stemmed more from her giving a damn than from the fact that they were still strangers to each other.

There was a first.

And you know what was scary about the whole thing? That Lisa had no idea he could hear her. She wasn't out to impress him, or even, he didn't think, to put off his mother: she simply meant what she was saying.

At that moment, even though he knew better, even though he knew nothing could possibly come of it, curiosity—there it was again—nudged aside caution, leading him to re-evaluate this avoidance business. To be honest, he enjoyed being around Lisa Stone. He liked hearing her laugh, watching how her brow puckered when she tried to figure out how to operate this or that electrical gadget, the way she'd chew on her bottom lip while helping Courtney with her math homework.

Lisa Stone was a nice woman. Okay, "nice" was kind of lame, but from him, "nice" was a compliment. And what could it hurt, letting himself enjoy her company, just for the few days she'd be here?

Yeah, yeah, he remembered all the sexual stuff. But he had that all under control. No, really, he did. Even though the thought of her marrying that guy made his stomach turn, Lisa seemed like the kind of woman who would do exactly that. The kind of woman who'd take on five kids just because she wanted to be useful probably *would* marry somebody just because he needed her to. So Steve wasn't about to do anything dumb, like come on to her again.

He didn't think, anyway.

But what was the harm in a little window-shopping?

Two-thirty. Rosie had conked out on the kitchen floor beside a snoozing George, where Sophie had decided to leave her; the other kids wouldn't be home for another hour at least. She ducked into her room, leaving her door open in case Rosie awoke and needed her, dragging her laptop onto the small desk in front of the window and plugging the modem into the phone jack, feeling a pang of guilt as she quickly, furtively, logged on to check her e-mail.

Four messages, this time. One each from her grandmother and Alek—who had, unbelievably, decided to stop traipsing all over the world and come back to Carpathia to roost—one from the secretary of the World Relief Fund, thanking her for her speech the week before and basically assuring her the Director's position was hers, if she wanted it, and one from Jason.

That one, she really didn't want to read.

She distractedly skimmed the messages from her family, telling herself she had nothing to feel guilty about. Nothing. After all, it wasn't as if they were engaged. She'd only told Jason she'd think about his offer. She hadn't given any promises.

So why hadn't she simply said "no"? Why was she afraid to open his e-mail?

"This is ridiculous," she muttered to herself, clicking on the "next" button. "Absolutely ridic...u...lous..."

She skimmed the message three times before it sank in. While he understood her ambivalence about his proposal, he said, for Andy's sake he thought it best that she be prepared to give him an answer, one way or the other, by the end of the month.

"Bloody hell," she whispered.

Not that he wasn't right: he deserved an answer. Which, frankly, she could have given him, right then, with all the appropriate apologies and well wishes concomitant to such things. Except an electronic refusal was so...so rude, she decided. So unlike her. And so unfair to a man who'd done nothing to deserve being given such a casual brush-off.

So, fingers trembling, she hit Reply, thanked Jason very much for his kind inquiry, and promised, yes, to give him her answer by then.

Then she closed up her laptop, tucked it back into the deepest recesses of the closet where she kept her Princess Sophie things and went looking for Rosie.

Who was no longer asleep where she'd left her.

Chapter 9

Since there were no more appointments, Steve had left the shop early to get in a little darkroom time before dinner. Maybe chat up his "housekeeper"—and yes, whenever he thought about the blowsy blonde with the prissy accent currently fulfilling that role, he put quotation marks around the word—while she did whatever in the kitchen. *Enjoy himself,* he thought it was called.

A thought that went careening off into oblivion the instant he pulled into the driveway.

The screen door slammed back against the house; her hair wilder than ever, her white pants blotched with dirt, Lisa came roaring outside, George hot on her heels. Her eyes shot wide open when she saw Steve, both from surprise and, he immediately realized, panic.

His own stomach clamped in response. "Lisa! What's wrong—?"

"Oh, God, Steven! It's Rosie! I can't find her anywhere in the house! She'd fallen asleep on the kitchen floor, I went to my room for maybe ten minutes, sure I'd hear her if she got up—" White as a sheet, she clamped a hand to her mouth.

Steve was up the steps in two seconds flat. "Lisa, Lisa, hey...it's okay," he said as much for his benefit as hers. "How long's she been missing?"

"Oh, gee—I don't know...fifteen, twenty minutes, maybe? Where on earth could she *be?*" she screamed, as freaked out as any mother who's ever turned around in the grocery store and discovered her kid wasn't where he'd been a second before. "Didn't you say there's a stream or something behind the house?"

"Way beyond the house, honey," he said, grabbing her cold, shaking hands. "And the back of the property is fenced and gated. Not even our clever little Rosie could negotiate that."

"But the road—"

"I just came up that way, remember? I'd've seen her." True, in theory, she could have crossed the road and headed across the field to the woods on the other side, but she'd never crossed the road before.... "She's got to be somewhere around. You know how she loves to fall asleep in strange places."

Except there were a lot of strange places to be found on ten acres. And both of them knew that. Lisa scrubbed her wet cheeks with the heel of her hand, smearing her mascara to kingdom come. "I'm so sorry, Steven, I'm so, so sorry...you were right, I shouldn't have done this, I had no business—"

"Lisa!" he said, grabbing her by the shoulders and pinning her terrified gaze with his. "Kids sometimes wander off! We'll find her, okay—?"

"Hey, what's wrong?"

Steve whipped around to Mac, who was coming up the driveway. "What're you doing home this early?"

"I told you, remember? They were shutting down early today for some teacher's meeting or something. I got a ride from Joey Hotchkin's mom. Why's she cryin'?" he asked with a nod in Lisa's direction.

"Rosie's apparently done it again," Steve said, trying to keep it light, trying desperately to keep Mac's protectiveness

in relative abeyance. "Gone off and fallen asleep somewhere—"

"You *lost* her?" Mac's gaze zinged to Lisa, his eyes black
with fury. And fear. *"You lost my little sister?"*

"Mac! She didn't *lose* her, for the love of Mike! Anymore
than you did that day I asked you to baby-sit and we found
her curled up underneath the kitchen sink!"

But the kid had thrown down his backpack into the dusty
road and taken off behind the house, not thinking, not planning, just reacting, while Lisa stood there hugging herself,
looking humiliated and horror-stricken. "Go back inside,"
Steven said softly, "and start looking again. I know you said
you already looked," he said to quell her protest, "but you'd
be amazed some of the places we've found her before. I'm
sure she's fine," he added, squeezing her shoulder. "And this
is not your fault, do you hear me?"

She hauled in a long, shuddering breath, then went back
inside the house.

His breath coming in ragged, painful pants, Mac tore around
to the back of the house, scaring the chickens so bad, some
of the dumb things flew right up into a tree.

How stupid could she be?

She'd only had one kid to look out for! *One.* His mother,
she'd had five, and he couldn't remember her ever losing any
of them, not even for ten seconds. Cripes, even that hag Hadley hadn't been this bad! Sure, Lisa looked real scared and all,
like she'd been crying, too, but…

Mac stood in the middle of the yard, his heart beating so
hard it hurt, staring out over the vegetable garden, past the
rabbit hutch and the goat's pen, willing his baby sister to pop
up from the wildflowers in the field beyond. He dragged the
back of his hand across his mouth, squinting from the sun;
sweat streamed down his face, his back.

Behind him, he heard Steve and Lisa, both, calling Rosie's
name. Lisa had gone back inside, he guessed, but Steve's voice
seemed to be coming from out front, maybe down the driveway or something.…

Please, God...nobody else, please. You got Mom and Dad, okay? Please...

He took off toward the back of the property, his high-tops pounding against the dirt, his blood making a weird whooshing sound in his head. Steven had put a chain-link fence around the back, like a week or something after they'd moved in. The gate was never locked or nothin', but it was enough to keep a three-year-old from wandering off.

That's what Steve had said, anyway.

Mac could tell, long before he reached the fence, that whoever had last gone through the gate had forgotten to shut it—

"Oh, God! Oh, *crap!*"

He swore, loud and long, using words he knew would get his butt in a sling for *weeks*. But he didn't care. Steve could ground him for the rest of his life for this one, it didn't matter, it would never matter....

They'd had a crazy cold spell last week, cold enough to use the woodstove, but they'd run out of firewood so late in the season. So Steve had said, go on down to the woods, see if you can find enough deadwood to get us through.

Mac's arms had been full. He hadn't shut the gate behind him. He'd meant to go back and do it, but he'd forgotten....

He nearly fell over when George shoved up against him, barking and whining. "Go away, you stupid dog!" Mac was surprised to discover he was crying, hated himself for being such a baby. "I don't want to play ball right now!"

He pushed through the open gate, struck out through the field toward the creek. But the dog grabbed hold of his sleeve and yanked at it, digging his feet into the ground to get enough leverage to knock Mac off balance.

"I said, go *away!*"

George let go, then bounded through the gate, yapping his dumb head off, then raced back to Mac, doing the sleeve-tugging number again.

"What is your *problem?*" Mac screamed at the dog. "I told you, I can't play! I've got to find Rosie!"

The dog let out an enormous *rowlf,* then latched on to the hem of Mac's baggy pants. Mac glowered down at the mutt,

who didn't look the least bit scared. Huh. Yeah, he was a dog
and all, but Mac could swear George looked almost like he
was saying, "C'mon, man—you gonna trust me here, or
what?"

So Mac followed the dog, who kept dashing ahead of him,
then back, up and back, up and back, the whole way back to
the garden, like he was saying, "Would you please hurry *up?*"
until they got to his doghouse, a great big wooden job about
twenty feet from the house, under the mulberry tree. Once
there, George dropped to his stomach, alternately peering inside and looking up at Mac as he wagged his tail and whined
his stupid head off. Once before, Mac had seen George act all
weird like this, when one of the cats had gone inside and
George was too much of a wuss to chase the animal back out.
Angrily, Mac swatted at the dog, then turned away, his stomach all knotted up about Rosie.

George rushed him again, nearly knocking him down this
time. "God, you are like *so* stupid," Mac said, trudging back
to the doghouse. "Why can't you—" he got on his hands and
knees to look inside "—just get the damn cat out by
your...self...oh, *crap,*" he finished on a shaky laugh which
was, if he wasn't real careful, going to turn into more tears.

"I found her!" Mac screamed, jumping up and running
toward the house. "Hey, guys—I *found her!*"

Steve had awakened the little girl and coaxed her out of the
doghouse—and George had run right in, settling in with a
relieved groan—only Lisa had grabbed Rosie right out of
Steve's arms, clearly not caring that the child smelled like
concentrated George, and hugged her so hard, Steve had been
surprised the kid hadn't burst into tears. Not that Lisa's reaction was all that surprising, considering. Mac's, on the other
hand, was.

The World's Angriest Kid had disappeared, somewhere
along the way, replaced by this quiet, and—if Steve wasn't
mistaken—contrite young man. Steve had been completely
prepared to fend off Mac's verbal blows, fully expected him
to rail at Lisa for what he'd consider her ineptitude. But he

hadn't. At all. In fact, after Lisa carried Rosie into the house and settled on the sofa with the little girl in her lap, Mac had bent down and given them both a hug, a gesture which clearly startled Lisa as much as it flummoxed Steve.

There was a story here, he was sure of it. But he figured the kid'd come clean when he was ready to. Maybe.

In the meantime, Steve had enough of his own jumbled feelings to deal with to last him a good long while. First off was the breath-stealing reaction he was having, watching Lisa with Rosie, remembering her anguished expression when she'd thought she'd lost the baby. Nothing faked about that, boy. And never would he have believed that a woman—a stranger—could bond as fiercely and, he thought, completely with these kids as she had.

If she did marry that guy back home, he'd be one lucky SOB, that was for damn sure.

The thought caught him up short, set his heart pounding so hard, it hurt.

"You okay?" he asked her now, wondering if his voice could be heard over that thudding heart.

She looked up over Rosie's dark head, gave him a weak smile. "I doubt I'll be 'okay' for a long time," she said. "But I can guarantee—" she hugged the child even more tightly to her chest "—it won't happen again. Not while I'm here."

Not while I'm here.

Right. She was leaving, possibly going to marry someone else, he didn't need the emotional mayhem getting involved with a woman—this woman—would undoubtedly entail.

"It wasn't your fault, Lisa," he said again, softly. "Kids slip away, even from the best parents. The thing to remember is, she's okay."

She stopped rocking the little girl for a moment, her gaze steady and cool. "So you're saying you weren't afraid? When I told you she'd gone missing?"

"Hell, honey—I was petrified. But that doesn't mean I blamed you, not for a second." He ducked his head, making sure he had her complete attention, that she understood. "Is that clear? You are not to beat yourself up about this, you got that?''

He saw tears well in her eyes, but she nodded anyway.

He stood there for another moment, hands on hips, then said, "Look…if you're okay, I could really use the extra time to get some darkroom work done—''

"Oh! Please, I'm fine as far as that goes!'' she said, shifting the child on her lap. "If you need to get to work, go right ahead. This one needs a bath, and I need to start dinner, and…'' She snatched a breath. "I'm fine, Steven. Really. And I think I can get through the next few hours without losing one of your children.''

Then she smiled, sorta, and it was everything—everything!—he could do not to go over to her and give her a hug. But the hormones were barely in check as it was; the slightest provocation would unleash those suckers, boy, sending them barreling through his bloodstream yelling "Yee-*hah!*'' and getting him into more trouble than a drunken cowboy on Saturday night. So instead, he just smiled back, sorta, and hightailed it down the hall toward the darkroom.

Thank goodness Steven was out of the picture for a little bit, Sophie thought as she wrapped the much-sweeter smelling three-year-old up in a big blue towel, rubbing her until she giggled. She truly didn't think she'd have been able to withstand that look on his face much longer. Not that she really knew what that look had meant, but it was bloody unnerving, that was for sure.

She stood with a grunt, the little one still in her arms, and headed toward the girls' room. Bad enough her heart was still racing from her fright at having thought she'd lost Rosie, but it never would have a chance to get back to normal with Steven around, would it?

She was exhausted, she was muddled, and for a brief spate this afternoon, she'd been frightened out of her wits. So why, she wondered, as she got fresh clothes for Rosie out of her dresser drawer, had she thought this would be such a good idea?

The screen door slammed downstairs; three voices, all talking at once, filled the house. Then, footsteps, pounding up the stairs. A second later, a breathless Courtney appeared in the doorway. Underneath dark, sparse bangs that had been stiffened to resembled a dozen or so wrought-iron curlicues over her forehead, chocolate eyes glittered with a combination of terror and excitement.

"Guess what, Lisa? I got my period!"

Even over his CD player, even in his room clear across the hall, Mac had heard his sister's announcement. A shudder streaked through him, sharp and cold, at the idea that nothin' was stopping them growing up, like normal kids. Didn't matter that Mom and Dad were dead, even though it felt like it should, you know?

It seemed...wrong, somehow, having other grown-ups taking care of them. Not that he didn't like Steve, it wasn't that. Steve was cool. But Steve wasn't family. Taking care of the kids, that was Mac's responsibility. Just like Dad had always said, right? That if anything ever happened to Mom and him, that he was depending on Mac to take charge. Except, the more time passed, the more Mac was beginning to think maybe he wasn't really ready to take care of four kids. Not that he'd ever let anyone know that—no way—but after what had almost happened this afternoon, when he saw that gate open and for a few really scary minutes thought maybe Rosie might've gotten out, could've maybe gotten hurt or somethin', he started to think that maybe he should stop acting all big and bad and stuff and instead just let the grown-ups handle things without him mouthin' off every five seconds like some hotshot know-it-all.

Because he didn't. Know it all. Like now. With Courtney? Hell, what did he know about all that girl stuff? Yeah, he'd been through sex ed same as everybody else, but that didn't mean he *understood* any of it. So at the moment, he was like really, *really* glad Lisa was here. Even if she wasn't goin' to be around for real long.

Trying to swallow past the damn lump in his throat, Mac got on his knees to dig out his math book from his backpack.

Outside the darkroom door, voices shrieked and George barked and various things thumped and banged, which meant the rest of the kids were home. Steve, however, kept his gaze riveted to the developing photo of Rosie snoozing in the girls' laundry basket, poised to pluck it out of the developing solution at just the right moment. Lisa was there, he thought. Lisa would take care of things for another hour or so.

Strange, the way a thought could be both comforting and terrifying at the same time.

He lifted out the eight-by-ten, frowning. But not at the print, which was, if he did say so himself, perfect. Oh, no. The frown was because, when he hadn't been thinking about Lisa—which was bad enough—he'd been mulling over that overheard conversation for most of the afternoon, especially on the long drive out to that new development Galen's husband Del was building on the north side of town. For a while there, he'd been concentrating so hard on what Lisa had said about his having to make his decisions on his own that he realized he'd missed the point, which was—hello?—he needed to be making some decisions, period.

His agent had called this afternoon. Said his royalties for the calendar he'd done the photos for last year looked like they were going to be pretty substantial, that the company wanted him to sign him a five-year contract, which Steve had to admit was damn tempting. And then, she was really after him to let her submit his portfolio to this children's poet who wanted a batch of kid and pet photos as illustrations in his next book. Basically, she said it was time to either commit or forget it.

But even Steve knew his limitations. There was no way he could stay on with his father *and* fulfill the contractual obligations to those publishers Cheryl was talking about.

Damn.

Marty Koleski had worked his butt off to turn Koleski's Electrical into the solid business it was today, a business that had paid for the family home and summer camp and two college educations and his sister's lavish, if doomed, wedding. And Steve knew his father fully expected Steve to take the reins, like passing on the crown to the firstborn. And for a long, long time, family loyalty—and the conviction that anything less would be selfish—had been battling it out with the need to follow his own dream.

Not his father's.

But somehow, listening to Lisa this morning, remembering that haunted look in her eyes as she told him about her marriage offer, he'd finally begun to get it through his thick head that if he didn't make himself happy, God knew nobody else would.

Because sometimes—he thought of Lisa again, wished his brain would stop doing that, already—an idea doesn't necessarily have to make sense to be *right*.

Since the red light was off over the darkroom door, Sophie decided it was safe to knock.

"Unless you're bleeding or the Publishers Clearing House guy is at the front door," the voice said from the other side of the door, "go away."

All right, so she'd been wrong.

"Just wanted to let you know, dinner will be in about ten— oh!" She let out a yelp as the door suddenly swung open. "—minutes."

From around Steven's white T-shirted shoulders billowed the pungent scent of developing chemicals, which not even someone in her advanced state of what she'd begun to peg as sexual frustration would find even remotely arousing. His grin, however—a little shy, a little cocky, and extremely endearing—was something else again.

"*You* may come in," he said, standing aside. "You, I can trust to keep your mitts to yourself."

She had to laugh. When she thought of all the palaces and high-level government buildings to which her position had given her entré, she couldn't recall ever feeling more honored—and more trusted—than Steven's letting her inside this precious, private world of his.

The all-white room was the smallest in the house, the window securely blanketed to prevent any light from seeping in. At the moment, the room was lit by a series of florescent strips tacked here and there, the stark, utilitarian light revealing various pieces of darkroom equipment, trays, shelves of solutions, packages of papers. And hanging like the morning's laundry on a line stretching over the trays, a dozen or so large black-and-white prints, at which she now glanced. And smiled.

"These are wonderful," she said, her hands laced at her back. From somewhere in the house, somebody yelled at somebody else. She tensed for a moment, then relaxed, a little, at the relative silence that followed. "George is remarkably photogenic, isn't he?"

Steve chuckled, and she thought, stupidly, what a wonderful thing it was, being able to make him laugh. "It's his smile," he said, and she laughed back.

And how wonderful it was to be around someone who made *her* laugh.

"You said something about, um, dinner?" he asked.

She turned, tilted her head at him. Realized with a start just how small the room was. "It's okay, Steven. Your mother was here. Gave me instructions to follow that, in her words, not even an idiot could screw up."

Wiping his hands on a towel, Steven let out a sigh. "The diplomatic corps will not be beating on my mother's door anytime soon."

Sophie shrugged. "At least one always knows what she's thinking."

"You, on the other hand," Steve said, his gentle gaze pinned to hers, "are. A diplomat," he finished when her brows lifted, questioning. "But honest, too. In your own quirky way."

She wasn't quite sure how to take that. Let alone what to say. And, not for the first time, guilt reared its ugly little head at her deceit. For there was no other way to describe what she was doing, keeping her identity a secret. True, she'd be gone soon enough, and what would be the harm? Still, it didn't seem right, not telling *this* man the truth. And yet...what choice did she have? She couldn't imagine he'd let her stay, knowing who she really was. This way, even though he knew she was being oblique about her life, at least he thought—she assumed he did, at any rate—she was pretty much like him.

And she intended to keep it that way.

"Speaking of honest," she said, moving on to the next photo, one of Dylan and the chickens (and what nasty, stupid beasts those were!), "Courtney has some news."

"Yeah?" Steve said, cleaning up something or other.

"Mmm, hmm. How shall I put this? She crossed the threshold into womanhood today."

Steve came to a total standstill, staring at her. "She got her *period?*"

His total ingenuousness both amazed and amused her. "This isn't a surprise, surely?"

"I just didn't think...oh, man." He sagged onto a nearby stool, rubbing his jaw. "A*lready?*"

"She is twelve, for goodness' sake. Which means Bree will probably start hers, too, fairly soon."

"I am not ready for this," Steven said, his hands lifted. "I didn't count on having to start toting the shotgun around for at least another two, three years."

Sophie leaned against another stool a few feet away, her arms crossed over her quaking stomach. Pride, vulnerability and protectiveness were a potent cocktail, she realized. "As long as Mac's around, I doubt you have anything to worry about."

Steven chuckled at that, but only halfheartedly. Then he looked up, embarrassment bringing a flush to his cheeks. "I take it, you, um—"

"All taken care of."

"And she's feeling okay?"

"Yes, as far as I know. She's very fortunate, in that respect. I remember being quite miserable."

Concern flickered in those sweet, green eyes. "Do you still—?"

"I apparently outgrew the worst of it," she said quickly, looking away. Silence floated between them for a moment, punctuated by Rosie's high-pitched squeal about something. Then she heard Steven's breath rush from his lungs. "Thank you, Lisa, for being here. From the bottom of my heart, thank you, thank you, *thank* you."

His gratitude was heartfelt, she had no doubt of that. If misplaced.

"I was glad to help. You know that. But if I hadn't been around, your mother would have been only to happy to fill in. Or Mala. Or Mrs. Takeda."

His brows plunged. "Who?"

"The woman the agency's sending? After…" Now, why couldn't she say *after I'm gone?* Curious. "The week after next. She rang today, said she might like to come out sometime next week for an hour or so, meet the children, get a feel for things. See if everybody 'clicked.'" Sophie glanced down at her hands, realized she had them knotted tightly enough to turn the knuckles white. "She seemed very nice on the phone. Good sense of humor, I think. But not at all silly, if you know what I mean. An older woman, I gathered…"

She realized, suddenly, that here she was, prattling on for all she was worth, while Steven simply sat there, staring at her, saying nothing. And the comfort of moments before simply went *poof.*

"I have a good feeling about her," Sophie said anyway. Driving home her point, perhaps. Keeping things…separate. "That she'll be perfect. That she'll care about the children as much as—"

She couldn't go on. Couldn't say "as much as I do." And wasn't that silly, since she hadn't even been there a week?

Her gaze snagged on Steven's.

Speaking of *silly.*

"I'm thinking very seriously of telling my father I quit," he said suddenly. Quietly.

Sophie jerked. "What?"

"I overhead you this morning. When Ma was here. I'd come home for a minute to change my shirt—long story—and heard you two in the kitchen. It was rude of me, I know, but sometimes…'' He slicked a hand over his hair, looked up at her. ''You know, all this time and I never knew Ma might take my side in this. Had no clue she thought anything other than that I should go into business with Pop. It's just that…'' He shrugged.

''That you're still not quite sure this is what you should do?''

Ambivalence shimmered in his eyes. ''There's a lot at stake here. The business is a sure thing, financially. And now that I've got these kids…'' He looked away for a moment, a frown creasing his brow, then back at her, his gaze steady. Intense. Mesmerizing. ''And it kills me to think I might hurt my father, Lisa. My taking over is what he worked for his entire adult life. It's not like I can just go up and give notice, and he's gonna say, okay, fine, have a nice life.''

No, she didn't imagine he would. And she'd never even met the man.

She screwed up her mouth, considering how much to say. How to say it.

''What?'' Steven said.

''It's not my place to try to influence you, Steven—''

''Yeah,'' he said on a soft laugh, ''I heard that part, too.''

''Oh. Well, then take this for what it's worth, all right?'' She sucked in a breath, carefully choosing her words. ''My grandmother has a small…business, too. One that's been in the family for several generations. So I understand your dilemma, believe me. The difference is, though, that in my case, I have no option about whether or not I wish to participate, at least on some level. Otherwise, it will eventually die. Which even I have to admit, would be a shame. You see, this thing I'm a part of…is strictly a family…enterprise, you see, not something that can be sold or passed on to someone else. And family ties are very strong, where I come from.''

''I got news for you, honey. They can be murder here, too.''

''Yes, I know that. But I still think, from what I understand of our two situations, that you have more…options, shall we say. It's not that I don't doubt what you say, that your father would be upset—''

Steven snorted.

''—maybe even very upset, but if he loves you, how could he not support what you really want to do? Would he want you to just waste your talent?''

He looked at her, long and hard, until she felt a shiver race up her spine. Then he said, gently, ''You're very naive, aren't you?''

For all their gentleness, however, the words stung just the same. And made her angry, to boot.

''Just offering an opinion, that's all,'' she said stiffly, getting up off the stool and heading for the door. ''After all, you brought up the subject—''

She gasped when his hands closed around her shoulders, turning her to him. ''That's why you really have to go back, isn't it? Not because of some dumb marriage proposal from some man who you clearly don't care about at all—''

''Well, that's not quite true—''

''—but because of this business?''

Suddenly, she saw something in his eyes she didn't want to see. And doubted Steven either knew was there, or wanted there if he knew. But damned if she was going to ask, was going to bring up a subject neither of them had any right to even be thinking about.

She'd said too much to a man too smart not to begin piecing together the puzzle she'd managed to dump out in front of him. And his grip on her arms, his breath, smelling faintly of butterscotch, she thought incongruously, stirred something so deep, so buried inside her, she couldn't even pinpoint its location.

And again, she felt like that child, her face pressed to the glass window, yearning for that bicycle, even though she knew the price was far out of her reach. Because, while she'd readily admit to being inexperienced about certain things, contrary to what Steven might believe, she wasn't naive. Not by a long shot. She knew, all too well, exactly what the stakes were, what she could and could not allow to happen.

Her home and work were in Carpathia. Her duty lay there. And always would. But, oh, what would it be like to *really* be Lisa Stone, to have the freedom to let all these stirrings and feelings for Steven Koleski take flight?

"Dinner's ready," she said quietly, pulling out of his grasp. "We'd better go."

Chapter 10

Each night since his mother's visit two days ago, dinner had gotten better. Tonight had been baked chicken breasts in mushroom soup, baked potatoes, microwaved peas. Nothing fancy, but more than palatable. From his end of the table, Steven raised his glass of iced tea in a toast. "This is very good, Lisa. Right, guys?"

Most of them mumbled something, but they were eating, so that's what mattered. And, true to form, less than ten minutes after they'd sat down, they all asked to leave.

Steve waved them away— "And that means you, too, mutt," he said to George—then squinted at his dinner companion. Ever since their conversation in the darkroom, she'd been quieter than usual. At least, around him. Brooding about something or other, would be his guess. And this was the first chance he'd had to ask her about it.

"Okay," he said, leaning back in his chair. "You wanna tell me what's bugging you, or you gonna pull a Francine on me and wait for me to guess?"

Her eyes, dark as midnight, shot to his, only to return almost immediately to her plate. She shoved a couple peas around for a second, then said, "I'm not sure I can. Tell you what's 'bugging' me, as you put it."

"Hmm." Steve took a swallow of tea. "Sure it wasn't something I did?"

Again, *zing* went that gaze. And this time, it held. Shakily, but it held. "No, Steven. It's not you."

He leaned back. Decided to be honest. "It bothers me when you're unhappy."

Her brows lifted at that, unfeigned surprise flickering in her eyes. And caution, as if weighing whether or not to say what she was really thinking. "But I'm not unhappy. In fact..." She got up from the table then, began briskly clearing plates. "In fact," she repeated, softly, "I'm happier than I've been in a very long time. So. Are you working in the darkroom this evening?"

He stood as well, scraping Dylan's and Rosie's leavings onto his plate, thinking that women were incredibly bizarre creatures. "I take it that means this conversation is over?"

She glanced over at him, smiling slightly. "If you know what's good for you, yes."

"Speaking of which...I thought I'd go have that talk with Pop tonight."

Her hands clamped around a stack of plates, she froze, staring at him. "Are you...sure?"

Her sincerity streaked right past the fifty million and one reasons why he'd be a fool to think of this woman as anything except someone nuts enough and nice enough to help out for a little while.

"Yeah. I'm sure. You'll be okay with the kids for an hour or so?"

She gave him an "oh, please" expression. Then she said, softly, "Steven?"

"Yeah?"

"Think of me, okay? Do this for...me."

Then she vanished into the kitchen.

Steven hadn't been gone five minutes when Dylan ran into the kitchen, holding up his hand. "I scratched my finger, Lisa!

Kiss it, kiss it!''

So she made a big deal of oohing and aahing over the non-existent injury, her heart cramping when the little boy threw his arms around her neck and gave her a fierce hug before running back out.

She stood for the longest time, staring after him, her hand pressed to her heart. What a bloody fool she'd been, so busy trying to ignore her attraction to Steven that she hadn't even realized she'd left herself wide open to falling in love with his children.

As if she could ignore her attraction to Steven to begin with. *It bothers me,* he'd said, *when you're unhappy.*

He'd meant that. And it had taken every atom of logic she had left in her not to blurt out that he was the first person other than her grandmother or Alek to give a damn about her feelings. To actually care about her.

But she hadn't been lying, either, when she said she was the happiest she'd been in a long time. It was just that knowing the happiness was temporary depressed the hell out of her.

And continuing in this line of thought would surely drive her over the edge. So, on a long sigh, she returned to surveying the battle zone of a kitchen. The children all had chores, certainly—Steven would have had it no other way—but the kitchen, in all its glory, was hers. On another sigh, she plunged the worst of the pans into a pan of soapy water in the sink.

''Lisa?''

She looked up to see Mac standing in the doorway, his hands stuffed in his pockets. ''Come in any further,'' she said, ''and run the risk of being put to work.''

''Oh. Okay. So, like—'' he walked in, looked around ''—whaddya want me to do?''

''Oh, Mac,'' she said on a laugh. ''I was just kidding—''

''Hey, it's not like you're a slave or something,'' he said quietly, starting to stack the dishwasher. ''Least, that's what my mother used to say, *all* the time.''

Sophie's breath caught: the ''dog'' had just taken a step closer to the food. ''Mac?''

He looked up.

"Just so there's no misunderstanding here…are you being *nice* to me?"

That merited this whole guy thing with the shrugs and head shakes. "Yeah, maybe."

"Why?"

He got the soap from underneath the sink, filled the dispenser. "Because I keep hearin' my mother's voice in my head, telling me to stop acting like such a jerk and stuff. And because…I got an apology to make. About the other day, when Rosie disappeared? I'm sorry I went ballistic on you like that."

Sophie went back to scrubbing the baking dish. "It's okay. You had every right—"

"No!" he said, slamming shut the dishwasher door. "I didn't." Then he explained about the gate and how he realized it could just have easily have been his fault and how bad he'd felt, getting so mad at her like that.

"And if…" He stopped, not looking at her, trying to control his shaking lower lip. "All I keep thinking is, what if Rosie had gotten out and something had happened? What if I'd screwed up again?"

"Again?"

"Like I did with my mother," he said, his voice gruff, and Sophie's heart broke.

"Oh, Mac," she said softly. "Do you really blame yourself for what happened to your mother?"

"If I'd gotten there sooner, I could have gotten her out in time—"

"Mac. No." She placed her hands on his shoulders, twisted him around to face her, even though he kept his eyes lowered. In her bare feet, he had at least three inches on her. "Steven told me the doctors said your mother…that there was nothing you could have done."

He just shook his head, his chin quivering.

Sophie stood there, counting her heartbeats, waiting out the rush of panic. What was she supposed to do now?

Stalling, she steered him to the kitchen table, offered him a can of soda, which he accepted. Then she sat at right angles to him, her chin sunk in her hands, and said, "I blamed myself for my parents' deaths, too."

Dark, incredulous eyes bored into hers. "I thought you said your parents died in a plane crash?"

"They did. But I managed to convince myself—for a while, at least—that, oh, I don't know...that I'd been naughty or ungrateful or *something* that somehow caused me to lose my parents."

"That's crazy."

"Is it?" She shrugged. "Life had been remarkably perfect, up to that point. Orderly, predictable. Safe." She watched recognition stir in Mac's eyes. "Suddenly, my world shattered, and I felt as if nothing would ever be right again. How could this have happened? *Why* did this happen?"

Mac took a swallow of soda, began rapidly tapping his heel against the floor. "Yeah," he said after a moment. "Yeah, I guess that's what I thought, too." His shoulders hitched. "Still do."

"And that's normal. Or so I eventually figured out. But what's also normal—which took even longer to figure out—is the human impulse to find a reason for everything, especially when something horrible happens. It's what we humans do, isn't it? Why police look for motives when a crime's been committed, why scientists spend years trying to discover what causes disease..." She tilted her head at the confused young man seated across from her. "Why children assume the blame for their parents' deaths. Because the alternative is admitting that sometimes, things just *happen*. And human beings don't do well with the concept of randomness. It's easier to accept blame, than to accept fate."

Mac stared at her for what seemed like a very long time, then let out a heavy sigh. "Life sucks, in other words."

"Sometimes, yes. But not always. Not if we don't let it beat us."

He frowned. "Whaddya mean?"

She took a deep breath. "What's the one thing all parents want for their children, Mac? For them to be happy, right?"

The frown deepened. "Yeah…"

"So how do you think your Mum and Dad would feel, knowing how miserable you still are?"

His eyes shot open. "I…I…" He ran a hand across his hair. "Man…I never thought of it like that."

"Neither did I, for months. I was so afraid to laugh after my parents died. As if that were wrong. But then I thought of my mother, how very much she loved life, and I realized that my refusal to be happy wasn't honoring her memory at all, was it?"

She got up from the table, took a sponge to the crumb-laden counter. Behind her, she heard the chair scrape against the floor as Mac stood. "You need me to do anything else?" he asked.

"No, thanks." Sophie turned. "I think I've got everything under control."

Mac nodded, then twisted around to leave. Only he stopped, looked back over his shoulder at her. "How come you don't talk to me like I'm a kid?"

She smiled. "How could I? You're taller than I am."

Two, maybe three seconds passed, then, slowly, a smile spread across the boy's face. Then he sort of chuckled—softly—and left.

And Sophie thought she would burst, not having Steven here to tell, right this very minute.

He'd come straight to the point.

So had his father.

"What are you, nuts?" His parents had been out to dinner at Galen's; Steve had caught them, just coming in. Tugging off his tie, Marty kept his dark brown gaze pinned to his son's, his mouth drawn into a tight line. Steve was taller than his father by maybe a couple of inches, but that didn't make the steel-haired, large-boned man any less imposing. "What kind of career is this, takin' pictures? I mean, I guess you're good at it and all—"

"I've been turning down work, Pop. Good commissions. The career is there for the taking. If I take it, that is."

Marty stomped across the room to hang up his tie in the closet, then jerked his shirt out of his pants. "I don't get it. You know this business as good I as do. You're good at it." Bafflement, and hurt, littered his eyes. "You got five kids to support now, I'm handing you a damn gold mine, and you don't *want* it?"

"Pop, I know how much the business means to you. I know *what* it means to you. And I know what I'm walking away from. I also know, if I stayed, twenty years from now I'd find myself financially stable, yeah, but miserable as hell."

With an exasperated sigh, Marty disappeared into the master bath. "All I know," he said over the sound of running water, "is my generation wasn't so, whatdyacallit..." He stood at the doorway, wiping his hands on the end of a towel. "Picky, that's it. We got a job, we were grateful for it, and if it was steady work, we didn't bail just because we got bored—"

"Oh, for the love of Pete!" Steve let out an exasperated sigh. "This has nothing to do with being bored. It's got to do with living my own life. Maybe you don't understand, but you gotta accept that. And it's not like the business really needs me—"

"*I* need you!" his father bellowed, making underused stomach muscles jump. "And I need to know I haven't spent the last twenty-five years of my life building somethin' up for you that's just going to go down the drain!"

"So groom someone else to take over! Joey would be dynamite. Or even Stanley—"

"This business stays in the family, Stevie. It's got our damn *blood* in it!"

Steve's hands shot up, right along with his blood pressure. "Are you even listening to me?" He swore, then said, trying to keep the lid on, "I was hoping to settle this amicably—"

"*Amicably?* What is this? A damn divorce?"

"—but since that clearly isn't going to happen...I'm giving notice, Pop. A month. That should give you plenty of time to get Joey or Stan in shape."

The fire in his father's eyes flared, only to suddenly die. "Hell. You'd already decided, hadn't you?"

"I wasn't asking for your permission, Pop," Steve managed over the knot in his throat. "I'm not going to turn down these jobs. The advance on the book alone would be more than I'd make in a year, working for you."

"So I'll raise your salary! And the whole thing's gonna be yours, you know that—"

"Pop, please…you're not gonna win this one."

Marty dropped onto the bench at the foot of the double bed he and Bev had shared for nearly forty years, one hand braced on his knee, the other forking through his thick hair. Steve thought he saw his father blink back tears, and felt like the biggest jerk on the planet.

"Pop—"

"Get outta here, Stevie," his father had said quietly, then looked up at him. "Now. Before I say something I'm gonna regret."

He nearly broke his hand on the door frame, he banged it so hard on his way out.

A half hour after her watershed conversation with Mac, and with both little ones down for the night, Sophie decided to take advantage of the relative quiet to slip into her room, thinking she might read for a bit.

As in, distract herself from thinking about Steven and his father and why an hour had come and gone and he still wasn't home and how she was worrying overmuch about a man who was, after all, only her employer.

Yeah, right, as Courtney would say.

Frowning, she reread the page she'd already "read" three times, only to realize there was a great deal of high-pitched giggling and whispering going on in the hallway right outside her open door.

"Girls? What's going on out there?"

Long waves bouncing around her face, Courtney stumbled into view, as if she'd been pushed. Her braces glittered in the light from the beside lamp. "Oh, um…you busy?"

Well, Sophie was certainly the popular one tonight, wasn't she? "Not really, no. What's up?"

Now Bree popped her head around the doorjamb, only the two went through this "Well, go on"..."No, you"..."You said you'd ask her"..."I did *not*" routine until Sophie again said "Girls!" loudly enough to make both heads swivel around.

"What?" she asked, hands spread.

Now a plastic makeup kit emerged, twice the size of hers, along with a curling iron. Eyebrows raised in question, Sophie looked from one to the other.

"We, um, just thought, since you've been so nice to us and everything? Well..." Bree tossed an agonized glance in her sister's direction.

"Look...there's just no tactful way to say this, okay?" the second girl said. "But your makeup needs some *serious* work."

"Yeah," Bree said, looking relieved that *somebody* had finally said it.

Fighting the urge to laugh, Sophie again looked from one makeup free face to the other. "But you don't wear makeup. Nor should you," she hastily added. "You're only twelve, after all."

At this, they both rushed into the room, planting themselves on either side of her on the bed. "But we've been practicing since we were like ten or something," Courtney said. "I mean, Uncle Steve is so old-fashioned, he won't let us wear even lipstick or anything until we're fourteen—"

"Even though we told him Mama said we could wear mascara and light lipstick for special occasions, once we turned twelve—"

"Which we did, like, *ages* ago."

"Anyway," Courtney said, slicing the air with her hands for emphasis. "So we practice on each other, sometimes, like when Uncle Steve's not around—"

"And our mom would sometimes let us practice on her, too—"

"Like kind of a treat, you know?"

"Oh," Sophie said, understanding probably far more than even they did. Her heart twisted in sympathy. And empathy.

Steven was a wonderful guardian—her heart twisted even more at that—but there were some areas in which he couldn't substitute. "I see. So…" She twisted, peering at her reflection in the mirror over the dresser. "You think perhaps my makeup is a little—"

"Lisa," Bree said, all seriousness, "don't take this the wrong way, but girls who wear that much makeup at school—"

"—don't, like, have the best reputations, you know?" Courtney finished.

"And you're nothing like that!"

"No, you're not!"

Now she did laugh, at their obvious horror that she'd take their concern the wrong way.

"All right," she said, and they looked at each other. "Well? What are you waiting for?"

With twin squeals of delight, they directed her to go into the bathroom and wash her face, then sat her down in front of the vanity in her bedroom and started in.

"So, like, when did you start wearing makeup?" Bree asked, smoothing something over Sophie's face.

"Hmm…a week ago?"

Now they *really* looked horror-stricken.

"God," Courtney breathed. "No wonder it looks so awful."

And this time, she didn't even apologize.

"Hey—you wear contacts, huh?"

"Mmm, hmm," Sophie said.

"So, like, what color are your eyes for real?"

Oops. "Mmm…not too much different than this, actually."

Which answer seemed to suffice, thank goodness. The girls refused to let her peek until they were done, which was perhaps a half hour after they started. While Bree did her face, Courtney tackled her hair, and all the while they smeared and smudged and curled and—ouch!—plucked, they giggled and talked about boys they thought were "cool" and those they thought were "dorks," and then, finally, about their parents, how they'd told them that once Mac and the girls started get-

ting big, how they'd missed having babies around, so they
decided to have Dylan and Rosie. And about how sad they
both still felt, sometimes, but—

"Mac is like, still so messed up," Bree said.

"Dylan, too."

Bree nodded. "And we didn't want to, y'know, make anybody feel any worse."

"Especially Uncle Steve."

"Right. Especially Uncle Steve." Bree let out a little laugh.
"He already looks at us like he can't figure us out."

"Besides," Courtney said. "We had each other."

"Yeah." Bree brushed something over Sophie's cheekbones. "So we could like talk it all out and stuff."

Sophie smiled. "I thought I'd have my brother. After my
parents died. But he was a bit like Mac, I think. He didn't
want to share his grief."

Courtney told Sophie to cover her eyes so she wouldn't get
hairspray in them. "Did your brother do this big protective
number on you—?"

"Like he was trying to take your father's place or something?"

Sophie thought a moment, then shook her head. "Not like
Mac does with you, no."

"You were like, *so* lucky, then." Bree stood back, squinting
like Michelangelo at her handiwork. "'Cause it's getting *real*
old. Okay?" she looked up at her sister, who nodded, then
back at Sophie. "You can look."

She twisted around, holding her breath, which she let out
in a delighted "Oh!" when she saw the results of the girls'
labor.

"Oh, my...oh, my goodness!" she said, lifting one hand to
touch a cheek softened by a rosy blush. That huge mouth she'd
always loathed suddenly looked...inviting, glistening as it was
with a tawny lipstick not much darker than her skin. And not
even great-uncle Heinrich's schnoz could withstand the soft,
floppy curls framing her face, flirting with her cheekbones.

She reached out, grabbed both girls by the hand and

squeezed. "Thank you, darlings. Thank you so very, very much."

"You really like it?" Courtney asked, still not sure.

"Oh, my yes. You'll have to show me what you did, so I can duplicate it myself, after—"

In the mirror, she saw both girls' smiles fade.

"Will you get mad if we said we wish you'd stay?" Courtney asked.

"Yes," she said. "But only because if you did, I'd cry. And then I'd ruin all your lovely work."

That got a couple little laughs out of the pair and kept things from a rapid descent into maudlin sentimentality.

"Uncle Steve says we're going to Wal-Mart tomorrow," Bree said. "So I can show you what I used, if you want to get your own stuff."

Sophie thought of the two-hundred dollars' worth of designer goo in her own makeup case and stifled a sigh.

The odd chicken or two squawked when Steve drove up in front of the house around eleven. He got out of his truck, slammed shut the door and yelled at the chickens to be quiet, for the love of Mike.

Fighting off that damn lilac bush, he stomped up the porch steps and banged back the screen door, nearing tripping over George who was busy doing his unconditional worship number. At the moment, Steve supposed there was a lot to be said for unconditional worship, if you didn't get it from anybody except your damn dog.

The keys clattered to the floor—twice—when he went to hang them up on the hook by the front door. He tore off his denim jacket, throwing it over the seen-better-days armchair closest to the door, then stood, hands on hips, breathing hard, for what seemed like forever.

Other than a light on in the kitchen, the house was dark. Good. Everyone was asleep, then. He stormed off in that direction, momentarily sorry he'd made that vow not to keep booze in the house because of the kids.

He yanked open the refrigerator: Mountain Dew or Caffeine-Free Pepsi. No contest. Downing half the can of Dew before coming up for air, he then tromped back out into the living room and sank onto the sofa, swearing softly.

"You were gone a long time," he heard from the doorway. He jumped, strained to see Lisa in the darkness. The words were gentle. Not accusatory. Not like Francine's would have been.

"I was driving around for a while. Needed to be alone."

"Oh, dear." She came closer, noiselessly, out of the shadows, her arms folded over her stomach. "That bad?"

He fumbled, a little, getting the soda up to his mouth. After his next swallow, he asked, "You get worried about me?"

"A little. Perhaps," she added, her smile evident in her voice. Even in the gray light, he could see she was wearing a long T-shirt, something light colored, maybe pink? Twin trickles of realization seeped into his brain: that he liked it, that she'd been worried about him, even if only "a little"; and that he doubted she was wearing much, of anything, underneath that shirt.

Then a third trickle, of regret this time, that he wouldn't be crawling into bed with her in a few minutes, just to be close, to feel her kindness and strength in his arms...to let himself float in the sweet, gentle comfort she exuded as naturally as breathing.

"Thought you'd be asleep," he said.

She laughed softly. "I was. Your entrance wasn't exactly silent."

"Oh, hell...I didn't wake the kids, did I?"

"I don't think so, no."

"They give you any trouble while I was gone?"

"No, of course not. Although..." He saw her settle into the armchair, wriggling into the jacket he thrown over the back earlier. To ward off the late night chill, he supposed. But her movements, the idea of her softness inside his clothing, did something to his brain he really didn't need to be dealing with right now. Then she told him about Mac's coming to her, his apology and their conversation afterwards, and her obvious pride and excitement at the breakthrough made him ache to hold her. Just…hold her. And her voice was soothing, that crisp little accent of hers like a balm. And the only thing, he realized, keeping him from putting a fist through something that would in all likelihood hurt him.

"Your turn," she said quietly. "Since I seem to be on call tonight, anyway."

Steve leaned back, wondering if he was really ready to let this woman inside a part of him he'd kept pretty much roped off for some time. Hadn't expected to re-open anytime too soon, either. If ever.

"I don't want to keep you from your sleep—"

"Steven. Talk to me."

"That a command?"

She tucked her feet up underneath her, leaned her head on her hand. "Just part of the service," she said, and he could feel that damned smile of hers clear across the room.

After he'd related the whole sordid story—during which she'd said little—she got up, crossed to him. "Let me see your hand," she said, kneeling in front of him and reaching to turn on the lamp beside the sofa. His other hand shot out, snagged her wrist. Her felt her pulse accelerate under his fingertips, felt his own follow suit.

"My hand's fine," he said through a dry throat. "Just stings a little, is all. Leave the light alone. Please."

Lisa gently twisted out of his grasp, sat back on her heels. Blatantly studied him in the half light, as if trying to figure him out.

As if she cared enough to figure him out.

A wash of moonlight, tender and benevolent, gentled the stark, strong planes of her face. Her hair—which looked less edgy, as well—seemed darker, her eyes lighter. And once again, that half-baked memory nagged at him, only to fade before it came fully into focus.

She smelled of flowers. And baby shampoo.

With just a hint of George thrown in for good measure.

His vulnerability swamped him, stealing his breath and damn near his reason as well. Loneliness and exhaustion and frustration all ganged up on him, taunted him, like a frenzied crowd yelling, "Jump! Jump!", to take a plunge from which there'd be no walking away in one piece.

He wished she'd get up. Go back to her chair. Go back to bed.

Go back to wherever.

"You did the right thing," she said.

He jerked. "What?"

She plopped on the braided rug in front of him, cross-legged, tugging the oversize T-shirt down over her knees. "I'm sure your father wants the best for you. He'll come round, eventually. And even if he didn't, you can't live your life pretending to be someone you're not, Steven."

He couldn't decide whether her comment ticked or amused him. "I wasn't pretending to be an electrician. And I'm pretty damn good at it, too."

"He said, modestly."

"Damn straight," he said, then kicked back the last of the soda.

"In any case—" now she brought her knees up underneath her chin, clamping her arms around them "—that's not exactly what I meant."

"I know what you meant, Lisa." He stood at that, crushing the can in his palm. "But it is too late and I am in no mood to get into some head-cleaning number with you, okay?" He held out one hand to help her to her feet; after a moment, she accepted.

And this time, damned if he didn't feel something like an electric charge pass between them, bright…soft…clear…

Terrifying.

He let go, stepped back as casually as he could manage, slipping his tingling hand into his back pocket. "Well. I suppose I'll see you in the morning."

"Oh, um…all right. Good night, then." She turned, one hand out.

"Lisa?"

His calling her back seemed to throw her off balance for a second. "Yes?"

"Just for the record, I've always known who I was, understood all the stuff that's made me what I am. That didn't mean I didn't have choices to make, but... I'm just an ordinary guy, and I know it. And I have to say, I've basically been pretty happy with that. Like George here." At his name, the dog scrambled to his feet for a scratch. Steve squatted and obliged, then peered up at the suddenly frail-looking woman standing barefoot in his living room wearing nothing more than a thin layer of cotton and a frown. "What you sees is what you gets."

After a moment, she said, "I'm afraid I don't—"

"Don't you think it's kind of odd that you're telling me that I need to be honest with myself when—" He stood, hauling in a breath. "Look, Lisa—or whatever your name is—if there's stuff in your life you don't like, if you don't want to marry this guy, for godssake, go home and deal with it. But what the hell good is it doing you, hiding out here?"

He heard her slight gasp, but her answer came hot on its heels. "It's giving me time to think, for heaven's sake. Surely you don't begrudge me that?"

"The time to sort things out? No." He took one, then another step closer, his thumbs hooked in his pockets, his insides churning at the balled-up expression in her eyes. "But why do you have to pretend to be somebody else? I just don't get it, Lisa. You're one of the most generous women I've ever met." At her widened eyes, he added, "It's true. But what you're doing galls the living daylights out of me. For the love of Mike—it's not like I'd know who you were any more if you told me your name. Or if it'd matter. But it's like I tell the kids—about the only thing I expect of them, is that they tell me the truth, whatever it is. That they be honest with me."

A beat passed. Then: "Please don't back me into a corner, Steven."

He crossed his arms. "Why not? Fair's fair, right? You pushed me into being honest with myself. I'm only returning the favor."

"It's not the same thing."

"Isn't it?"

Silence hovered between them for several seconds before she finally said, "No, it isn't. And I know I have no right to ask you to trust me about this, when I can't do the one thing that *would* gain your trust. But believe me when I say…" She glanced out the window, hugging herself so hard Steve wondered how she was breathing. "I just wish things were different, Steven." She looked at him. "That I could be what you want me to be. That I could do what you have every right to demand. But I can't. And it breaks my heart to know that *because* I can't, you'll always be disappointed in me."

She spun around to leave, whacking her shin on the coffee table.

"Lisa!" Steve got to her in two strides, grabbing her hand. She tried to jerk away; he held fast. "You okay?"

"Yes, I'm fine. Now please let me go—"

"Look—your not being straight with me is one thing. Like I said, I don't like it, and I don't get it. But *disappointed* in you? Where the hell did that come from?"

That frantic pulse beneath his fingers was his only answer. This time, when she pulled away, he let her go, watching her feel her way out of the darkened room.

Shaking like George during a thunderstorm, Sophie dropped onto the edge of her bed, still coddling the complaining shin, grateful she hadn't done herself an even bigger mischief navigating the dark room without either her contacts or her glasses. But when she'd heard Steven thrashing about, she hadn't wanted to take the time to put in the contacts, and wearing her glasses—as in, letting him see her in them—wasn't an option. Which meant, during that whole far-too-cozy scene in the living room, she hadn't been able to see his face all that well.

But then, she hadn't needed to.

How ironic, that she should feel closer to this man than any other she'd ever known when there was this impossibly high wall between them. Except, what Steven didn't understand was that, should she elect to tear down that wall, another would only spring up in its place:

The truth.

Major obstacle, that. Major, major reason why she shouldn't be feeling what she was feeling. But she couldn't help it, couldn't help the yearning to put her arms around this strong, proud man, just to show she cared. Understood. In his own hardheaded way, he was hurting. A don't-touch-me kind of hurt. An I'll-get-through-this-on-my-own kind of hurt. And all she wanted, was to simply be a friend.

S-sex didn't have anything to do with it.

No, really.

Well, maybe just a teensy bit. She was inexperienced. Not brain dead.

And now we come to the crux of it, boys and girls. Of all her muddled thoughts, this one was the muddliest.

Heat raced up her neck, flooded her cheeks. She didn't have to see, or even hear, particularly clearly to know that Steven still wanted her. Even though he was clearly fighting it, if not outright denying it.

But he wanted her honesty more than he wanted her body, she was sure. And without the former, the latter, as far as he was concerned, was off-limits.

Sophie sucked in a breath, sharp and needy: there was nothing more erotic, was there, than a man torn between what he wanted and what he knew he shouldn't have?

She should know.

Heart pounding, Sophie lay back down, irritably yanking the sheet up over her shoulders, taking precious little comfort in knowing that her continued silence about her identity was very possibly all that was preventing somebody jumping somebody else's bones.

Chapter 11

Sunday, Steve had told her, was her day off. Her first order of business, she therefore decided, was catching up on at least a few of the trillion or so hours of sleep she'd missed since taking on this…project.

"You *doodyhead!*"

So much for that. The rooster, she could have got through. The dog barking at the wind, she could have got through. Five children yelling at each other every five minutes, however— and throwing things: what was that all about?—completely annihilated any chance of having a lie-in. Besides, unless her nose was deceiving her, somebody was fixing breakfast. And it wasn't she.

That, and the oh-goody!-let's-*play* sunshine ramming through the slightly crooked miniblinds, finally rousted her from her covers. Such as they were. A week ago, it had been freezing. Yesterday, a heat spell had come from out of nowhere, instantly turning the old house into a bloody oven. Steve apologized, said he'd really meant to get the wiring finished up to accommodate the new central air-conditioning before this, but…

He'd shrugged and she'd sighed.

Well, she'd hardly melt, now would she? What was she? A princess?

She dragged herself from the bed and into the bathroom, plugging in the hair curler as she yawned, just as glad her myopia prevented her from being able to see her reflection. It occurred to her, obliquely, that should she ever marry, perhaps choosing a mate with equally morning-fogged vision might not be such a bad idea.

Ten minutes later, face on, hair done, dressed in a pair of baggy shorts and an absolutely adorable embroidered cotton blouse she'd picked up at this amazing Wal-Mart place—although she'd found it a bit disconcerting trying to keep an eye on Rosie and Dylan in a store only minimally smaller than her entire country—she followed her nose toward the scent of freshly brewed coffee and something cooked on a griddle.

A paper airplane nearly clipped her chin when she entered the kitchen, which was positively rife with children. More than usual, in fact, two of them with bright red hair.

"Morning," Steven said from the stove, Rosie on his hip, spatula in his hand, one of those white T-shirts hugging his torso and disappearing into a pair of low-slung denim shorts.

She called herself smartly to attention and dragged her gaze back up to his face, where she saw that same odd mixture of heat and caution and gentleness and perhaps a little regret that had been there ever since That Evening.

"Good morning," she murmured in return, scuttling across the crowded floor to the coffeepot. By mutual but unspoken consent, they'd gone back to the keeping-out-of-each-other's way routine. Sort of. No more chats in the dark in one's nightie, that sort of thing. Except when they were together, they'd fallen into this truly horrid habit of joking with each other, instead of actually *talking*. Strictly to diffuse the tension, Sophie had assumed at first, both about the unspoken subject of his father—who hadn't yet, as far as she knew, reconciled himself to his son's plans for his life—and about the equally unspoken subject of the snap, crackle and pop between her and Steven. The kids loved the clowning around. Well, all except Mac, who just kept giving them these I-thought-you-were-supposed-to-be-the-grown-ups? looks. A look he had clearly taken great pains to perfect.

In any case, what had happened was that instead of ameliorating the tension, their bantering-from-a-safe distance was only making things worse. From her angle, at least. What was going on in Steve's head—or anywhere else—she couldn't say. But the more she was around him, the more her mouth went dry.

Unlike other sectors of her anatomy.

She was, she decided, turning into a wanton hussy, right before her eyes.

Housecleaning, she'd come to realize, provided one with a lot of time to think. After all, there was little to engage the brain while vacuuming or mopping floors or changing beds. And with her ample opportunity for introspection—not to mention a socially acceptable way to work off sexual frustration—came a gradual understanding of something she would never have thought true about herself, until a few days ago: that her…power, for lack of a better word, to attract a man stemmed from something so basic about her, she couldn't even name it. Instinct, perhaps? Who knew. But it had nothing to do with anything on the surface, not her looks—good or bad—not her position, or lack thereof. Even though Steven knew nothing about her, not really, he was still attracted. Extremely attracted, if the heat in those bright green eyes as they took in her abbreviated outfit that morning meant anything.

Hands shaking, she poured her coffee, scuttled back across the room.

She felt almost drunk. And more than slightly reckless. She felt…

Sexy.

Sexy? *Her?*

Yes. Her. And you know what? She jolly well liked it.

"You've been holding out on me," she finally said to Steven, settling in at the table so Dylan could scramble up onto her lap, *oof*ing a little when an elbow or two landed in places she'd rather they'd not. The little boy, reeking of pancake syrup, lunged across the table to drag his plate in front of them, then wiggled around to wrap his arms around her neck, plant a sticky kiss on her cheek.

"I didn't wet last night," he said with a grin.

"Oh, love—that's *wonderful!*" She reared back enough to smile into the dark brown eyes. "You must be so proud of yourself!"

"I am. Didn't have no bad dreams, neither."

She hugged him back then, perhaps more tightly that she ought, catching Mac's scowl from across the table, accompanied by an odd look she couldn't quite define. Then she caught Steven's look, which was no less odd. And no more easily defined. "I didn't know you cooked," she finally said as he lowered a shrieking Rosie to the floor.

"Uh, no. I make pancakes." He reached over, held up a box. "From a mix." Box smacked back onto the counter. "My sole claim to culinary fame—"

"Uncle Steve, I asked for three pancakes! You gave me four!" This from the female redhead, who, at the moment, was not going to win any civility awards. Steven's niece, Sophie remembered finally. And the boy, who had exactly the opposite complaint, as well as the same new penny hair, his nephew.

"So sue me," Steve answered mildly to Carrie. "Eat what you can."

"But I *said*—"

"Deal with it, honey. And you never eat more than two pancakes, Lucas, so be grateful for the three I gave you—"

"And there's fuzzies in my orange juice!"

"Carrie, I strained the juice myself. No fuzzies, I promise. Whoa, Rosie—" He swooped down just in time to right a bowl of something in the little girl's hands as she made her way across the kitchen, George in tow. "Hang on tight, munchkin, okay? Hey, Dyl—think you might leave some syrup for the rest of the world?"

Air traffic controllers had nothing on this man.

"I'm full," Lucas announced, blue eyes batting owlishly behind little wire-rimmed glasses.

Steve glanced over at his nephew's plate. "You only ate two bites."

The child shrugged, scratching his nose. "C'n I leave the table?"

"*May* I, and I suppose—"

"'S'okay if we go to Heather's house?" Courtney asked, yanking open the dishwasher to put her plate inside.

Steve poured out six circles of pancake batter. "You got all your chores done?"

"Yes!" both twins said in unison.

"Okay, sure. Just be sure to be home before Christmas, okay? Oh, Rosie," he said on a sigh as a thousand Fruit Loops went flying everywhere. Rosie promptly burst into tears as George gleefully moved in to rectify things.

"It's okay, honey," Steven said, shoving the mildly snarling dog away with his knee. "Mac—would you mind getting her some more, then taking everybody outside to start weeding?"

That was met with many groans.

"Hey—you want me to take you guys down to the creek later, you weed now. So…how many pancakes do you want?" Steven asked Sophie over the ensuing melee.

Perhaps there were a few more creases framing his mouth than might be there otherwise, but clearly, this was a man who thrived on chaos. If not insanity.

And what was scary was that Sophie completely understood.

"Oh, you don't have to make anything for me…."

A bemused grin tugging at his lips, Steven glared at her over the sea of heads and limbs flailing about as Mac finally got all the little ones lined up and out the back door.

The relative silence—one could plainly hear kids and dog and chickens and an occasional goat bleat through the open window—was, as they say, deafening.

"How many pancakes would you like?" Steven repeated quietly. "And don't you dare touch the mess on the table. It's your day off."

The tone of his voice brooked no argument.

"Six, I think. And I promise to eat every one of them."

His grin made her insides go all a-quiver.

Steve spent the next few minutes concentrating for all he was worth on making sure Lisa's pancakes didn't get burned.

If only *if* were as easy to make sure *he* didn't.

Ten days ago, if somebody had told him he'd be going through this head trip over a woman he hardly knew, he'd have laughed in their face. Especially as he hadn't planned on letting himself feel this sort of thing for anyone, ever again. But when she walked into the kitchen a little bit ago, snuggling up to Dylan the way she had, he found himself thinking how normal and natural and just plain good it seemed, having her here. You know, like she'd always been around?

And that's when he knew he was in major trouble.

He flipped the pancakes. She'd changed, since he'd first seen her. Like she was still trying to figure out who she was or something. But at least she was down to wearing enough makeup for only one person, not five. And her hair, too, was no longer lethal. In fact, it even bounced when she moved.

He'd heard her singing, a couple times when she thought he couldn't hear her. God, her voice was terrible. But that wasn't the point. The point was, since she'd arrived, she'd relaxed enough *to* sing, which made him feel pretty good, if you want to know the truth.

Even if things were wound just as tight—tighter—between them as ever.

His mind refused to wrap itself around the idea of her as his *housekeeper*.

And never mind what his body was doing.

Forget the physical attraction—well, okay, it wasn't like he could actually *forget* it, let's not get carried away here—this went way beyond reacting to little specks of salacious-driven matter. He was falling—oh, *hell*—for *her*. Even though it made no sense, even though his head kept hammering away at all the reasons why this was like the dumbest thing he could be doing, should be doing, even though he still didn't know who the blazes she really was, the thought of this woman leaving in a week, that he'd probably never see her again, was seriously making him crazy.

But why? Was it her pluckiness in taking on this job to begin with? The odd combination of insight and innocence that made second-guessing her impossible? Her natural affinity for the children?

All of the above, he supposed. And something else he couldn't define.

And it was the something else that had him seriously worried.

He handed her pancakes to her; she smiled, said thanks. "So what's with the extras?" she asked.

"Excuse me?"

"Your niece and nephew?"

"Oh." *Just…go back to the stove. Don't sit down…don't—* He yanked back a chair, dropped into it. Tried, with absolutely no success, to keep his eyes of her…anything. "My parents and I alternate taking them off Mala's hands every Sunday. To give her a break."

She looked up, a forkful of pancakes poised in front of her mouth. "You've already got five kids of your own, yet you take on hers, too?"

He shrugged. "It's family. You do what you gotta do."

He wasn't sure, but he thought that might be admiration glimmering in those enormous blue eyes. Since nobody but George had ever looked at him like that, he supposed he could live with this. "What happened?" she asked, then stuffed the pancakes into her mouth. Steve dragged his gaze somewhere else. Landed on her neck. Oh, boy. "With Mala's husband?"

"Mala's been a single mother for more than two years now. Her choice." At Lisa's lifted brows, he explained. "My sister might be generous to a fault, but sharing her husband with various and assorted bimbos was not on her list."

"Oh. Yes, I could see where that would be a problem." Lashes lowered, black and thick against her pale skin, she swirled a piece of pancake in a pool of syrup for a moment, then asked, "And your wife?" She looked up. "Or don't you talk about her?"

Steve leaned back in his chair, his wrist propped on the edge of the table. "Perhaps we could make a deal."

"Oh?"

"Yeah. My life story for your real name."

She stilled for a moment, then pushed herself up from the table, carrying her dish to the counter. No surprise there.

"I can't tell you that," she said softly, not facing him. "But I do have a grandmother, and a brother, my parents really did die in a plane crash when I was ten, a man really did ask me to marry him, and I really don't know how to drive a car. And I'll tell you something else that's the whole truth and nothing but." She turned, tears shimmering in her eyes. "Do you remember the other night, when I told you I was the happiest I've been in a long time?"

He nodded.

"Well, that was true, too. But what I didn't say was that I've never been so miserable, either, as I have been since coming here."

He got up, slowly. Moved toward her, even more slowly. Speared her gaze with his and hung on for dear life. Knew he was being a fool, didn't really give a damn anymore.

"Why have you been so happy?"

She linked her arms across her middle, shrugged. "Oh…" She drew out the word, then tried a smile. "In no particular order…Rosie's hugs. The twins' giggles. Learning to cook. Knowing when I look at a clean bathroom, it's clean because of my own efforts." She looked away, and the smile dimmed. "The sound of your truck pulling into the driveway at dinnertime." His heart stuttered as she faced him again. "Seeing you walk through the front door every night."

Steve swallowed. "And what's made you so miserable?"

"The same things."

His heart pounding, Steve lifted a hand to her cheek, expelling a harsh sigh when she leaned into his palm.

"You got any idea how much I want to kiss you right—?"

Ka-*blam!* her mouth was plastered to his, her arms entwined around his waist.

Now, this wasn't exactly something he wanted broadcast

about, but her move had so thrown him that it was a good
second or two before he started kissing back. God knew how
long it was going to take before she came to her senses, so he
figured he'd better damn well take advantage of her moment
of weakness for as long as it lasted.

Which turned out to be a lot longer than he'd at first guessed
it would be.

This was one of those kisses meant to be remembered for
the next decade or so, one of those slow, deep, almost messy
numbers that could light up towns in another state. He hadn't
known she could kiss like that. Hell, he hadn't known *he* could
kiss like that. And he'd done some serious lip-locking in his
time.

Her face was soft as cotton against his roughened palms;
her breath, sweet and maple-flavored; her mouth pliant, hot,
demanding. And giving.

So very giving.

He wasn't sure what she was after, if anything, but damned
if he wasn't willing to sacrifice just about anything to give it
to her. Including what little was left of his sanity.

She pulled away with a soft cry, clasping her hands on top
of his, still bracketing her jaw, her almost savage expression
setting off a scalp-singeing, blood-boiling, God-am-I-gonna-
live-through-this? blaze of desire like nothing he'd ever known
before.

Maybe, for whatever reason, she couldn't tell him who she
was, but damned if that was going to stop her from showing
him what she *felt.* And that meant everything she was feeling.
Not just the longing, but the shock and confusion and terrifying joy of a woman in the process of, he surmised, discov-
ering a thing or two about herself.

He kissed her again, damn near shaking with restraint, realizing as she opened to him she was the most honest woman
he'd ever met.

Sophie braced her hands on his chest, reveling in his solid-
ity, the way his heartbeat pounded against her fingertips. She
was playing with fire, playing the fool, knowing all too well

that a few kisses weren't about to quench the need shredding her control. He smelled, felt so delicious. So real. So everything she'd ever dreamed of, even if she hadn't known that's what she'd been doing. If only she could somehow crawl inside him, came the irrational, immature thought. If only she could somehow make this—*him*—her reality.

She broke away a second time, nestling against his chest, rubbing her cheek against the softness of his T-shirt. "I'm afraid I'm not very good at this," she whispered, smiling when she felt his chuckle in her hair.

"Says who?" he said, hooking his knuckle underneath her chin and once again bringing his mouth down on hers. A sweet, achy longing stirred and stretched luxuriously inside her as the kiss lengthened and deepened and drugged the lonely little princess into believing in fairy tales.

She began to tremble, from need, from fear, from the anguish of impossible situations. Steven released her just enough to brush soft lips against her forehead. "Honey...don't look now, but I think we have a problem."

"You think?" she said, echoing one of Courtney's favorite expressions. She extricated one of her hands, skimming her fingers along Steven's morning-smooth jaw, marveling that she'd nearly completed her third decade on this planet without having simply touched a man's face. Still shaking, she let her fingers trace every angle and contour, awed at the sensation swirling thickly through her, just from the rasp of male skin against fingertips. How easy it would be to fall in love with this man—

As if burned, she yanked away her hand.

Steven had been, if not exactly betrayed, certainly hurt by his wife's walking out on him, not all that long ago. For Sophie to let him think...to use him to stoke her own pitiful ego...

Her common sense might be crumbling to pieces at her feet, but damned if she was going to let the same thing happen to her integrity.

Agony as brutal as any she'd ever experienced tore through her as she slipped from his embrace, walked back to the table to start clearing away. Her lungs felt stiff, brittle, as though they would crack if she took too deep a breath.

"I told you," he said behind her. "Don't do that."

"Please, Steven," she said quietly. "It gives me something to do. At least…" Her eyes burned. "At least this is honest."

She gasped when his hands gripped her shoulders, pulling her around. "The kisses weren't honest?" he asked quietly.

That, she couldn't lie about. "What do you think?"

He stroked the pad of his thumb over her bottom lip, sending a shudder straight through her. "Yeah," he said, his breath fanning her cheek. "That's what I figured, too."

"I'm sorry," she said, her eyes stinging.

His brows dipped. "For?"

"For sending mixed signals like this."

"'S'okay," he said at last, then turned and walked back to the sink. "So," he said, yanking open the dishwasher to begin stacking plates, "you up for going down to the creek later with me and the kids?"

The hard edge to his words nearly broke her heart. "Are we pretending, Steven?"

He twisted around, incredulity straining his features. "Are *we* pretending? This from the woman who won't even tell me her damn *name?*" He rammed the last plate in the rack, slammed shut the dishwasher door.

"I never meant to hurt you—"

His back to her, he sliced the air with an open hand. "You haven't *hurt* me, okay? A couple kisses aren't going to alter my view of the universe, for the love of Mike. It's more that…" He swiped his palm across his jaw, then turned, squinting at her. "You're confusing the hell out of me, Lisa. But here's the crazy thing…I know you're not doing this on purpose. You may be stubborn as hell, but you're not a tease. Or a manipulator." His tone softened, as did the expression in his eyes. "I know you're just as mixed up as I am."

She didn't think she could bear the tenderness, the understanding, one more second, even as she knew she'd cherish the feeling for the rest of her life. "So…" Her eyes lowered, she traced the outline of a rose on the vinyl cloth with one fingernail. "What do we do now?"

"We go down to the creek and forget about everything for a couple hours."

She looked up. "And when we get back?"

He blew out a long hiss of air, then shrugged. "Dunno. Maybe something will start making sense by then." One side of his mouth pulled into a half grin. "Or, if we're lucky, one of us will do something really stupid and the other one will get hit with a strong dose of reality."

"One can hope," she said, smiling back.

"Yeah," he said, hooking her gaze in his. "One can."

The soft, just-turned dirt warmed Mac's knees through the threadbare denim of his jeans. In some ways, he really was beginning to feel better. Even though it still felt weird. He just kept thinking about what Lisa said, though, about how his folks wouldn't want him to be unhappy…well, he guessed she had a point. But it was still weird, that's all he had to say.

Except now other things were bothering him. Like how it just seemed so stupid, that here somebody'd finally come along who was so nice and stuff, but she wasn't going to stay.

He looked up at Dylan's approach, managing a grin for his baby brother who held his hands behind his back, teasing. Mac held out his hand.

"You get it?"

"No," Dyl said, giggling as he shook his head, his long, dark bangs swishing across his forehead.

It was good to hear the kid laugh again. Almost made things seem, y'know, normal and stuff. He'd sent Dyl up onto the back porch to get a trowel—somebody had left it up there instead of in the shed where it belonged—a couple minutes ago. Getting the kid to give it up, however, wasn't gonna be easy.

"C'mon, Dyl—gimme the trowel."

"What's the magic word?"

Mac batted away the twinge of sadness, hearing Mom's words coming out of his little brother's mouth. He glanced over at Carrie, Lucas and Rosie who were busy throwing limp weeds at each other at the other end of the garden, close enough for him to keep an eye on, far enough away not to bug him. Kids didn't help worth squat, but at least they were out of his hair for a few minutes.

Breathing in the scent of freshly turned earth, Mac surveyed the kinda large plot, which Steve had rototilled just last week, thinking that, right at this moment? he could almost believe maybe he'd stop hurting, eventually. Steve and him had done this whole plan for the garden, where to plant what, getting all kinds of pamphlets and stuff from the country extention service. Not that Mac cared all that much for vegetables, but he thought he could maybe get into eating ones he'd grown himself. Radishes and broccoli and lettuces and three kinds of squash and a whole bunch of other stuff…they'd started the baby plants from seed a couple months ago, and now they were big enough to put into the ground.

But he needed a trowel for that.

"Dylan…" When the kid shook his head, Mac sighed. "Please?"

Smack, went the trowel into Mac's outstretched hand.

Dylan squatted beside him, scabbed knees poking out of the hems of his shorts. "C'n I help?"

"Sure. Hand me that purple pot over there."

"What's this say?"

Mac pointed to the letters on the Popsicle stick in the dirt. "Pepper. See?"

"Pepper," Dylan repeated, then asked, "How come boys and girls kiss?"

Mac shot his little brother a glance, then said carefully, "I dunno. I guess because they like each other, you know?"

"But it is okay? I mean, it's not wrong or nothin', is it?"

Where the hell was this coming from? Mac shrugged. "Depends. Most times, yeah, it's okay. Long as both of them want to, I guess. Why?" He grinned, but his stomach felt funny. "Somebody at school try to kiss you?"

Brows knotted in a serious little scowl, Dylan shook his

head. "Uh-uh. But when I went up on the porch to get the trowel, I saw Lisa 'n' Uncle Steve kissing in the kitchen."

A feeling like a hot knife ripped through Mac. "Yeah?" he said, trying to sound calm. Like it wasn't any big deal or nothin'.

"Yeah. Was that okay?"

"They're grown-ups, Dyl." He jabbed the trowel into the dirt, wondering why his eyes were burning. "If they want to kiss, they can."

"You think this means they like each other? 'Cause if they like each other, maybe Lisa will stay. And then we wouldn't have to get somebody else to come take care of us—"

"Forget about it, Dyl." Mac yanked out the tiny plant, stuck it into the ground. He'd watched his mother, plenty of times, when she'd plant little flowers in the window boxes in their apartment. She'd had plans, too, for the new house.

Next spring, Evan, she'd say. *Next spring, you and I are going to turn this yard into Eden, aren't we…?*

Something choked him, made it hard to breathe, to get his words out. "I don't know why they were kissing, okay? But Lisa ain't staying, so you might as well stop thinkin' along those lines. I heard her say, lots of times, how she's got all this stuff to take care of back where she lives. She's just helping Uncle Steve out. That's it. Hand me that next pot, wouldja? Please?" he added, beating Dylan to the punch.

"Mac?"

"What?"

"Why don't you like Lisa?"

The question startled him. "Who said I don't like her? I mean…she's okay, I guess."

"Then don't you *want* her to stay?"

He twisted his head to frown at his brother, ignoring his churning stomach. "Look, Dylan—it doesn't matter what any of us wants, okay? Ever. You got to understand that." Mac heard his voice begin to rise, but it got away from him like a kite snatched by the wind. "Stuff happens, whether we like it or not. Stuff we can't control. Stuff that hurts. So you might as well get used to it, bro, because *that's just the way life is!*"

A foot away, Dylan's eyes brimmed with tears. "Oh, cripes, Dyl," Mac grabbed the little boy, hugging him close. "I didn't mean to yell, I swear. I'm sorry, okay? Stop cryin', buddy… it's okay…it's okay…"

After a moment, Dylan wiped his eyes and sat back on his heels, poking at the soil with Mac's abandoned trowel. "Mac?"

"Yeah?"

"I didn't know you was scared, too."

Mac looked away, making sure the other kids were okay. "Everybody's scared of somethin', Dyl."

"Even big boys, huh?"

"Whatever." Mac wiped his sleeve across his eyes. "Now would you stop acting like a little wuss and hand me that watering can?"

After that scene in the kitchen, the last thing Sophie felt like doing was plastering a smile to her red face and going down to the creek. But there was no getting out of it, at least not without upsetting the children, so down to the creek she went, through a field of wildflowers and butterflies, clutching a half-dozen worn beach towels to her chest and doing her level best not to look at or listen to Steven. Which was tantamount to trying not to blink.

The twins were still at their friend's house, and Mac—his characteristic glower now gone downright surly—had opted to continue working on the garden. So four shiny heads now bobbed ahead of them, two dark and sleek, two fire-red and bristly.

"Hey! Guys!" Steven yelled. "Slow down! Creek's not going anywhere!"

The children, of course, didn't pay the least bit of attention, which left Steven and her alone for the rest of the walk, which they accomplished in a sort of staticky silence. However, at the edge of the woods, Steven suddenly said, "By the way, I wasn't quite being truthful about something this morning."

Her gaze shot to his, just long enough to get singed. "Oh? About what?"

"Those kisses. Actually, they altered my view of the universe quite a bit."

Another stretch of charged silence followed, peppered with birdsong and the gentle susurration of wind-tossed pines. "Oh," was all she could come up with, even after several seconds, and that was probably more due to her stumbling over a root than anything else.

Steven caught her—naturally—holding on at least a half minute longer than necessary.

Naturally.

The children's shrieks of laughter nearly drowned out the burbling creek, which was obviously very close by now. "This isn't a good idea," she said.

"What?"

"What you're doing."

"And what is that?"

"He said, skimming his fingers along her rib cage."

Steve laughed. Then he let go.

But only physically.

"Later," he reminded her. "We'll sort it all out later. Right now, let's just enjoy the afternoon, okay?"

Easier said than done. But after a moment, she nodded, and they continued their walk. Suddenly, the pines gave way to willows as the small, noisy creek popped into view. Sunlight lanced the green-gold, silkily humid air, making the erosion-slick rocks jutting out of the gently churning water sparkle like gemstones.

"Oh...it's beautiful," she whispered.

"It's why I bought the place," he said, spreading out a tablecloth in a shady spot nestled between a pair of rough, gray roots the size of elephant legs. "Well, that, and the house itself." He plopped down on the ground with a soft grunt, digging out a camera from the depths of his multipocketed camera bag. He seemed so...relaxed. Nonchalant. As if he hadn't just said what he had.

"You like it?" he suddenly said, startling her. "The house?"

"I take it you want an honest answer?"

He suddenly seemed very intent on checking aperture settings and the like. "Sure. Knock yourself out."

She walked away, rubbing her arms as she watched the children cavorting in the water a few feet away. "It feels like home," she said, unsuccessfully quelling a surge of melancholy. The crunch of twigs and dead leaves behind her told her of Steven's approach; she flinched, both dreading and praying for his touch. Only he kept going, down to the water's edge, snapping pictures every few seconds. He seemed to be concentrating on Carrie, whose bright red curls blazed in the thick, apricot sunlight.

"I take it those are in color?"

He turned, grinning. "That red hair among all the green should be something, huh?"

She only nodded.

"When I'm done this roll—" Click. Click, click. "—we can go in, too."

Her head whipped to him. "Oh, no, I don't think—"

"You can go in on your own—" click...click... "—or I can throw you in." He looked over, the very devil in his grin. "Up to you."

And her heart just fell in two, right then and there. How, how was she going to be able to leave this man?

To leave any of this?

Sophie turned her gaze back to the water so he wouldn't see her blink back tears. "And here I thought you were a *nice* man."

He stopped clicking long enough to toss her a glance. "Whatever gave you that idea?" he said, and the funniest little chill ran right down her spine.

An hour's hard play in the water, combined with the sultry air, soon knocked all four kids out. And while they napped, dry and warm like a clutch of wood sprites in the dappled sunlight, Lisa and he sat on towels underneath the shivering willow, a good body's length apart from each other, munching Cheetos, avoiding eye contact, and talking quietly about stuff. Kid stuff. House stuff.

Safe stuff.

The better part of an hour had passed before he realized he'd been doing the lion's share of the talking. And how weird was that? He'd never met a woman who could get through an entire hour of conversation without talking about herself for at least fifty-three minutes of it.

Okay...so how many positives were we up to, here? She liked kids. She liked dogs. She was a good listener. She was a good kisser.

A damn good kisser, he thought, stuffing another Cheeto into his mouth.

And she blushed whenever she caught him looking at her.

And the negatives? Well...other than the minor point that he was clearly setting himself up for a serious fall, none that he could see.

Suddenly, the Cheetos weren't sitting too well.

Lisa leaned back against the tree trunk; a sliver of light winked through the trees, illuminating her face. Steve leaned over, grabbed his camera.

She went absolutely white, quickly covering her face with her hands. "Oh, no, you don't." Her fingers parted only enough for her to peer through them. "I absolutely hate to have my picture taken."

That was worth an exasperated sigh.

"Lisa. Lisa—look at me."

"I am," she mumbled from behind her hands.

He reached over, yanked her hands to her lap. "You have, without a doubt, one of the most intriguing faces I've ever seen. But I'm not going to give you some line about how beautiful you are, because you'd know it was bull and then you'd never believe anything else that came out of my mouth."

Her mouth fell open, followed by a startled laugh.

"Huh? Am I right?"

She let out what sounded like a pained sigh, then nodded. "Very. I have, after all, seen my reflection."

"Oh, for the love of Mike..." He raised his hand to graze her jawline with his thumb, watched as her eyes went wide, her breathing shallow. And he stilled, forced his own breathing to stabilize. "Just because you don't look like some preconceived notion of what 'beautiful' is doesn't mean I don't find you attractive. Okay—look over there." He pointed off across the creek. "See those two trees, right next to each other? The one's just about perfect, isn't it? Straight and symmetrical, about as flawless as it could be. The other one, though…"

He glanced over, made sure she was looking. "The other one looks like God wrung it out after a rainstorm, then plunked it back into the ground, just like that. Some people might think it's gnarled, even ugly, but I absolutely love that tree. I could sit and stare at the damn thing for hours and still find something about it I missed before. The other tree…" He shrugged. "Once you've seen it, you've seen it. Yes, it's pretty, but it's ordinary. Boring. You see what I'm saying?"

"That my face reminds you of an old, gnarled tree?"

"Dammit, Lisa, that's not what I meant—"

Her laughter cut him off. "It's okay…I know what you meant. And thank you."

"You're welcome," he said, trying not to think of how much—how very, very much—he wanted to kiss her again. How much he loved hearing her laugh. "But that's not the point. The point is, when I look at you, I see goodness. Generosity. Hell—you're the most genuine person I've ever met. *That's* what I see when I look at you. *That's* what I want to photograph."

She looked away, her brow puckered. "How can you say that when—"

"I didn't say it made sense, honey." Underneath the frown, her eyes shifted to meet his. "Let me take your picture. Let me show you what I see. Let me…" He shifted his gaze before he drowned in those incredible blue eyes. "Let me take your picture so the kids will have something to remember, okay?"

Their gazes locked, for several very scary seconds, the tension shattered by Lucas's sleepy, "Uncle Steve?"

They looked over to see a quartet of yawning children, Lucas and Rosie stumbling in their direction like a pair of pups.

"I'm hungry," Lucas said, twisting around and plopping into his lap, his hair looking like a wheatfield at sunset.

"Oh, you are, huh?" Steve said, sending the child into gales of laughter by tickling him. "Then I guess we have to go back."

Then he glanced over to catch Lisa's attention fixed on his hands. When she realized she was being watched, her gaze darted to his, and a deep flush swept up her neck.

It took everything he had in him not to laugh.

But you know what? Wanting Lisa Stone—and yes, he wanted her, more than ever—and pressuring her were two different things. He'd never crowded a woman before, and damned if he was going to start now. Her reticence wasn't unreasonable. There were valid, substantial reasons why they shouldn't even have kissed, let alone even begin to contemplate anything more.

Criminy—he was having a hard enough time dealing with the idea of not having Lisa in his *house* again. How dumb would it be to let her anywhere near his *bed?*

Chapter 12

A little later, Steve was in the kitchen making peanut butter sandwiches to feed the hungry hordes when he heard a strange, and extremely rude, noise from the living room, intertwined with gales of laughter and George's frantic barking.

"Do it again, Lisa!" he heard some small person or other beg.

Silence. Then, again, that rude noise, this time accompanied by squeals of delight and more laughter and more barking. So, curiosity being what it is, he peered out the kitchen door to see Lisa huffing and puffing as she blew up a balloon—now, who had had that?—then letting it go so that it took off in an erratic, noisy journey around the room, the idiot dog going nuts trying to catch it. By this time, all five were breathless and red-faced from laughing so hard.

You know, if she didn't want him to like her so much, maybe she should stop doing stuff like that.

Turning away from the scene before he made himself crazy—crazier—he finished up the sandwiches, then carried them out to the living room. Everyone had collapsed on the sofa in a panting heap, all the kids looking happier than he'd seen them look in a long time. Dylan and Rosie, bless them, each took half a sandwich, no problem. And said thank you, no less. His dear, darling, high-maintenance niece and nephew, however, had a sudden—and unfortunately all-too-common—picky fit.

"I don't want peanut butter," Lucas announced, never mind that he'd just asked for it five minutes before. "Do you gots any cheese?"

"No, I don't *have* any cheese—"

Behind the wire-frames, blue eyes immediately went liquid. "But peanut butter makes me choke!"

Dylan, who'd long since learned the wisdom of leaving the scene of a scene, wandered back outside to presumably see what Mac was up to in the garden. And Rosie picked that moment to drag Lisa away to go potty. Leaving Steve with two very strong arguments for birth control. Not that he didn't love Mala's spawn, most of the time, but he'd take his five over these two, any day. Carrie, who had actually taken her sandwich, had duly inspected it, frowned at it, then stepped up to the Complaints desk, declaring the bread was hard.

"I just took it out of the bag, Miss Princess. From a loaf I bought yesterday. It couldn't possibly have gone stale in thirty seconds."

One prissy little finger, daintily edged in pink, poked again at the bread. With a royal toss of those auburn curls, she handed it back to Steve. "Yuck."

Nope. Not buying this little number, not today. Steve straightened up to his full height, the plate of sandwiches held aloft. "Okay, here's the deal, guys. Either you eat the sandwiches, or go hungry. This isn't a restaurant."

"You *have* to feed us," Carrie declared, crossing her arms over her chest and doing that pout thing she did. "Mama said. And if you don't, I'll tell."

Lucas stared at his sister for a moment, clearly judging the merit in this argument, then crossed his arms, too. "Yeah. You gots to feed us."

Steve glanced at the quivering dog, who was licking his chops and whimpering and doing everything in his power to convince Steve *he* had no problem with hard bread, never had, never will, send it on *down*.

One eyebrow raised, he glanced at the kids. "Last chance."

Carrie shrugged. Lucas eyed his sister, not sure, then shrugged, too.

Steve tipped the plate. George got the first two pieces before they even hit the floor.

Both kids screamed.

"You *stupid!*" Lucas bellowed at his sister. "Now look what you did!" *Wham*, went the balled up fist, right in Carrie's arm.

No shrinking violet she, Carrie slugged him back. Which made it Lucas's turn again. The dog, the offending food efficiently dispatched, jumped from one to the other, barking his fool head off, unable to decide whose side he was on.

Dylan wandered back in to see what was going on. The twins, apparently returned, came in from the kitchen, took one look and headed up the stairs.

And Lisa was nowhere in sight.

"Lucas! Carrie! We do not fight— Hey, cut it out! Lu-cas! *Ow!*" Rubbing his thigh, which had inadvertently taken a lob intended for his nephew, Steve grabbed the flailing Carrie and more or less shoved her down onto the sofa. "Caroline Vanessa Sedgewick, sit down and act like a lady—" that got a priceless look "—and for the love of Mike, George, *shut up!*"

"Mama says it's not nice to say shut up," Carrie said.

Dimly, Steven heard a car door slam, the sound distracting him just long enough from the banshees howling at his knees for Carrie to get in another punch. The front door popped open as Lucas let loose with a wail that could probably send folks for their tornado cellars.

"Well, for heaven's sake!" his mother said. A blur of light blue polyester made a beeline for Carrie, who'd burst into prize-winning crocodile tears the instant she saw her grandmother. "What on earth is going on in here?"

Steve shot Carrie a look he hoped she'd remember to her grave as she fell, sobbing prettily, into her grandmother's arms, the better position from which to relate the horrors that had befallen her under mean old Uncle Steven's neglectful care. Which, unfortunately for her, she had to share with an equally hysterical Lucas, since if it was one thing he could say for his mother, it was that she spoiled all her grandchildren, blood or ipso facto, equally.

Someone paused to take a breath; Steve jumped in with, "So, Ma—what are you doing here?"

"Oh—" quick, dead-giveaway smile over the top of Carrie's curls "—we just thought, you know, it had been a while since we'd seen the kids and all. And since we knew Carrie and Lucas would be here, too—"

We?

Dread suddenly burned through Steve's stomach like a slug of bad booze.

"Ma."

Now seated on the sofa, Bev pulled Lucas into her lap, looking everywhere but at Steve. "Okay, okay. I thought you and your father should talk."

Ah. "And what did you do with him?"

"I didn't *do* anything with him. He's out in the car."

On a heavy sigh, Steve crossed to the window, glanced out at the fifteen-year-old Grand Marquis he was beginning to think his father was going to ask to be buried in. Pop sat inside, arms crossed over his chest, face folded into a glower fierce enough to wilt plants.

Steve tilted his head back toward his mother.

"Well, I—" Mouth open, she looked down at the children, who had suddenly gone stone silent, their beady little eyes darting back and forth like fireflies between Steve and her. "Hey, kids—go on out and get Pop-Pop, huh? *Now,*" she added, swatting Carrie on the rump.

They clumped out—reluctantly—giving them twenty, thirty seconds tops.

Steve skimmed a palm over his hair, watching as the kids, who'd collected Dylan along the way, tried to pry his father out of the car. "Hate to tell you this, but I don't think Pop's exactly going along with your scheme."

"Honestly, Steven—" He jumped when she suddenly appeared at his side. "Between you and your father, you're gonna take five years off my life. Took me three days as it was to finally worm out of Marty what was bugging him." She smacked him in the arm. "And what's up with not bothering to tell me what you were doing, huh? I could've paved the way—"

"I don't need my mommy to fight my battles for me, Ma."

"You got a smart mouth, Steven Michael Koleski, you know that?"

"Hey—I learned from the best."

That actually shut her up for a second or two. But, as he fully expected, she recovered quickly. "Well, I got news for you, buddy, whatever you did, it ain't working. And damned if I'm going to just sit by and watch the two of you grow apart over this, like what happened between Frank and Izzy Mellon, you remember that?"

Steve turned to her, steadily met her gaze. "And you don't think this isn't making me sick, working with a man who's not talking to me? Knowing I've hurt him is eating me alive, but I can't—"

"*I can't, I can't, I can't.* That's all I hear, from the both of you." Steve looked down at his mother, his heart twisting when he saw tears shining in her eyes. "Look, I don't give a horse's hiney how you work this out. Or who gives in to who. But, dammit, I want this resolved, today, because I'm not spending one more night with your father so miserable like that. He snores something awful when he's upset—just look at these bags under my eyes. So you two, you just go somewhere and talk this out, you hear me?"

At that moment, Carrie, Lucas and Dylan dragged a grumbling Pop-Pop in through the front door just as Lisa returned with Rosie, who took off shrieking with joy into Nana Bev's arms, the twins came downstairs and even Mac poked his head in to see what was going on.

Five seconds later, his mother and Lisa had cleared everyone out, leaving Steve and his father glaring at each other like a pair of wolves.

* * *

"Did you know Steve's birthday's this comin' Saturday?" Steve's mother asked, finishing up some grilled cheese sandwiches for the twins because she refused to let Sophie anywhere near the stove since it was her day off.

"Oh?" Sophie pulled out a milk carton from the refrigerator. "No, I didn't."

"Nothin' fancy, just family, y'know? At our house. I hope you'll be there?"

The milk sloshed over the rim of one of the plastic cups Sophie was trying to fill. "Oh, um...I'm not sure..." She grabbed a nearby napkin, cleaned up the spill. "I mean, since it's family and all."

Mrs. Koleski snickered. "And you don't think you're one of the family?"

"Well, I...no."

That got a spatula swat in her direction. "Well, you are, far as I'm concerned. So you'll come."

Well, that seemed to settle that, didn't it? Then the older woman said, "You know...you've got one of those faces."

Fortunately, the kitchen was momentarily devoid of small people because said face went very red. "Oh?"

"Yeah. You know—whatever you're feeling, it shows?" She cut the sandwiches in two with the edge of the spatula. "I suppose I'm like that, too. But my point is—" She tromped over to the back door, stuck her head out. "Girls—your sandwiches are ready! And for heaven's sake, Carrie, Lucas—leave the poor chickens *alone!*" She tromped back, looked at Sophie. "What was I saying? Oh, right—that I can tell you're worried about what's goin' on in the other room. Between Steve and Marty."

The girls swooped in, chattering like starlings, thanked Bev for the sandwiches, and swooped right back out, giving Sophie just enough time to realize that one simply did not talk one's way around Bev Koleski.

"Well, of course I'm concerned," she said, nibbling on half a peanut butter sandwich someone had left on the table.

"Uh-uh," Steve's mother said, grabbing the still smoking griddle from the stove to stick it underneath running water in the sink. *"Concerned,"* she said over the sizzle, "is what you feel when you hear about some earthquake on the other side of the world. Yeah, you feel bad, but it don't affect you personally. What I see on your face is *worried*, hon. Like you care."

Sophie folded her arms across her chest, sternly instructed her facial muscles to keep still. "Well, of course I care…"

"But it's too early to tell, if something might blossom between the two of you?"

Under other circumstances—though what those might be, she had no idea—she might have laughed. "A few days ago, you said you'd be 'ticked off' if you thought I was after Steven—"

"That was a few days ago."

"Mrs. Koleski—" Sophie leaned forward, her palms flat against the table top "—a week from tomorrow, I'm going home, as I'd planned all along, and there's nothing anyone can do to change that. And besides—" she straightened up, crossed her arms again "—how can you possibly even consider me as suitable for your son when you haven't the foggiest idea who I really am?"

Bev pursed her lips again, then crossed to stand at the other end of the table. A face-off. "Y'know, after fifty-nine years, I think I'm a pretty good judge of character, and I don't need to know where you come from or what your real name is to know who you are. That comes from inside. You're a good woman, hon, as good as my own kids." She smiled. "Maybe even better. Secondly, I'm a firm believer in things working out if they're meant to. I could tell you stories that would curl that bleached blond hair of yours, the crazy ways even the most impossible situations can get straightened out. But, frankly, this has nothin' to do with whether *I* think you're suitable for my son. You think I didn't see the look on his face when you come into the room just now?" She angled her head. "Or the look on yours—?"

"Lisa!" Carrie ran in, eyes wide, awkwardly holding a screaming, bleeding Rosie in her arms. "Rosie fell down and hit her lip on something!"

Both women reached for the panicked little girl at the same time; Sophie won, almost overcome by the rush of tenderness that swept through her at the thought of a child she'd come to care about so much being in pain.

"Is she okay?" Carrie said behind them, clearly distraught.

Until that very moment, Sophie wouldn't have thought Carrie had it in her to worry about anybody but herself. "She's going to be fine," Sophie reassured her, then directed her attention to her Rosie.

Her Rosie?

"Oh, now…shuush, baby, it's okay," she whispered, carrying the sobbing child to the counter. She ducked her head to peer at the tear-and-blood-streaked face. "You want your lovey?" she asked as a diversion while she quickly inspected the boo-boo, which, as she suspected, revealed more blood than injury, just a bumped lip, nothing more. Without further prompting, Carrie dashed off to fetch Rosie's quilt from her bed; barely a half minute later, a much calmer little girl, lovey in tow, was happily sucking on a freeze-pop—Steven bought them by the caseload, always kept a couple dozen in the freezer—none the worse for wear. Then, not being a total fool, Lisa dispensed additional freeze-pops to whoever wanted one, which of course included refereeing a minor skirmish over the last red one, and sent them all back outside.

Then she turned and met Mrs. Koleski's appreciative—and worried—gaze. "You're meant to be here, hon," she said.

Sophie didn't have the heart to disabuse the woman of her notion.

Steve stood across from Pop, his thumbs hooked in his pockets, torn between wanting to storm into the kitchen and keep his mother from hooking her claws into Lisa and wishing the Smarts Fairy would smack him with her wand so he'd know what to do about his father.

Who was staring out the window like the Pope was pruning the rose bushes.

"Your mother's something else," Marty said at last, his voice worn down. He folded his arms across his protruding middle. "Got this bug up her butt about us comin' to some sort of understanding."

"She tell you you'd have to sleep in the guest room unless we did?"

A weary sigh. "Yeah." Then, "Don't suppose you've changed your mind?"

"Nope," Steve said softly.

Finally, his father looked at him. His mouth was tight and his brows nearly met, but for the first time, Steve saw neither anger nor pain in his eyes. "That whaddyacallit? The advance? It could really be that big?"

"Yep."

"Huh." One hand came up and rubbed his chin. "And you don't think this is a one-shot deal or nothin'?"

"Well, there aren't any guarantees, if that's what you're asking. But I trust my agent. She's been around for a long time, knows the business. She seems to think things could go very well."

His father nodded, then looked back out the window. "Just so you know, anytime you want, you can come back."

"If I failed, you mean?"

"Oh, for the love of—" On a weary sigh, Marty turned, his hands stuffed in the pockets of his madras shorts. "Now you listen to me, Stevie, and you listen good. Maybe some fathers would do that, but I ain't one of them, you got that? You're a good son, been good to me and your mother all your life. Well, most of it anyway. We won't talk about your senior year of high school. But my point is, maybe I don't understand what it is you feel you gotta do, and maybe I don't even agree with it, but like you said—it's your life. And I got no right to get in your way and tell you how to live it."

Before Steve could recover from this about-face, Marty said, "I ever tell you about when I was courting your mother?"

Steve shook his head.

"Well, my own mother had been gone a cuppla years already, and my father, he wanted more than anything for me to hook up with Amy Belewski down the block. Not that he was totally off base—she was a sweet girl, and quiet, and looked a lot like my mother did when she was younger, y'know? Unfortunately for his plans, within twenty-four hours of meeting your mother, I knew there was no other girl for me.'' He grinned. ''I think she bowled me over, if you wanna know the truth. In any case, no way I was gonna go for Amy Belewski now. Well, that didn't go over so good with your grandfather, let me tell you. And when I said me and your mother was getting married, he blew his stack. Told me, if we went through with it, I was out of a job, that I couldn't ever set foot in the shop again.''

Stunned, Steve sat on the arm of the sofa. ''You're kidding?''

''The truth, so help me God. Anyways, so I go to your mother, tell her if we get married, I have no job. And she says she wants me, job or no job, she don't care. So I realize, it's no contest. I could get another job, but I couldn't get another Beverly Paskowitz. When I tell my father this, he's furious. Tells me to get out, he don't ever want to see me again, that I've betrayed him.''

A wry grin slid across Steve's mouth. ''Hmm. Sounds familiar.''

''None of your lip, Stevie,'' Marty said, but his mouth was twitching, too. ''Except, not a month after we got married, who should show up at our apartment but my father, begging me to come back. And tellin' me, if I loved your mother half as much as he loved mine, enough to buck him the way I did, how could he not respect that? So I'm saying to you, if you feel strongly enough about this photography of yours to buck me, how can I not respect that? And something you said, about waking up one day and realizin' you weren't happy…that really hit home, kid. I don't want that on my head.''

After a moment, Steve got up from the arm of the sofa, walked across the room. He and his father had never been particularly demonstrative with each other, and he didn't figure now was the time to turn the scene into a Hallmark commercial.

A thought which had apparently also occurred to his father,

who now looked around the room, as if seeing the framed photos for the first time. He walked over to the one of Del and Galen in the restaurant that Lisa had admired. ''Not that I know squat about any of this, but you know something? You're good.''

''Thanks, Pop.'' He came up beside him, held out his hand.

After a moment, Marty took it, only to pull him into a bear hug like he hadn't given Steve since he was a little kid. Then he held him back, intensity burning in those dark eyes. ''If somethin' ain't worth puttin' your butt on the line for, what's the point, huh—?''

''So,'' his mother said behind them. ''Is it safe to come out yet?''

Steven turned, ran right smack into Lisa's big, blue eyes.

And felt his butt inch closer to that damned line.

Over the next few days, things between him and Lisa got both better and worse, depending on how you looked at it. He didn't dare touch her—that was sure to send her scurrying away like one of the chickens whenever they caught sight of George—but there were plenty of other things that just kept his heart in knots. Like he'd come downstairs in the mornings to find her already up, coffee made, chattering with Rosie— who clearly thought she was one of the chickens—and Rosie would run into his arms and Lisa would offer him coffee with one of those damn smiles of hers, and Steve would, just for a moment or two, think, *''This is the way it should always be.''*

Or they'd all go bike riding after dinner together, like a real family.

Or she'd finish a sentence he started, which was really freaky since his parents did that but they'd been married a million years already.

Or he'd come home after work and shuffle into the kitchen with a little kid clamped to each leg, and she'd turn around from the stove and laugh and laugh and laugh, and all he could think of was how much he wanted to always make her as happy as she seemed to be right now.

How much he wanted to take her to bed, to make slow,

sweet, mind-drugging love to her, to feel her honesty and generosity flowing around him, through him.

Fact was, he liked Lisa Stone more than he'd ever liked any woman.

And he was falling so deeply in love with her, it hurt.

And the days ticked off, one by one by one, and still, she refused to tell him the truth.

Which was what really hurt.

"Don't forget," Lisa said on Wednesday morning as she fixed the kids' lunches. She seemed more subdued this morning, but she'd passed it off to not sleeping well because of the heat. "Mrs. Takeda is coming this afternoon."

"Four, right?" Steve said, downing the last of his coffee.

She only nodded.

He got up to carry his mug and cereal bowl to the sink, turned to leave. Turned back again. The kids were still all upstairs, except for Rosie who'd already planted herself in front of the Teletubbies out in the living room.

Watching Lisa stiffen with awareness as he approached, Steve crossed the kitchen until he was no more than six inches behind her. Close enough to smell her shampoo, to make a wisp of hair shudder on the back of her neck when he breathed. "Lisa?" he whispered.

Her movements stilled. "What?"

Revealing the depth of his feelings would only make things worse, he knew. But not revealing at least some of them was being dishonest. "I just want you to know how much I appreciate everything you've done. I don't think I've ever seen the kids this happy, not since… Well, they've been doing a lot better, is all. I just wanted you to know that. And to know…"

Aching to touch, to make contact, he lifted one hand toward her shoulder, only to drop it. "And to know I haven't exactly been suffering either."

He saw her hand knot on the counter, wanted to roar in frustration.

But he didn't.

"Thank you for telling me that," she said, the words clipped. Fearful.

"Uh, sure. Well." He turned to leave, just as the older kids came barreling into the room. "Four o'clock, right?"

Now she turned, a bright, unnatural smile plastered to her face. "Yes."

He left before he throttled the living daylights out of her.

Del removed the electrical blueprint from Steve's hands, glanced at it, said, "Uh-huh," and handed him another one. "Might help to look at Model 17's plans when you're standing in Model 18, doncha think?"

Steve frowned at the plans, then swore softly. "Sorry," he said on a sigh. "I suppose I would've figured it out eventually."

"No doubt." Del clapped him on the back, grinning. Except Steve managed to roust himself from his own worries to notice his friend's smile seemed a little worn around the edges. "But spacing out is a dead giveaway, you know."

"For what?"

"You, buddy, are one smitten man."

Furious at feeling his face heat, Steve returned his attention to the plans, having no earthly idea what he was looking at.

"No comment?" Del asked.

"Nope."

"You eat yet?"

"Nope."

"Good. Then you can help me do in this veal parmesan sub the size of the Upper Peninsula Galen gave me." He started out of the framed model, only to pivot back when Steve didn't follow. "What? You don't like veal parmesan?"

Steve sucked in a lungful of sawdust-scented air, then stabbed the space in front of him with the plans. "You know, sometimes the way everybody in this town looks out for each other irritates the hell out of me."

"What are you talking about?"

"Aw, c'mon, Del—when was the last time you asked me to have lunch with you? Who got to you? Mala? *Talk to him,*

Del," he mimicked his sister's higher voice. "*Maybe you can talk some sense into him.*"

Del just stared at him for several seconds, then gave an uncharacteristically subdued half laugh. "And women think they've got the market cornered on paranoia. Cripes, Steve— all I do is ask you to have lunch and suddenly there's this whole conspiracy thing going down. Get over yourself, Koleski. It's not all about you. So you coming or not?"

Del started off again, his work-booted feet resounding against the bare floorboards. This time, Steve followed. Grumpily, but he followed. A light, dusty breeze teased them as they left the house, then trudged in silence across the rutted, as-yet-unlandscaped lot toward Del's trailer. This was a serious hooky-playing day, the high, noontime sun searing uncomfortably through T-shirts and jeans and heavy shoes.

Steve thought again of the wiring he hadn't yet gotten around to fixing in his own house, how hot it was, how valiantly Lisa was putting up with it. Francine would have had a royal hissy fit by now.

"So," Del said. "You got a thing for Lisa or not?"

Steve wiped a beat of sweat off his forehead as they walked. "She's leaving in less than a week, Del."

"Not what I asked."

"I don't go after long shots."

Del glanced at him. "No, of course not. So…how long until you quit?"

Steve wondered about the subject switch, decided to be grateful. "Another couple of weeks. Right after we get these babies done."

Del nodded. "I know how it goes, telling your father you don't want the silver platter he's spent his whole life polishing for you." Del had insisted on scavenging for all his own work when his contracting business was new, even though his father was a hotshot developer.

"Except you ended up taking it anyway."

"On my own terms, at least," Del said amicably as they clomped over a wooden bridge spanning a water main trench. "And only after I'd proven a few things to myself."

They reached the trailer, clanged up the metal steps. Even with all the windows open, it was stuffy inside.

"Man, it's hot for May," Del muttered as he flipped through a handful of "While You Were Out" slips his secretary had left for him, then went into the cramped kitchenette at the back of the trailer, where he pulled out an enormous, butcher-paper-wrapped package from the half-size refrigerator. "Damn," he said, jostling some aluminum cans. "Marylee keeps buying this cheap store-brand junk. What the hell is Dr. Fizz? Oh, hang on—" more rummaging "—yes! Wanna Coke?"

"Yeah. Sure." Steve sank into the folding chair in front of Del's desk, thinking for the thousandth time about Lisa's forlorn expression this morning. At this rate, and as much as the thought made him sick, maybe it was better that she was going away in a few days. He didn't think he could take the torture much longer, that was for damn sure. For a man who liked to keep things simple, life had sure gotten complicated, somewhere along the way.

Del loosened the wrapping on the sandwich, stuck it in the microwave in the kitchenette. Within seconds, the trailer smelled like heaven on earth.

A can of soda and a paper plate landed in front of Steve. Del sat heavily in the rolling chair behind his desk, withdrew an army knife from his back pocket, glanced at the blade, wiped it off with a napkin, then efficiently cut the sub in two. "Gimme your plate." Steve did; half a steaming sandwich thunked into it. Del pushed the plate over to Steve, then raised his Coke in a toast. "Cheers."

For several blissful seconds, nothing could be heard except chomping and slurping, punctuated by an occasional soft groan.

"And to think," Steve finally said, studying what was about to be his last bite, "how many men have to pay for this. And you get it for free, every night."

"Yeah. Guess I'm one lucky sonuvabitch, huh?"

Something in Del's voice brought Steve's head up sharply. His sandwich finished, Del was leaning back in his chair, staring out the window, one hand angled behind his head. All the muscles in his neck and jaw were tight as drums.

"Del?"

The deep brown eyes shifted to look at Steve for a second, then focused again outside. "Galen's pregnant."

Steve's soda thunked to the desk. "How—?"

Del shrugged, then rubbed one eye with the heel of his hand. "Who knows?" The hand slapped onto his thigh. "Somebody screwed up, didn't put the clamp on right…if there's a way for the wrong thing to happen, it's gonna happen to me. Or someone I love."

The bitterness tainting Del's words took Steve by surprise. Yeah, Del had been through a lot—his mother's death when he was young, then his first wife's in childbirth as a result of a heart condition she hadn't told Del about, his daughter's deafness as a possible result of complications from that birth—but Steve had never known anyone more optimistic than Del Farentino. And his marriage to Galen had certainly seemed to be a turning point in his luck. Now, however, his friend simply looked defeated.

"Hey." Steve wadded up a napkin, threw it across the desk. "It's going to be okay."

Del just looked at him. "She could *die,* Steve. She got the tubal in the first place because one of her pregnancies nearly killed her."

"Nobody's going to let her die," Steve said quietly, his insides knotted at the raw fear etched in Del's lean features. "Maybe you should think of this as a miracle instead of a threat."

"Please, Steve," Del said. "No platitudes."

"So whaddya want me to say? You want me to agree with you, that you just got sucker-punched again and that this couldn't possibly, maybe, be a *good* thing? Look at how much you have, for godssake—"

"And look at how many times I'd had it all yanked out from under me! Life isn't a goddamn fairy tale, Steve! There might be happy middles, but I'm seriously beginning to wonder about happy endings. And no matter how much you might want to, you can't always protect the people you love from getting hurt—'' He clamped his jaw shut even as he slowly banged his fist against the desk.

Only Steve's came down harder, driven by a raging frustration he hadn't even realized existed until that moment. "Would you listen to yourself? Cripes, Del, some of us have yet to have one happy marriage. You've had *two*. And you've got a terrific kid, your business is going like gangbusters.... You *are* one lucky sonuvabitch, and I'll be damned if I'm going to let you forget it!''

All Del did was to lower his head into his hands.

"Del—'' Steve leaned forward "—I know you're scared. And I don't blame you. But it's gonna work out. You just gotta trust, y'know?''

On a ragged intake of air, Del looked up, anguish crumpling his features. "But things don't always work out, Steve. No matter how much we *trust*.''

Suddenly galvanized, Steve stood up and grabbed the plans, shaking them in his friend's face. "Then forget about trust— take action! Dammit, Del—this isn't like what happened with Cyndi! Galen's not going to keep anything from you, or do anything to put her life in jeopardy! So you make sure she gets the best care possible, and then you make sure those doctors tell you exactly what her options are! But sitting around and stewing about what might or might not happen is just plain dumb, you know?''

Del's deep brown eyes lifted to his. "And just letting Lisa walk out of your life without a fight *isn't?*''

Oh, several beats passed after than one. Then Steve smacked the plans on the desk, muttered "thanks for lunch'' and walked out.

Chapter 13

Mrs. Takeda was barely as tall as the twins, with a mild voice and a tinkly little laugh that reminded Sophie of a delicate wind chime. But the fiftyish woman conveyed a deep inner strength and serenity that Sophie immediately respected, and knew the children would, too.

It wasn't Mrs. Takeda's fault that Sophie resented the woman with everything she had in her. But then, she would have resented anyone sitting across from her right now in that club chair, in this living room she'd just spent two hours cleaning, being interviewed as the person to replace her.

"The other children will be home soon?" the smiling woman asked.

"Yes. Any minute." She glanced at her watch, a Timex she'd picked up at Wal-Mart, figuring the Cartier her grandmother had given her for her twenty-first birthday would probably raise an eyebrow or two of suspicion. "And Mr. Koleski should have been here by now—"

The house shuddered from the back door opening, shuddered again when it closed.

"And there he is."

She stood, only to nearly topple over when Steven strode to her, put his hand at the back of her waist and kissed her on the temple. "Sorry I'm late. Last appointment was trickier than I thought it was going to be." Then, while she stood there with her contacts about to fall off the edges of her bugged-out eyes, he extended a hand and a broad smile to Mrs. Takeda and basically took over the interview.

Which was as it should be, after all. The children were Steven's responsibility, as was their care. In a few days…

Unable to finish the thought, Sophie quietly excused herself.

He found her a half-hour later, out back feeding carrots to Butthead, the goat. Kneeling by the animal's pen, she looked up at his approach, tried to smile. But the clumped lashes kind of gave it away. An old metal milk crate lay on the ground near the goat's pen; Steve walked over, sat down. "C'mere, you," he said softly, holding out one arm.

She looked at him, turned her attention back to the goat. "What good is that going to do?"

"I have no idea."

After a moment, she tossed the last carrot to the beast and got up. Hesitated. Finally went to him, settling onto his lap. *Really* settling onto his lap, head tucked against his chest and the whole nine yards.

"Is this as good for you as it is for me?" he asked, and she gave a little hiccuppy laugh underneath his chin.

"But this is wrong," she said.

"Why?"

"Because. It just is." But she didn't move, he noticed. "Rosie still asleep?" she asked.

"Mmm, hmm."

"And Mrs. Takeda?"

"Well, she looked pretty wide-awake when she left, but that was ten minutes ago." Lisa gently slapped his chest; Steve grabbed her hand, kissed her knuckles, then stupidly said, "I think she's gonna work out real well."

Lisa trembled for a second or two, then collapsed into sobs, going on about how everything had gone wrong and how she'd made such a mess of things when all she'd wanted to do was *help,* for goodness' sake, only now she saw how naive she'd been to think that she wouldn't get involved or attached....

Steve snagged her chin on that one, reeling in her watery gaze. "Just how attached are you?"

She sniffed. "You have to ask?"

Awkwardly, he reached around, patting his pockets until he came up with a clean tissue, which he handed her. "So don't go back," he whispered, watching her eyes go wide over the tissue held to her nose, even as his brain screamed, *"What?"*

"What?" Lisa mumbled from behind the tissue.

"You heard me. Don't go back. Stick around. Not as the housekeeper though. As...as..."

Lisa lowered the tissue. "As what? Your lover?"

"That could work."

She almost laughed, but it died before it fully blossomed. "You really want me to stay?" she whispered, amazement flickering in her eyes. As if she couldn't quite believe anyone would care whether she came or went. And irritation flashed through him, that she should doubt him.

"You have to ask?" he echoed, watching as her brow crumpled. She looked down at her hands clasped in her lap, nodded.

"Thank you," she said.

He craned his neck to peer up into her face. "I wasn't being polite, honey. I really meant it."

"I know that," she said on a harsh sigh, her mouth twisting. "But..."

His stomach did a slow turn. "Don't tell me you decided to accept that guy's marriage proposal?"

"What? Oh...no," she said, shaking her head. "No. I have at least enough sense to know *that* wouldn't work."

"Thanks for cluing me in."

She looked at him like he'd lost it. "I'm sorry, Steven—I didn't tell you because I didn't think it mattered. Not in the long run."

He tightened his grip around her waist, shaking her slightly. "Trust me, honey. It matters."

She lifted a hand to his face. "What are you saying?"

That I love you. The words were right there, straining to get out. But she was the one with the most garbage to work out; she'd have to be the one to go first, this time.

"That it matters," he repeated, his heart in his throat. On his damn sleeve.

"Oh, Steven…you mean more to me than any man I've ever known. But I can't afford to…to let myself fall in love with you. Or you, me. This—" she pointed back and forth between them "—isn't going to work. I've always been very up-front about that—"

"I know, but—"

"But nothing's changed." New tears welled in her eyes. "Which is why I'm so bloody miserable, because I've been raised to always do what is right. And until now, *right* was easy to identify. Until I met you, *right* had never felt wrong before. Oh, dear…" On a sigh, she lay her head against his chest again. "Does that even make sense?"

"Yeah," he said, skimming his hand up and down her smooth, cool arm. "Only, in my case, it's just the opposite. *Wrong* feels so, so *right*."

She sat up then, linking her hands around his neck, intensity blazing in her eyes. "Explain."

He smoothed a lock of hair off her face, his brow knotting slightly at the dark roots. "Okay, one—I don't know who you are. And—two—you still won't tell me. And whoever you are—or choose to let me believe you are—I've known you for less than two weeks. Which I suppose makes three, since, while I have no qualms about sticking my neck out when I feel it's necessary, I'm not by nature an impulsive person. And four—I've been divorced less than a year. So for all I know, what I'm feeling could well be nothing more than the effects of loneliness and deprivation. Yet in spite of what I think we can both agree are very valid reasons for running like hell in the opposite direction, I've never felt more like wanting to move forward in my life."

"Damn you," she said softly, looking out over the garden. They sat and listened to the goat's bleating, an occasional chicken squawk, for a minute until she said, "I had no idea I could be torn in two like this, Steven. None. But you're absolutely right about one thing."

She looked at him. "You don't know me."

"Well, see, honey…that's the part I'd like to work on. But I suppose that's up to you, isn't it?" Then he drew her closer, just to comfort. And be comforted. Except her scent flooded his senses, for one thing. And then there were her breasts, lurking right on the other side of that little cotton top she was wearing, soooo damn close to his lips, they were practically begging for a nuzzle. *Just a little one. Pleeeease?*

And just as Steve was reminding himself that he wasn't the type of guy to take advantage of…things, Lisa leaned into him. Slid her fingers through what there was of his hair.

Sighed.

Oh, what the heck—it wasn't as if the goat was gonna tell.

Now, see, Steve had had this thing for breasts for, well, a long time. Probably longer than his mother would like to know, certainly. And this thing wasn't about size or anything like that—nor had he ever touched a woman unless he was damn sure she wanted to be touched—but about responsiveness. As in, he really got off on watching and listening to a woman whose breasts he was courting. He supposed it was all tied in to his wanting to make people happy, you know? And, from what he'd gathered over the years, done right, this was a surefire way to make a woman downright ecstatic. So, with that in mind, he very slowly, very carefully, pressed his lips to the tantalizing, delicately perfumed swell peeking out over the neckline of her top. She let out *just* the faintest gasp, then swallowed. Thus encouraged, he very slowly, very carefully pulled back that neckline. Oh, man—flesh-colored lace. Yowsa.

Okay, okay, so there were perks in this for him, too.

Her hands tightened in his hair.

"You want me to stop?"

She did this little whimpering thing. He took that as a "no."

So, with just one finger, he traced the outline of that pretty lace on that even prettier breast for, oh, about ten seconds or so, until her breathing got nice and choppy and her eyes drifted closed, before he very slowly, very carefully, slipped two fingers underneath the lace and made contact with ground zero.

She actually sobbed. Except then nature did its thing in his part of the ballpark and her eyes popped open, big as saucers.

Lisa tried to wriggle off. He wouldn't let her. "Hey. Sweetheart. It's okay. That's what's supposed to happen."

A single fat tear jumped over her lower lashes and streaked hell-bent-for-leather down her cheek. "This is so incredibly un*fair!*"

He reached up, grazed the tear from her cheek. She was so soft, so incredibly soft.

And he was so incredibly…not. "To…whom?" he finally got out.

She pushed out a sigh, then looked at him. "When you touch me, I can't think. I don't *want* to think. I only want you to keep touching me. But who wants to start something they can't finish?"

He managed a weak grin. "Oh, I have no doubt that we'd finish—"

"Oh, Steven—" She squirmed off his lap and headed back toward the house, tossing "Don't be such a bloody idiot!" over her shoulder as she went.

Of course, the kids came home soon after that, so there was no way to continue the conversation. Let alone anything else. And then Lisa disappeared into her room right after dinner, claiming a headache. But Steve—who, when push came to shove, actually could figure out a thing or two—realized what she was doing was pulling away. From the kids. From him.

From something neither of them could handle.

Still, something nagged him about her resistance. Maybe *he* was being naive—it had been known to happen—but since the "other guy" was out of the picture, and, frankly, he didn't completely buy this going-back-for-the-sake-of-the-family-business number, he figured there was something else going on here.

And that, whatever that something else was, he'd be a fool

to pursue it. Yeah, taking action was all well and good, but he was hardly going to bonk the woman over the head with his Nikon and drag her back to the farmhouse by her dyed blond hair, was he?

Along about midnight, he heard a knock on the darkroom door. He opened it to find Lisa standing there in that little sleepshirt thing she wore, her arms carefully folded across her breasts. Her face was scrubbed. And splotchy, like she'd been crying. Steve refused to react. To make things worse.

"I just thought you should know...I made my plane reservations for Sunday morning."

"Oh," he said, somehow. "Uh...well, I suppose we can take you to the airport then—"

"You've got to be kidding?" she said on a strangled half laugh, her hand at her throat. "I'd never live through that, Steven. And I think it would be easier on the children if we...if we said goodbye here. So I'll just take a taxi."

He hooked his hands on his hips, tamping down his anger. "Never mind what anyone else wants—"

Then she startled him by laying a hand on his arm. "Don't," she said softly, then stood on tiptoe to kiss him briefly on the lips. Except he grabbed her hand as she tried to walk away, snaring her gaze in his.

"If we could turn back the clock to ten days ago," he said, "would you have made the same decision you did then?"

Underneath the thin cotton, her shoulders rose with the force of her sigh. "Not a fair question."

"Why not?"

"Because it's one I can't answer," she said, slipping her hand from his. Then he watched, unable to breathe, as she padded barefoot back to her room and softly shut the door.

Friday afternoon, Sophie opened the door to a grunting Mala, her arms loaded with what looked like photo albums. "Where can I put these?"

"Oh, um...on the coffee table, I guess."

"Great."

Sophie stood and watched as Steven's sister, dressed in a

baggy, floral romper and backless sandals, her hair pulled back with a pair of tortoiseshell combs, lunged toward the table, dumping the albums before the rest of her got there. "Where's the Rose?"

"Down the road, playing with the neighbor's little boy." Sophie glanced outside. "Where are yours?"

"School," Mala said, untangling herself from her shoulder bag, which she then flung onto the sofa before rushing down the hall toward the bathroom, tossing off something about her mother and a project for Steven's birthday that she'd put off until now because she was simply *swamped* with work and she hoped Lisa wouldn't mind helping her.

The bathroom door slammed shut, leaving Sophie staring at the tower of albums and feeling very much like throwing up.

If it hadn't been for the children, she would have left five seconds after Steven's foray into her brassiere two days ago. Oh, not because she was offended, far from it. But because she liked it far too much. And because she'd ached for more. Not just more sex—although she would hardly have been averse to that—but for *more*.

Steven Koleski was more than she could ever want. Or would ever be able to have.

The bicycle that would never be hers.

The old pipes groaned as the downstairs toilet flushed; a minute later Mala came zipping back down the hall, looking much less stressed.

"Okay," she said, "Ma's got this idea that it would be 'cute'—her word—to make up a little photo retrospective of my brother's life for his birthday. You are coming, aren't you?"

Sophie sat on the sofa, hitching her errant bra strap back into place underneath her sleeveless blouse. Steven had finally gotten around to installing a ceiling fan in here, although she honestly didn't think it made that much difference. She nodded to Mala's question, hefting the top album onto her lap. "Your mother extracted my promise in blood," she said distractedly, leafing through the brittle pages. "This is Steven?" she said, laughing in spite of herself as she pointed to a studio portrait of the chunkiest baby she'd ever seen in her life.

Mala glanced over, chuckled. "Yeah. Guess how old he is?"

"Oh, mmm…a year?"

"Four months."

"Four months!"

"Kid weighed eleven pounds, nine ounces at birth. Biiiig sucker."

Sophie laughed again, only to sober as she continued turning pages. It seemed so unfair, that she should be privy to all the important events of Steven's life—including the ubiquitous naked baby pictures—when he knew nothing, really, about her. Yet, even as her heart bled with each page she turned, she was grateful for the illicit glimpse into the life of a man with whom she'd—illogically, improbably, and irrefutably—fallen completely in love.

A man she'd never see again, after Sunday morning.

"Oh, I think this one, definitely," she said, pointing to one of him wearing a football helmet. And nothing else.

Mala glanced over and hooted with laughter. "Definitely. He was three or four when that was taken, something like that. Here—" She extended a hand. "Give it to me."

During the next half hour, the two women fell into an easy conversation that tugged at Sophie's heart even as it filled her with a quiet, sweet pleasure. She'd never had a girlfriend, not really, and she found she both cherished the easy camaraderie that she and Mala seemed to enjoy and dreaded its passing. Along the way, they accumulated a couple dozen priceless pictures of the hapless birthday boy, until they'd come to the last album, an old, brittle, leather-bound number filled with assorted newspaper clippings.

"This one was my grandmother's," Mala said, leaning closer to Sophie as she carefully leafed through the fragile pages. "Ma used to send her all the family announcements and stuff. I doubt we'll find anything we can use in it, but I thought it would be fun to look at, anyway… holy cow, Lisa! What is it? You're white as a ghost!"

If she'd had any idea this was coming up, she could have bluffed her way through it, simply turned the page and not said a word, and Mala would never have been the wiser. As it was, however, the sight of the newspaper photo stunned her into paralysis.

Nearly twenty years old, it was. And Sophie remembered the day with extraordinary clarity, how much she'd hated being stared at, being dragged around and forced to smile at people she didn't know, didn't want to know. Her shyness had faded with time and maturity, but at ten—gawky and plain and painfully introverted, especially when compared with her vibrant, beautiful mother—the goodwill trips her parents forced her and Alek to make with them were sheer torture. As anyone could see from looking at this photograph.

"The Crown Princess Ekaterina of Carpathia, with her husband, Nobel prize-winning physicist Sir Lloyd Hastings and their children, Prince Aleksander and Princess Sophie, pay visit to tiny Carpathian community in Detroit."

"Lisa? What—?" Mala scooted closer, turned the album a bit to get a better look. Her gaze shot to Sophie's face, back to the photo. "Wow—the little girl looks enough like you to be—" Her hand flew to her mouth, then dropped. "Holy crud—that *is* you!" Steven's sister looked back at her, her eyes wide. "You're a *princess?*"

After her initial shock, Mala seemed to take it all in stride. She set a plate of Oreos on the table between them, then sat down in the kitchen chair across from Sophie, who'd gone more or less catatonic.

Mala took a bite of cookie, then said, "My grandmother lived in that neighborhood, back then, until Ma convinced her to come live out here with us. I'd forgotten all about that day until now. We'd gone in to see Baba, and she insisted on going to the little church where you and your parents were supposed to visit."

They'd brought the album into the kitchen with them; Mala now pointed to something in the photo. "I'm pretty sure that's

Steve's arm," she said on a laugh. "Our family's claim to fame."

"I call my grandmother 'Baba,' too," Sophie said, then let her head fall forward onto her arms.

"So," Mala said, "what should I call you? Your Highness or what?"

"How about…stupid."

"Can't. I already laid claim to that title years ago."

Sophie laughed a little, then rested her cheek on her arms. "Please promise me you won't tell your brother."

"So you can, you mean?"

Sophie shut her eyes against the twinge of pain Mala's words provoked. "It's all such a muddle." She pulled herself upright, more or less, then heaved a great sigh. "I ran away to straighten out my life. Not screw it up more."

"You didn't answer my question. About telling Steve?"

"I know I didn't."

That, apparently, merited Mala's taking a good-size chomp of the cookie and several seconds of intensely thoughtful chewing. "He's gonna have a cow when he finds out, you know."

"Oh, Mala—why do you think I don't want to tell him? My plan was to just disappear, that he'd never know…" She looked away, blinking back tears that refused to cooperate.

"Oh, hell," Mala said gently. "You're in love with the nut, aren't you?"

After a moment, Sophie nodded.

Then Mala's face clouded. "But you can't let anything come of it because we're, whaddyacallit, commoners?"

Sophie's stomach plunged at Mala's frosty words. She leaned forward, capturing the brunette's suddenly cooled green gaze in hers. "Mala—your brother is one of the finest men I've ever met. His kindness and integrity and innate goodness are worth far more than any fortune or title I could even think of. And for him to be attracted to *me* is beyond flattering. It's mind-boggling. And all the sweeter because he *doesn't* know who I really am."

"But…?"

"But that doesn't change the fact that I can't *not* be who I am. I can't change the fact of my birth." She got up to get a napkin from the dispenser on the counter to blow her nose. "I can't change the fact that I have obligations to fulfill that someone like Steven would undoubtedly find boring or insipid or stupid."

"Then maybe you're underestimating him."

"Oh, for heaven's sake, Mala—*I* detest half the things I have to do, so I know Steven would. Besides, in the less than two weeks I've known your brother, the one thing he's made extraordinarily clear to me is that he's not going to change for anyone. Which is probably what I love best about him, how comfortable he is inside his own skin. I couldn't make those kinds of demands on anyone, but especially not him." She paused, her hand pressed to her stomach. "But my position would. And that wouldn't be fair to him."

Mala studied her for several seconds, then said, "So what you're saying is, there's nothing says you two *couldn't* get together. Just that you won't let that happen?"

Sophie averted her gaze for a moment, then let out her breath in a long, shaky sigh before looking at her again. "My father's parents were good people, heaven knows, and hard-working—his mother was a schoolteacher, his father a factory foreman in Manchester. So whatever prestige Father enjoyed derived solely from his work, his achievements. Still, I know he always felt that he didn't quite fit within our circle, that he was always pretending, always playing catch-up. I know my parents were seriously considering a separation, just before they were killed. And I'll always wonder, if they'd lived, whether or not the marriage would have survived in any case."

She shifted, shrugged. "I didn't intend to fall in love with your brother, but that doesn't make it any less of a mistake. But to let things go further…" She let the sentence drift off.

Mala toyed with another cookie for several moments, finally letting a short, succinct curse put an official end to the conversation.

Chapter 14

"C'mon, guys—everybody in the van!" Fighting his way into a windbreaker which, he'd discovered too late, had one sleeve turned inside out, Steve stood in the doorway, shooing assorted juvenile bodies outside. It took a good half hour to get to his mother's. According to his watch, they had fifteen minutes. No, fourteen. "Wait—where's Lisa? Where's *Rosie?*"

"I'll go look for her," Courtney said, doing an about-face in the doorway. Steve grabbed her, spun her back around.

"Forget it. At least this way, I know where four of you are."

He tramped through the house, ignoring George's maligned expression—he couldn't go, this time—banging open the screen door to see Lisa clomping about in those killer shoes after the chickens, flapping at them with the hem of her sundress like a toreador taunting a bull. In the west, black clouds threatened a corker of a storm. "What the hell are you doing?" he called over the wind.

"They shouldn't be left out if it's going to rain, should they?"

Steve sighed, then said, "The rest of the kids are in the van, but I can't find Rosie anywhere."

"Well—go on, shoo! Shoo!—she's not out here..." Lisa took off after Frieda, the orneriest one of the lot. Her face was flushed, her hair a holy mess, and Steve fought down a pang of almost overwhelming sadness that, by this time tomorrow, she'd be gone. "And yes, I know she's not in George's house. Did you try the basement?"

"Yep. And the pantry and the laundry room, too."

"Well, she's got to be *somewhere,* for heaven's sake." Unlike last time, her words was laced with annoyance, not panic. Knowing the end was in sight had made them both pricklier than porcupines around each other these last two days, although they'd tried to keep things on an even keel whenever they were with the kids. Who'd been, come to think of it, just as prickly.

"Oh, you *stu*pid thing!" Lisa cried as Frieda shot across the vegetable garden.

God, he was gonna miss her.

He went back inside, racking his brain. George moseyed on over and sat down in front of him, panting, wearing a so-what-can-I-do-for-you? grin.

"I don't suppose *you* know where Rosie is?"

The dog yawned, then trotted off down the hall toward Lisa's room.

And sure enough, her door was ajar. As was the door to her closet, which in the humidity was too swollen to shut tightly anyway. Yet another item to add to the To Do list, Steve thought, tugging it open. Sure enough, soft snoring alerted him to Sleeping Beauty's presence, all the way in the back by a shelf. To reach the little girl, Steve had to fight his way past what looked like a dress and a trench coat, both very beige, very conservative, which he'd never seen Lisa wear.

"Hey, munchkin," he whispered as he scooped Rosie into his arms. She yawned, slinging an arm around his neck. "You ready to go? Oh, shoot!"

In picking her up, he'd bumped the shelf, knocking over a shopping bag and Lisa's tote. And something else...a laptop computer, he now saw. Frowning, Steve squatted clumsily, the child clinging to him like a koala bear, quickly picking everything up and putting it back where it had been. He'd always been fanatic about respecting his housekeepers' privacy. Even when his hand landed on what was obviously a passport.

Man, oh, man…temptation had never, ever screamed so loudly in his ears.

Never.

And the only thing that made him stuff the damn thing back into the tote without looking at it, even then, was the sudden realization that it wasn't so much that he wanted to know who she was, as it was that he wanted her to *tell* him.

Of her own free will.

Steven's parents' house was small and obsessively neat. Not to mention obsessively coordinated. Everything was in shades of blue, including the carpeting, the pictures on the walls, the furniture. At one end of the living room, one of those super-large televisions was turned to a baseball game, even though no one was watching at present.

The children had all dispersed like seeds in the wind the moment they arrived, apparently oblivious to the lack of conversation between the two so-called adults in the front seat. But then, considering the noise level from the back, no wonder.

"Oh, there you are," Steven's mother said, hustling from the kitchen in a voluminous tropical print dress. She glanced from one to the other, lifted her eyebrows, blessedly said nothing. Except, "Stevie, get out there and keep your father from having a coronary. Honest to God, you'd think the man hadn't done barbecue a thousand times before, the way he gets himself into a state."

Steven glanced back at Sophie, only to have his mother swat him in the arm. "Go on. I'm not gonna eat the woman, for godssake." Once he'd disappeared out the back door, Bev Koleski turned to Sophie with a smile and open arms. "I'm so glad you came," she whispered as she hugged her. Then she let her go, shaking her head. "God, what I wouldn't give to be able to get into an outfit like that, huh? So, what's that you got there?''

''Oh—'' she held up the present ''—it's for Steven.''

''Well, I certainly didn't figure it was for me,'' his mother said with a loud laugh, then led her into a small, but excruciatingly formal, dining room, overblown crystal chandelier and all. A mountain of presents sat on the gleaming mahogany table; a huge ''Happy Birthday'' sign in metallic letters had been taped, a little crookedly, to one wall.

Sophie had to smile.

''Just put yours up there with all the others. If you want, you can stick your bag in the little bedroom right down the hall there.''

She did as she was told, placing her bag on the dark blue corduroy bedspread in what had obviously been Steven's room, complete with a complement of sports trophies lining a ledge along one wall and a collection of framed photos taken at various ages, in various uniforms. Arms folded, she walked over to the wall, her gaze lighting on one in particular. Steven was about twelve or so, she guessed, in a filthy football uniform. He looked straight into the camera, an enormous, cocky grin splitting his face.

''You like potato salad?'' she heard from down the hall.

Blinking back tears, Sophie followed the voice to the blue-and-bluer kitchen. From outside, she heard the kids shrieking and running around, which drew her to look out the window over the sink. The wind plastering the thin windbreaker to every muscle he had, Steven stood next to his father at the grill on the redwood deck, a soda clamped in one hand, quasi-arguing with his sister about something.

''Sophie? Potato salad?''

She faced Mrs. Koleski, remembered she'd been asked a question. ''I don't think I've ever eaten it.''

Eyebrows shot up over silver glassframes. Then she scooped up a glob of the creamy-looking mixture and held it up to Sophie's mouth like a mother would to a baby. Obediently, Sophie took the offered bite, then smiled.

''It's good, huh?''

"Ma's potato salad is the best," Steven said from the back door, making her choke. She whirled around, coughing. "At least you got to sample *that* before you left," he said, expressionless, before snatching a bag of hamburger buns off the counter and disappearing.

Two hours later, Sophie was surprised to discover she'd been enjoying herself. The food was wonderful and totally unhealthy, the kids had kept them all entertained, and she truly adored Steven's parents. Especially Marty, who, just as she suspected, was basically a soft touch. And as dedicated as his son to bringing healing to Ted and Gloria MacIntyre's five children. A wonderful family, one any woman would be thrilled to be a part of…

"Okay, let's see here…" Steven said, rubbing his hands together behind the loaded dining room table. It had finally started to rain, conveniently when they'd been about to move back inside for presents, anyway. And she thought of the Ansel Adams book of photographs she'd found for him online—and had held her breath would arrive in time—and how pitiful it was as a present, considering that she knew what he really wanted from her was the one thing she couldn't give him: the truth.

Not much longer now, she thought, slipping into a corner in the back of the room. Soon, there would be no more lies, no more guilt…no more Steven in her life.

Major bummer, as Bree would say.

He opened the kids' presents first—various mugs, T-shirts, and no less than three truly awful ties which he wrapped around his neck with much fanfare and flourish, swearing he loved them all. Then he opened the Ansel Adams book, thanking Sophie until she blushed furiously. The next present he picked up warranted a whole routine of exaggerated shaking and listening gestures until his father said, "For godssake, just open the damn thing already!" which provoked a swat from Steven's mother and an injunction about little pitchers and big ears.

Except Steven tortured everybody by carefully undoing

each flap, then slowly peeling the paper away…until a stunned expression fell across his face.

He looked up at his father, who was trying not to look embarrassed.

"It was your mother's idea—"

Steve's mother smacked him again. "The heck it was, Marty. Honest to God." She shook her head. "Took him two weeks to pick it out. He must've gone to a dozen stores until he found just what he was looking for."

"But that don't make no difference, Stevie. I got the receipt. You don't like it, we can take it back—"

"Pop," he said softly. "Shut up." After a deep breath, he lifted the digital camera from its box. "I can't believe…" He stopped, blinked a couple of times. "It's perfect, Pop."

"You really like it?"

Steven looked at his father, and the affection in his eyes brought tears to Sophie's. "Thank you," was all he said, but clearly it was enough. Marty beamed. "Yeah, well, I remember you saying somethin' about how it would be nice to be able to put your stuff up on the computer so you could mess with it, y'know. Not that I understand a lot about that, but I figured, with you doing this full-time and all…" He ended the sentence with a shrug.

Steven just raised the camera again in a salute, and was reverently slipping it back into its box when Mac, who'd been keeping an eye on some sports news show, cried out, "Oh, *crap!*"

"Hey, Mac!" Steven yelled through the open archway between the rooms. "How many times am I gonna tell you not to use that kind of language—"

"Oh, yeah, sorry. But you know that race car driver I was tellin' you about, Jeff Henderson? The one who's been doing so good in Formula One this year? He was killed today in a racing accident in France somewhere. It's on the news."

Sophie's head whipped around to the TV, which she could easily see from where she stood. Jeff Henderson…wasn't that…?

"*…one of America's most experienced race car driv-*

*ers...more than eight hundred races under his belt...leaving
behind a wife and young son...also injured in the freak accident was Henderson's original sponsor and long-time friend,
Crown Prince Aleksander of Carpathia...''*

"Alek!" Sophie screamed, then clapped her hand over her
mouth.

Her brain gone numb, she was barely aware of Steven's
clasp on her arm, even less aware of the confusion in his voice.
"Hey, honey—you know that guy?"

Then she felt Mala's arm slip around her waist, lead her to
a chair moments before her legs gave way. "You know what,
Mac?" Mala said. "Why don't you get Sophie something to
drink?"

"Sophie?" Steve's mother said. "Who the heck's Sophie?"

"She is," Mala said softly, handing Sophie the glass of
water Mac brought, except her hands were shaking too much
to hold it. "Sorry, sweetie," Mala said, holding the glass to
Sophie's lips, as she might a child. "But I think you just blew
your cover."

"So, like, do you live in a castle and stuff?"

Since "blowing her cover," as Mala put it, Steven had yet
to say anything to her. The children, however—especially the
twins—more than made up for their guardian's taciturnity, and
Sophie felt as though she'd been answering questions for
hours.

At least, her mind had been put somewhat at ease about
Alek. Steven's parents had insisted she call her grandmother
from their phone, never mind the expense. So she did, to find
out that Alek had been taken to a hospital near Nice, that he'd
called Baba to let her know his injuries weren't life-
threatening. She could tell, though, how relieved her grandmother was to know Sophie was coming home. And she knew
Alek, who would back in Carpathia within the week, would
undoubtedly be grateful for her support, as well. Jeff Henderson had been one of his closest friends when they were
younger, during her brother's "wild" days, and Alek was
bound to take Jeff's death very hard. And very personally,

since he'd been instrumental in getting Jeff's racing career off the ground.

Now, several hours later, they were back at the farmhouse, Dylan and Rosie long since asleep, the twins and Mac sitting with her in the living room, bug-eyed and curious.

"Well, not a castle, exactly. But definitely a palace. Perhaps, someday…" She hesitated. "Perhaps you can come visit me."

Both girls' eyes went even wider. "You serious?" Courtney asked.

"Absolutely—"

"Girls. Mac." Everyone but Sophie turned at the sound of Steven's voice. "The kitchen could use some straightening up."

"But Uncle Steve—"

"Scram," he said, very, very quietly.

They left.

And Sophie was tempted to wish she'd never been born.

The only thing keeping Steve from losing it was Lisa's—Sophie's—obvious concern about her brother. That, and the fact that, as mad as he was, he couldn't exactly pinpoint *why* he was so mad. Wasn't as if she'd lied to him, exactly. She'd told him she was hiding out. She'd told him she'd have to return, and why, even if obliquely. She'd told him that nothing could come of their attraction. Now he knew the reason. He should feel…what? Relieved? That the mystery had been solved? Instead, he just felt sucker-punched.

With a heavy sigh, he sank into the club chair across from where she sat cross-legged on the sofa, her bare feet tucked up underneath the long dress, picking at a chipped fingernail.

"You know," he said, "I kept thinking you seemed familiar, somehow. Except I convinced myself I was hallucinating. Then Mala showed me the newspaper photo—"

"Please don't be angry with her." She quirked her mouth. "I made her promise not to tell you."

Slouched in the chair, he laced his hands across his stomach, decided to leave his sister out of this, for the time being. "You've changed quite a bit since I last saw you."

The corners of her mouth twitched. "Twenty years will do that."

Silence yawned between them for what seemed like forever, until Steve finally said, "You weren't planning on telling me at all, were you?"

Lisa—no, Sophie—glanced up, then back down, shaking her head. "No."

"Why?"

Her hand shaking, she tucked a strand of hair behind her ear. "Because…because of exactly this. Oh, God, Steven— I'm so sorry."

He crossed his arms, his stomach churning. For both of them. "So what was this? Some sort of game? Let's play peasant for a couple weeks—"

Hurt flared in her eyes. "Oh, for pity's sake! You know that's not true!"

"Then why couldn't you tell me? What possible threat could I have been to you, Lis—Sophie? What did you think I was going to do? Take out an ad in the *Spruce Lake Gazette?* Sell tickets to see the princess in disguise?"

"Of course not!"

"Then *why wouldn't you tell me?*"

"Oh, please—would you have let me clean your toilets if you'd known who I really was?" Her gaze met his, her voice softened. "Would you have kissed me?"

His gut twisted. "Sure. Why not?"

Her laugh was hollow, disbelieving. "No, you wouldn't have done. Because to most people, I'm not a person. I'm a *princess*. Unapproachable. Untouchable. Even your mother, the instant she found out, suddenly began straightening up the living room, as if I'd find a stray cup or crookedly placed magazine offensive. And this was the woman who, not two hours before, was spoon-feeding me potato salad!"

Her eyes met his; for an instant, they shared a smile. But she looked away immediately, her face crumpling. "For the first time in my life, I saw the chance to feel like a real human

being. And I grabbed it. Granted, I will regret deceiving you
for the rest of my life. But I will never regret what these two
weeks have meant to me. While I was here, I felt…a part of
something.'' Her eyes lifted to his, her hand flat against her
chest. ''As though I mattered, on a very basic level. Yes, taking care of a house and children can be exhausting and boring
and repetitious, but it can be exhilarating, too. And fun. *You*
make it fun, Steven. You are just the most extraordinary
man….''

He damn near forgot how to breathe on that one. All he
could do was watch her as she reached up, swiped a tear from
the corner of her eye. ''I love this town, the way people are
judged for who they *are,* not what they *have.* I love the kids
and this crazy, wonderful old house and George and the chickens and…''

Her mouth clamped shut, she again lowered her eyes, swallowing repeatedly. ''It felt so damn good to be ordinary,'' she
said at last. ''To be around people who say what they really
think, instead of what they think they should say. What you
and your family and your friends have is so very precious.
And all I wanted was to share some of that, just for a little
while. Just to borrow a little bit of…normalcy. I certainly
hadn't planned on…''

She wrapped her arms around herself, shaking her head.
''Oh, Steven—'' Anguish flooded her features, threatened to
drown him as well. ''What on *earth* made me think I could
slip into someone else's life, then slip out again without any
consequences?''

He had no answer for that. He had no answer for any of it.
But the hopelessness of the situation finally hit him:

She was a princess, for godssake. And the closest his family
came to royalty was the deck of cards Pop used when he
played poker with his buddies.

She was watching him, he realized, her gaze intent. ''So
now that you know who I really am, tell me, Steven—are
things the same between us? When you look at me, do you
see the same person you—''

''Fell in love with?'' he finished quietly.

Her eyes flooded with a new round of tears before she buried her face in her hands.

He stood, swallowing pretty damn hard himself as he stared down at the top of her head while she wept, wanting nothing more than to hold her close.

Wanting nothing less than to be able to hold her forever.

"No," he said at last, answering her question, then forced himself to leave the room.

The taxi came at eight the next morning. Sophie had been ready since six, never so grateful in her life to see dawn as she had been that morning. Sleep had been out of the question, but her thoughts had tormented her more than any nightmares could have done. Despite her grandmother's reassurances that Alek would be fine—she'd called, again, at four in the morning, Michigan time—she was worried sick about him. And then there was…everything else.

"Taxi's here," Courtney said stiffly from her post by the window.

"Oh. Well, then…" It was raining again, just as it had been two weeks ago when she'd started this whole charade. Underneath her trench coat, Sophie wore the black Capri pants, a cotton sweater. And the shoes she knew Steven hated so much. She gathered up her few things and walked through the door Bree held open for her. They all followed her out onto the porch.

Except for Steven, whom she hadn't seen since last night.

Somehow, even though she knew how upset he was, she hadn't expected him to simply ignore her leaving. Not that she didn't deserve it, but still.

She started with Mac, who wasn't quite as tall as she in these shoes. She squeezed the thin arm through his unpressed plaid shirt. "You've got to promise me—and I intend to check up on you, so you really have no choice—to live your own life, do you understand? And let your siblings do the same?"

He looked everywhere but at her, but he nodded.

"And to forgive me someday?"

His dark gaze shot to hers, moments before he hugged her hard enough to leave bruises, she was sure.

Next were the twins, who she made repeat her e-mail address with promises to write at least once a week, without fail.

And then the little ones. Rosie was too small to fully understand what was going on, but Dylan did. And his tears were nearly her undoing. She hugged them both, for a very, very long time, then kissed them all, all over again—except for Mac who just shook hands—then slipped into the waiting taxi, about to tell the driver to go ahead when Steven came running out of the house, shouting "Wait!" and waving an envelope or something in his hand.

He grabbed an umbrella off the porch and tromped down the steps, holding the envelope close to his chest. "These are for you," he said, his voice flat over the thrum of rain on the taxi roof. Taking great care to not touch her, he handed her the envelope through the open taxi window, then stepped back, rain streaming off the umbrella.

Not caring that she might get wet, she tore open the envelope, extracted a pair of photos that still smelled of developing fluid. The top one was of her, grinning broadly into the camera, and she sucked in a breath at how happy she looked. And almost pretty, in her very own gnarled tree sort of way.

The second was of the children, and George, taken out back by Butthead's pen. They were all mugging for the camera, even Rosie whose head was tilted back as she laughed, her lovey clutched to her chest.

"Thank you. They're wonderful," she said over the lump in her throat, then looked at Steven, holding up the one of the children. "But you're not in the picture."

One last time, those kind, wonderful green eyes met hers. "I was never meant to be, was I?"

She snapped her head around, her vision blurred. "Please," she managed to the driver over her breaking heart. "Just go. Now."

Chapter 15

"Hey—anybody home?"

A lesser man—or a stronger one, Steve wasn't sure which—might have ignored his sister. Especially as he needed the interruption like he needed a gall bladder operation, since he had less than four hours to get these slides FedEx'd to his agent.

But ignoring Mala was like ignoring a volcanic eruption. He shifted a couple slides around in the light tray set up on the dining table—he really was going to have to do something about setting up a real studio, now that he was doing this "for reals," as Dylan would say—and called out, "In here."

A moment later, the shrieks from outside escalated as Mala's two joined the melee; a moment after that, Mala waltzed into the room, fanning herself with the mail. "The postman got here the same time I did," she said, tossing the mail onto the end of the table. "Geez, Louise—the kids are driving me insane." She yanked back a chair, plopped into it, readjusting her underwear underneath her white tank top. "Isn't it September yet?"

Steve glanced up, then back at the transparencies spread out on his light table. "School just let out on Friday, Mal."

"More's the pity," she said, picking up one of the slides, squinting at it in the sun coming in through the window. "I really like this one."

Steve grunted.

Mala replaced the slide. "You still mad at me?"

"That why you're here? To mend fences?"

"Nooo," she said, shifting in the chair, not looking at him. There wasn't a Koleski alive who could lie worth a damn, but that didn't keep some of them from trying. "Ma sent over a couple loaves of banana bread."

"Mmm. Well, to answer the question you didn't come all the way out here to ask—" Steve placed the slide his sister had just looked at into the "possibles" pile "—I'm not mad at you."

"Like hell. Look, I said I was sorry, but Sophie made me promise not to tell. And you know my finding out was an accident—"

"Mal—forget it. It's over, it's done with, and I'd like to just get on with my life, if you don't mind." He tossed one slide into the "yes" pile, three others into the "no."

Her nails drummed against the table for several irritating seconds. "So tell me something—are you ticked because Sophie *is* a princess or because she didn't *tell* you she was a princess?"

"I'm not ticked, I'm…"

"Miserable?"

"Tired of everybody giving me dirty looks. Like you all like Sophie better than you like me."

Mala's smile wrinkled her slightly sunburned nose. "At the moment, we do."

Another slide bit the dust. "And I suppose all of you think I'm supposed to do something about it, right?"

"Since it's probably a safe bet the Fairy Godmother ain't gonna intervene—yeah. I don't suppose it's occurred to you to call the woman?"

He almost laughed. "Palace numbers aren't exactly listed, you know."

"So the kids have her e-mail address. That would work."

"Dammit, Mala!" He slammed one palm down on the table, making the slides—although not his sister—jump. "Nothing's going to *work,* got it? This isn't a fairy tale, and I don't turn into a prince at the end of the story!"

"So that's that?" Mala said, sitting back in the chair, her arms folded over her ribs.

Steve nodded.

Outside, a roar went up from the kids. When it subsided, Mala said, "You know, you are the biggest reverse snob I ever saw."

Steve's head shot up. *"Snob?"*

"Yeah, snob. All you could talk about, before you found there was a title attached to her name, was how wonderful it was to have finally met someone regular. Normal. So suddenly she's changed, just because now you know she has blue blood?"

"She was pretending, Mala!"

"Oh, please—you know as well I do she wasn't *pretending* to care about your kids! And I know for a fact, Mr. She-Done-Me-Wrong, that she sure as hell wasn't pretending to care about *you!* For crying out loud—did it ever occur to you that she didn't tell you who she was because she was afraid of being rejected?"

Again, his gaze zinged to his sister's.

"Yeah," she said, getting up and tugging at the seat of her shorts. "I thought maybe you'd missed that part." She walked over to the window, called out to her two to come on, they had to get going.

"But that doesn't change—"

"Who she is? No, it doesn't." She crossed to the door. "But maybe you should go back and read some more fairy tales, Steve. 'Cause it seems to me I remember that it's not always the prince who gets the princess's hand in marriage, but the guy with enough balls to buck the odds."

* * *

At midnight, Mala's words still ringing in Steve's ears, Mac knocked on the open darkroom door.

"Hey, bud." Steve casually slipped the photos he was looking at into a folder, laid it on the counter. "What's up?"

Mac sauntered—he seemed to be sauntering more and more these days, which Steve took as a good sign—into the darkroom, casually removing the photos from the very folder into which Steve had just placed them. "Nothin'," the kid said, which Steve knew was a crock but also knew better than to mention. "I really like this one where she's laughing." He held up one of the pictures so Steve could see it.

Steve glanced over—casually—as if he'd already forgotten about the photos. "Yeah. It's okay. A little underexposed, though."

Then he noticed Mac scrutinizing the newspaper photo, which Steve had taken from the album and encased in an acetate sleeve to preserve what was left of it. "Man, she looks, like, *totally* pissed, doesn't she?"

It was hard not to smile at that. Except then, after putting the photos back, Mac propped his baggy-shorted butt on the edge of a stool and graced Steve with one of those looks every parent, or reasonable facsimile thereof, dreads. So Steve did the only logical thing: he ignored it.

"Got that contract offer today," he said. "For the children's book?"

"Yeah?" The boy nodded a couple of times. "Cool."

Silence settled between them like an old, wet blanket.

"The girls got an e-mail from her today," Mac said, sliding his knuckle up and down the counter. "Her brother really wasn't hurt too bad. Some broken bones and stuff, but he'll be okay."

"Oh. Oh, that…that's good."

"And she said she really, really misses us."

Steve waited until the cramp around his heart eased. "She misses you guys—"

"That's not what she said. She said she missed *all of us.*"

"Mac…"

"You know, I've been thinking about some things Lisa—I mean Sophie—said to me. About how it's, like, human nature and stuff to try to find some reason for why things happen? That the human mind doesn't like chaos, stuff like that. Anyway, don't you think it's like totally weird, the way you met Sophie all those years ago, then she ends up coming here to stay?"

More than a little stunned, Steve plunked his own posterior on another stool and cocked his head at the teenager. "You telling me you believe in fate, Mac?"

"Maybe. I dunno. But it just seemed really good when she was here, y'know? Like things were finally starting to feel right. So we took a vote, me and the girls and Dylan, and we decided you need to go over there. You know, talk to her or something. And before you ask, Mrs. Takeda said that would be fine with her."

Steve opened his mouth, his brain fully prepared to spew out all the reasons why he couldn't do that. Except his heart jumped up and intercepted all those logical, practical, *fearful* reasons and basically pulverized them, so that, instead of "That's not possible," Steve heard, "You really think I've got a shot?" come out of his mouth.

Mac tried desperately to keep a straight face as he said, "Sure beats sitting here in the middle of the night staring at her pictures, don't you think?"

Less than a week later, Steve found himself seated on a fancy chair in a honest-to-goodness palace, Bree's birthday necktie strangling his seventeen-inch neck, facing a tiny, white-haired woman flanked by a pair of handsome white Alsatians. Princess Ivana's long, black dress may have been simple enough, but a blind man couldn't have missed the pear-shaped dinner ring the size of Rhode Island that glittered fiercely whenever she moved.

The old woman seemed to take his sudden appearance in stride, even if her brows had lifted at his question.

"Yes, Sophie's father hailed from a working-class background," she said, a maze of delicate wrinkles bracketing her smile. "Why do you ask?"

Steve grinned when one of the dogs bumped his hand for a scratch, then met Sophie's grandmother's gaze before telling her what he'd managed to get out of Mala, that Sophie was convinced her parents' marriage had gone on the rocks because her father had never felt he'd "fit in."

The light from a large, Chinese-looking lamp nearby flickered in her snowy hair as the princess studied her hands for a moment, then looked up. "Mr. Koleski, Sophie's father was a brilliant man. And a good man, as well. As I know you are." At his raised brows, she quietly laughed. "My granddaughter obviously cares for you a great deal. She may even be in love, if an old woman's intuition on these things can still be trusted." A smile blossomed across her face. "Your arrival wasn't exactly unexpected, Mr. Koleski. And since Sophie doesn't have a frivolous bone in her body—despite her recent escapade—I trust she wouldn't lose her heart to someone of less than impeccable character. On that score, there is no impediment whatsoever to your interest in my granddaughter, if that's what you're asking me."

One side of his mouth hitched in an embarrassed smile. "But…?"

"But," she said on a sigh, "there is a reason for the term 'social barriers,' arbitrary though they may be. And crossing them isn't always easy. It wasn't for Lloyd, who truly hated the social obligations that came with his marrying into a royal family. Nor did it help that Katya—the Princess Ekaterina, my daughter—not only had the attention span of a hummingbird, but she absolutely adored being a princess and all that word implied. So it never occurred to her that her husband craved the normalcy, the simplicity of his upbringing. That he might have enjoyed an occasional quiet night at home, a dinner alone, an afternoon playing with his children…"

She smiled sadly. "There were two people to blame for the eventual rift in that marriage—Lloyd, whose naiveté, even though he was fifteen years Katya's senior, prevented him from clearly seeing what he was getting himself into, and my daughter, who refused to grow up. And to compromise. It was as simple, and as tragic, as that."

The dog gave Steve's hand a little "thank you" lick, then walked across the room to join her companion on the ornate rug in front of the fireplace. "What exactly do you think you can offer Sophie, Mr. Koleski?" the elder princess asked gently.

A question Steve had asked himself about a thousand times during the past week. After a moment, he said, "Happiness, I would hope. Peace." He grinned, shrugged. "A place to hide out when things get rough." Then he sobered. "My heart."

A inscrutable smile played around the princess's lips. "And what do you think she can offer *you?*"

"What she's already given me," he said simply. "Herself."

Princess Ivana nodded in apparent approval, then leaned back again, her hands knotted in front of her, softly banging her knees as she spoke. "For a marriage to work, there must be common ground, common interests and goals, a common devotion to each other's happiness, even if that means the occasional sacrifice of one's own. And I truly believe that last—that devotion to each other's happiness—is far more important in determining whether or not a marriage will stand the test of time than whether or not the partners hail from the same socioeconomic background. So, young man…does my granddaughter's happiness mean more to you than your own?"

"Yes."

"You didn't even hesitate."

"I didn't need to."

After another nod, Ivana rose, the soft fabric of her dress swishing against her frail body as she crossed to the open, leaded windows. "Considering the state she's in, I would say her answer would be the same as yours. Although…"

The princess turned, her hair trembling in the gentle spring breeze. "Sophie is free to make her home anywhere. But if you're looking for a woman who will be there to share dinner with you every night, you will be disappointed."

Steve got to his feet as well. "I understand that. And I'm not. All I want, Your Highness, is to share as much of my life with Sophie as she wishes to share. If she'll have me."

"Ah, yes. And there's your problem, isn't it?" The princess let out a sigh. "My granddaughter can be very stubborn, as you may have already guessed. If you wish to court her, not only can I not stop you, but I wish you well. I just cannot guarantee the outcome."

"I didn't come here looking for a guarantee. Just an opportunity."

"That, I think we can arrange," the elderly woman said with a soft smile.

Sophie had just taken a sip of wine when the servant gave her the message. The excellent vintage went down the wrong way, provoking a coughing fit and a dozen heads whipping in her direction.

"Yes," she rasped after an embarrassing ten seconds, holding a napkin to her watering eyes, but carefully, so as to not smear her makeup. "Yes, of course I'll see him."

Alek, seated at the foot of the table directly to her left, laid his uncasted hand on her wrist. She glanced over at her older brother, the crisp lines of his white silk dinner jacket echoing the sharp planes of his still bruised face, which in turned echoed the melancholia that had dulled his quicksilver eyes since her return. His physical injuries had indeed turned out to be relatively minor—a broken wrist, some cracked ribs, a few cuts and bruises—but the blow to his soul was not so easily mended. "Him?" he asked.

But at the moment Sophie had her own heartaches to deal with. With trembling fingers, she carefully folded the linen napkin, set it by the gold-leaf charger. *"Him."* With a shaky but—she prayed—gracious smile, she excused herself from the dinner party, expertly maneuvering the full taffeta skin of her mother's favorite Givenchy gown as she swished dramatically from the dining room. Perhaps the ugly duckling had learned enough tricks to at least pass for a swan, but inside she was a mess.

What the bloody hell was she supposed to do now?

He was waiting for her in the library, the room her father had used as his study, complete with leaded windows and rich oak paneling, tan leather furniture and an enormous tooled leather globe dating from the seventeenth century. The windows stood open in the warm night, flooding the room with the scent of roses and newly mown grass. Seeing Steven, inhaling that scent, flooded her memory with a thousand bittersweet images, cramping her heart.

The sight of that massive frame constrained by a suit— and oh, dear, Bree's tie—startled her. She hadn't even known he owned one. At the most, she would have expected a sportcoat, perhaps, over a pair of khakis. An ordinary outfit for an ordinary guy. But how could she ever have thought him ordinary? The air around him vibrated with a confidence that made her catch her breath.

And wish he hadn't come.

He glanced up at her entrance. And smiled, which just about did her in. "Nice place you got here—"

"The children? How are they?"

His whole face lit up. "They're…good. Out of school now for a week and already bored. They, um, like Mrs. Takeda."

"Yes," she said, managing a tiny smile over the earthquake going on in her stomach. "I knew they would."

"And Mac took a job as a day camp counselor in town. And Dyl hardly wets at all now."

"Oh! Oh, that's wonderful." She smiled through a scrim of tears. "And Galen—how is she?"

Steve stuffed his hands in his jeans pockets. Grinned. "It looks like she's getting her miracle. So far, it looks like a normal pregnancy. Of course, Del's nuts with worry, and she's going to have to cut back on her hours at the restaurant, but we've all got our fingers crossed."

"I'm so glad, Steven. Honestly."

"I know you are," he said, and she watched as his expression gentled into something that was equal parts apprehension and adoration, sizzling desire and almost worshipful respect. Then, as if the smile wasn't bad enough, he whistled, a long, low one that did very bizarre things to her nerve endings.

"That is some dress," he finally said, taking a step toward her. And then another.

She backed up, stumbling into a chair. "It was my m-mother's. I never thought I could pull it off before. Thought my shoulders were too bony for strapless. And the red seemed so…"

"Maybe you don't want to know what the red does to me," he said softly. "Let alone what the image of *pulling it off* conjures up."

"Oh?"

"Mmm. And your hair." He was close enough to touch her—how had that happened?—his hand skimming the short, feathery style she'd finally settled on, in a shade close to her own. And since glasses really didn't go with Givenchy gowns, she'd decided to continue wearing contacts, albeit clear ones.

She backed away, her vision blurred. Except he caught her, folding her into his arms, gently cradling her head against his chest. And because she knew she'd never have this opportunity again, she simply stood there and relished the feel of his arms around her. Regrets were pointless, she knew, but right at that moment, she'd have given anything to have slept with him before she'd left. To at least have the memory of what it would feel like to have nothing between them except heated skin.

And trust.

He didn't want the moment to end. But the only chance he had of making her his meant risking losing her forever. He brushed his lips over her hair, knowing the next minute or so could well be the most important of his life.

"Sophie…" His heart began pounding high in his throat; he swallowed it down. "Sophie, look at me."

She did, questions littering those quicksilver eyes.

"Do you love me?"

Her eyes widened. "Yes," she whispered.

"Do you love *me,* plain old ordinary Steven Koleski from plain old ordinary Spruce Lake, Michigan?"

"Yes," she repeated, more strongly.

"So, in theory, you have no problem with getting emotionally involved with a regular guy."

"Steven—"

"In *theory*."

She nodded.

"And do you love five certain kids who also happen to live in plain old ordinary Spruce Lake, Michigan?"

Her expression softened. "Oh, yes. With all my heart."

"And isn't it true that, since you're not in direct line for the throne anyway, you can actually live anywhere you want?"

"Well, yes, I suppose—"

"And don't you already handle many of your responsibilities long-distance via fax and computer?"

A wary comprehension dawned in her eyes. "Yes."

"Then listen to me, Sophie, and listen hard, because I didn't travel a million miles just for one of your smiles, okay?" Except she did smile, a little, at that, which both terrified and encouraged him all at once. "The thing is, maybe I don't speak a half-dozen languages and I doubt at my age, that's gonna change. And maybe I only know how to use more than three utensils at a time—well, four, if I'm eating at Mala's 'cause she always has a salad fork. And I hate opera and the only time I went to the ballet, I fell asleep. But, hell, I'm not untrainable, you know? Hey—the last time I wore a dinner jacket, I thought I looked pretty damn good, if I do say so myself. So I think it's reasonable to assume I could get up to speed enough not to embarrass you—"

"Oh, for heaven's sake, Steven!" A mixture of horror and genuine astonishment streaked across her features. "The setting might show off the stone to better advantage, but it doesn't make it more valuable! You don't have to *get up to speed,* as you put it! I would never ask you to change on my account—"

"I'm not talking about changing. I'm talking about adapting." He cupped her face in his hands, touching his forehead to hers. "If you can do it, so can I." He sucked in a quick breath, and leapt. "Let me be your refuge, honey. Forever. Marry me."

She pulled back so quickly she stumbled over the hem of

the dress. Her balance, if not her equilibrium, regained, she now stood less than a yard in front of him, her hand pressed to her stomach, her eyes enormous. "Did you just ask me to *marry* you?"

"Well, shoot, sweetheart—I didn't come all this way just to ask you to the movies."

"Oh, for heaven's sake, Steven—this is nothing to joke about."

"Who's joking?"

After a stunned moment, she turned away, shaking her head. "It's not that easy. And I know it sounds patronizing to say that, but it's true."

He'd been determined, when he'd made this decision, that he wouldn't lose his cool. A resolution being sorely put to the test in the face of this woman's obstinacy. "Let me get this straight—you can fit into *my* world, win over my kids and my family, steal my heart, dammit, but I can't fit into *yours?*"

She twisted back around, her expression tortured. "Even on a part-time basis, my world can be hell. Which few people outside of it understand. I might be able to hide out from who I am from time to time, but I can't turn my back on it completely. Even if..." She shut her eyes for a second, opened them again. "Even if I were to accept your offer, even if I put you and the children first in my heart, I doubt I'd be able to put them first the way a normal wife and mother would."

One trembling hand, the nails tinted the same shade of red as the dress, lifted to her breastbone. "Having money and position rarely confers freedom, despite what people think. If anything, it can be a prison. And I love you too much to let you take that risk, to sit by and watch my so-called life eventually destroy what we feel for each other. To watch the children's affection wither to resentment because I have to be away from them so much."

"That won't happen, Sophie."

Tears welled in her eyes. "You don't understand—"

"Yes, I do, you little twit! I know all about taking risks! And yeah, they're scary as hell, but without them, what've you got left? Dammit, Sophie—you're talking to a man who took on five traumatized children because I loved them and they needed me, never mind that I didn't have a clue as to what I was doing. And then, if that wasn't crazy enough, I quit my job to pursue a career in which you're only as successful as your next contract.''

He took a step closer, taking perverse pleasure in watching her back up a step. ''Next, some crazy lady pops into my life, says she wants to help take care of my kids, and even though I don't know her from Eve, I risk trusting my instinct that she's okay, and hire her anyway. Then, even though I've been through hell and back with an ex-wife I wouldn't wish on my worst enemy, I let myself fall in love again, harder than I've ever fallen before. And to top it off, since clearly I'm either the bravest or dumbest man in God's green earth, I spend several thousand bucks I don't even have yet to get my butt halfway across the world in the hope, slim though it may be, that maybe I can convince this crazy lady that if she'd just stop putting up a thousand damn roadblocks, maybe we could figure how to work this out, because there's a whole bunch of people where I live who *need her!*''

He took another step closer. And this time, she didn't move.

''Especially me, Sophie,'' he said softly, lifting a hand to stroke her cheek. ''Oh, God, honey, I love you. I love *you,* the wonderful, generous woman who somehow made five confused, unhappy children fall in love with her, too. And maybe that's all I have to offer—besides a run-down house, a chicken-chasing mutt, and a batch of noisy kids—but at least it's genuine. And it'll last forever.'' He lowered his hand. ''But I'm just sorry that woman—the one with the guts to dress up like a bimbo and run away from her bodyguard, the one with the guts to hire herself out as a housekeeper when she didn't even know how to *cook,* for godssake—got lost somewhere between Spruce Lake and Carpathia, because that woman sure as hell wouldn't get her panties in a twist about whether or not I'd be able to handle a few state dinners or hold my own with some ambassador or something, every once in a while.''

He waited for a moment—for what, he wasn't sure—giving her one last chance to say…something. Anything.

When, after a good ten seconds, silence still vibrated between them, he stormed from the room.

Chapter 16

"The poor man traipses a third of the way around the world to see you, and you throw him out on his ear?"

Swiping tears from her face, Sophie twisted around to see her grandmother standing in the doorway. "I did *not* throw him out!"

"As good as, judging from his expression."

"Oh, Baba," she said on a trembling sigh, sinking onto the love seat. "What have I done?"

The elderly princess sat down beside her, taking her hand in hers. "Would you say I'm a fairly good judge of character, child?"

Sophie shrugged. "I suppose."

"Then would my assessment of the young man perhaps influence you, even a little?"

She turned, frowning. "When did you—?"

"Oh, your Steven and I had quite a nice little chat, before you were summoned. And I have to say he is, without a doubt, one of the most delightful, bullheaded young men I've ever had the pleasure of meeting."

Sophie simply stared at her grandmother until the older

woman laughed. "To come after the woman he loved like that, in spite of the tremendous odds against his quest being successful? How many men do you know with the courage to simply knock on a palace door and request an audience with a princess? With *two* princesses?" She leaned toward Sophie, nudging her with her shoulder. "Impressed me no end, I can tell you. I think…" Amusement glittered in her dark eyes. "I think, perhaps, you could do far worse than to be seen on that young man's arm, don't you?"

"Oh, Baba…but you know—"

"Yes, I know what you told him. The door was open, after all." Warmth flooded Sophie's cheeks as her grandmother continued. "Letting Jason go, I can understand. I was wrong to push that alliance, and I apologize. But this Steven…he's a keeper, child. One who met and matched every one of your arguments. And still you let him walk away. Why, child, when he clearly loves you so very much?"

Sophie pulled away from her grandmother's clasp, then stood and walked to the open window to stare up at the cloud-blurred moon. "But that's the problem, don't you see?"

"What is, child?"

"Who he fell in love with." She turned, her hands linked in front of her. "It was overwhelming, and thrilling, the idea that this wonderful man had apparently fallen in love with me. Not my title or my money or the potential to influence his way in the world, but with *me*. Except…"

Her eyes flooded. "Except, I finally remembered something very important, which was that he no more fell in love with *me* than the man in the moon. He fell in love with a woman of my own creation, someone I made up. An illusion. A woman who wore cheap, funny clothes and too much makeup and bleached blond hair. A woman with…with a sense of humor! He accused me of pretending, when he found out. And he was right, wasn't he? Even if we could figure out the horrendous logistics, how could we possibly build a relationship, a marriage, on something that never had a foothold in reality to begin with?"

"In other words," Ivana said, her gaze riveted to Sophie's,

''you're afraid to trust that this wonderful man had the good sense to see through all that? That he's...forgiven you?''

''Oh, Baba—'' Tears breaching her lashes, Sophie clamped one hand over her mouth.

Her grandmother stood and walked over to her, once again taking Sophie's hands in hers. ''Darling girl, only you can search your heart and decide whether your fears are viable. Even though, as I'm sure you know, few fears have any power except what we give them. But just remember this—if you let this man go because of those fears, you may regret it for the rest of your life.''

She reached up, fussed with Sophie's pearl necklace. ''You told me, in that first voice-mail, that you'd stolen that time in order to reassess your life. Your priorities. To find yourself, you may have even said. And isn't that precisely what happened? Oh, child, the freedom to choose whatever life you want has *always* been yours.'' Then her cheeks feathered into a hundred tiny creases as she smiled. ''And did it ever occur to you that the person underneath the funny clothes and wild hair and makeup *was* the real you? The one you were afraid to let out all these years?''

Her parting shot having effectively hit its mark, Princess Ivana started toward the door. ''Our guests will really be wondering what has become of us. But I will give them your apologies. Let's see—a sudden headache, will that do?''

On a sniff, Sophie said, ''Yes. That will do quite well, thank you.''

''I thought it might. Oh, I nearly forgot—Steven happened to mention that he was staying in the inn in the village. And something else...about the midnight train back to Budapest?''

The Duprok family had run the tiny apothecary shop in the village since the sixteenth century, give or take a few decades. While their wares had undergone some dramatic changes over time, the shop's importance to the village—and to the monarchy—hadn't. Being called upon in the middle of the night in order to provide an ailing monarch with a tonic to ease digestion or soothe inflamed bronchial tubes was simply part of the job description. So when the ringing phone nearly cost plump little Gerta Duprok, the chemist's rosy-cheeked wife, five years of her life as she approached the climax of the particularly gruesome horror novel she was reading, she took it completely in her stride.

"Oh, yes, Your Highness," she said, nodding as if the younger princess could see her. "Certainly. Ten minutes, you said? Da, I will be waiting."

And so, while her husband blissfully slumbered on, she threw on a pair of slacks and a blouse, tucking her arms into the sleeves of her white smock as she trundled down the stairs that separated the living quarters from the shop to unlock the front door.

Good as her word, Princess Sophie arrived on her bicycle precisely ten minutes later, at half-past eleven, her cheeks flushed, her new short hairstyle—and very becoming, it was— wind-tossed. She looked just like that Audrey Hepburn in her slim black pants, little black top, black flat shoes. And she wore a little makeup these days, too, just enough to enhance that pretty mouth of hers, those dramatic gray eyes.

"Thank you so much for opening the shop for me," the princess said in Carpathian, looking around. "If it weren't an emergency, I certainly would not have bothered you."

"Think nothing of it, Your Highness. And if there's anything I can help you with—"

"No, no—here they are."

Gerta's hand automatically lifted to her face to cover her flush as the princess—smiling broadly—brought her selection to the counter.

"Oh," Gerta said, equally unable to look at the princess or away from the item in front of her. She cleared her throat. "Should I…add these to palace's account?"

But the princess had already pulled out a bill from her wallet and was shaking her head. "Mmm, I think not." As Gerta took the princess's money with a nervous little smile, the princess picked up the box, then frowned at it. "These are good, I trust?"

Gerta coughed a little, made the princess's change. "We have had no complaints."

"Excellent. No, no bag. I'll just drop them in here." And she did, right into a large tote bag dangling from her right hand. "As I said. If it hadn't been an emergency..."

But Gerta waved her hands. "No, no, is all right. I understand." As the princess headed back toward the door, she called out, "Have a good evening, Your Highness!"

"I fully intend to!" the princess called back before vanishing into the night.

Her heart thumping, poor Gerta sat with a thud on the little stool behind the register. "Oh, my," she whispered to herself. "Oh, my, my, my..."

Then, grinning with sudden inspiration, she popped off the stool and went upstairs to surprise her husband.

The concierge was extremely apologetic. And irritatingly obsequious. "Da, Your Highness, Mr. Koleski was here, but he left about fifteen minutes ago."

Sophie forked her hand through her hair. "Do you know if he went to the train station?"

"I am truly sorry, Your Highness, but I was not at the desk. I did not actually see him leave."

"Oh," she said on a sigh, then offered a lopsided smile. "Well, then. Thank you. If he should come in...oh, never mind."

Feeling quite like a child whose birthday party has been canceled, Sophie dragged herself outside. She'd parked her bike in the rack fronting the inn, but the last thing she felt like doing was going back to the palace. She glanced up the narrow street toward the closest thing the village had to a pub and thought, oh, why not? A half pint would hardly kill her, and maybe it would relax her enough so she could sleep.

The tang of lager and cigarette smoke smacked her in the face when she entered the dark, wood-paneled room, her ears cringing at the roar of conversation dulling some female American country-western singer's wailing lament from the jukebox by the front door. The crowd was a godsend, though, since nobody paid her any mind. Dodging one of the day staff from the palace, she wedged herself up onto a bar stool and placed her order, only to have the oddest, prickliest sensation that she was being watched. One hand lifting to the back of her neck, her gaze darted around the overly bodied room, until it landed right on a pair of amused green eyes, twinkling at her through the smoke and a dozen conversations in languages he couldn't possibly understand. The suit and tie were gone, replaced by a dark knit shirt that let his broad shoulders breathe.

Her lips parted in a silent, "Oh!" before she slid back off the stool and began fighting her way through the pack, as if petrified he'd vanish before she could get there.

They met halfway. And then she was in his arms, and his mouth met hers—just your average mouth—but there was nothing even remotely ordinary about the sensation that mouth produced. Over the pounding music, the thrum of conversation and laughter and clanking glasses, her heart thrummed and laughed and clanked, as well. Her soul keened for him, even as her body made itself more of a nuisance than George did whenever someone was eating. They broke the kiss—at last— but their faces were the only parts of their bodies not touching.

This was home.

And Carpathians had always been known for their hospitality.

"They'd told me you'd left," she shouted over the din.

His breath fanned her cheek as he bent close enough for her to hear him. "I decided to wait until morning."

"So…" She moved even closer. "Does that mean you still have your room?"

Now *that* was a cocky grin.

They were both breathless and giddy by the time he sneaked her up to his room.

She'd kicked off her shoes and had her hands on the bottom of his shirt, tugging it from his jeans before the locked door finished its click.

"Shouldn't we talk or something first?" somebody said, but the other one said, "No," and that was that.

Chuckling over the knot of panic lodged in his chest, Steve grabbed her wrists, kissing her quickly when she lifted puzzled eyes to his.

"You wouldn't be taking advantage of your position, now would you?"

Her entire face blossomed into a wicked, wicked smile as, being the resourceful type—since her hands were trapped— she shifted her hips to settle nicely against his arousal. "Oh, I have every intention of taking advantage of any position either of us find ourselves in for the foreseeable future."

"So tell me…am I about to ravish Lisa Stone, or Princess Sophie?"

Except wickedness morphed into wistfulness as she said, "Me, Steven. Just…me."

Then, leaving him half brain-dead, she twisted out of his loose grasp and walked over to the chair where she'd thrown her bag. She extracted a small, telltale box from it, tossing it to him. "And you've got thirty-six opportunities to get it right."

"Uh…" He walked over to his open duffel bag on the floor, pulled out another box. "Seventy-two."

She hooted with laughter even as wonder flooded her eyes. Silver eyes, as soft and changeable as a cloud. "Why, you sentimental old thing. But wait a minute…" She crossed the room, snatching the box out of his hand, her mouth pursed as she quickly inspected it. "Oh, all right. You pass." Then she handed it back to him.

"Huh?"

"The seal. It's not broken. Just wanted to make sure you weren't planning on sticking me with your leftovers," she said, only to burst into laughter as Steve groaned at the bad double entendre. Then he reached out, gently sweeping a loose strand of hair off her cheek. And he silently thanked all those people back home who'd given him a collective kick in the keyster to get over here. Not to mention his father who'd reminded him, again, what he'd been willing to give up, in order to be with Steven's mother. And even, he realized, Mrs. Hadley, whose walking out on him had led, amazingly, to this moment.

Yeah, Mac. Fate can be pretty damn cool, if you don't fight it.

"I won't pretend there weren't women before Francine," he said softly. "Not a lot, but a few. And then there was Francine, and only Francine, for nearly four years. Then no one. At all—" he brushed his lips over hers "—until now—" and again "—until you."

His earnestness drove home the implications of what she was about to do. And that, in this at least, disingenuousness didn't have a prayer. She braced her hands on his chest, captured his darkened gaze in hers. "Perhaps now would be a good time to tell you I, um, have never done this before."

Steven grinned. "Kissed a slightly crazy American man in his hotel room?"

"Well, that, too. But—"

He took her hand in his, brought it to his mouth to graze his lips over her knuckles, which certainly heated things up quite nicely. "I'd already figured that out, honey."

Her brows shot up. "How—?"

"Sometimes a guy just knows these things, okay?"

"And it doesn't bother you?"

Steven's eyes crinkled at the corners when he laughed. "Everybody's got a first time at some point, right? So this is yours."

"In other words, no big deal?"

His expression sobered. "Oh, I didn't say that." He shifted to pick her up, carried her to the bed where he laid her gently down on top of the blue-striped down comforter. "When it comes to big deals—" he lay down beside her, tucked her hand in his against his chest "—this is one of the biggest. The only stipulation is, you have to be completely honest with me, okay? No lying here in silence, wondering if this is the way it's supposed to be. If something feels strange or awk-

ward, my feelings aren't going to be hurt if you tell me to
stop. Got it?''

He looked so bloody serious, it was everything she could
do not to laugh. "Got it," she said, then melted into his kiss.

A half hour later, she was still waiting for something to feel
awkward or strange. Now, *marvelous* had wandered through,
a time or two. As had, in no particular order, *amazing, wonderful, mmm* and *oh, my.* Not to mention the ever-popular
yes!!!! But, no, no *awkward* or *strange* here.

What she felt, was beautiful.

They had both been quite naked for some time now, una-
bashedly exploring each other's bodies with something ap-
proaching reverence. And a heartbreaking tenderness unlike
anything she'd ever known. Her lack of experience certainly
didn't seem to be a problem, as far as she could tell. Sometimes Steven would guess at what she might like, sometimes
he'd just come right out and ask. And, so far, things seemed
to be working rather well.

Oh, all right. Extraordinarily well. He truly had the most
amazing hands. And mouth. And, well, everything. And if the
amount of attention he was lavishing on her breasts—which
were most appreciative, by the way—was any indication, he
certainly seemed to think she was pretty bloody amazing, too.

She could live with this.

Or rather, how could she live *without* this?

When she mentioned that she thought she might explode if
he did what he was doing a second longer, they broke open
the seal on one of the boxes of condoms—much like one
might pop a champagne cork—and worked together—team-
work and all that—to get it on. Then he slowly…gently…
tenderly slipped inside her and her breath caught at the joy
that swept through her at being able to express love so completely. So intimately. So perfectly.

And to think…perfectly ordinary people did this every day.

What an extraordinary thing life was.

And wasn't it remarkable, that the one thing she'd nearly
accepted as never being within her grasp—being loved for
herself—was actually hers, for real and forever.

If she had the courage to take it, that is.

She shut her eyes as her hands drifted over her head, letting the sensation swirl and climb, ebb and flow and tug at her heart, her soul. Steve linked their fingers, his breath sweet on her face, her breasts. Through a haze of what she could only call rapture—although she doubted she'd ever actually admit that to anyone, lest she sound completely barmy—she heard words of love. Of promise.

Of trust.

Then he pulled back. She opened her eyes to find his gaze pinned to her face, his expression at once tortured and hopeful. She wriggled one hand free to smooth her fingers over his brow, skimming one knuckle down his roughened cheek, feeling so full of love—in every sense of the word—she could hardly get her breath.

"Husband," she whispered with a smile. He smiled in return, briefly traced his tongue over her lips, then filled her sharply, thoroughly, exquisitely, sending the last of her fears spiraling into sweet oblivion.

"What time is it?" Sophie asked.

Steven's answer rumbled underneath her ear. "You really want to know?"

"No." One arm draped over her lover's—soon to be her husband's—chest, Sophie hugged him more tightly. They'd been talking—believe it or not—for some time. About her new appointment as Director of the World Relief Fund and his photography and how they'd manage being parents and their schedules and holidays and what would happen if—when—she became pregnant. And although they hadn't sorted everything out, they'd at least come to a point where they could see that they could. And that was all that mattered. She softly laughed. "I would have been extremely annoyed if I'd missed you. Missed this."

"Not as annoyed as I would've been," Steven said, chuckling at her shiver when he began tracing lazy circles at the small of her back. "Although perhaps annoyed isn't the word I would've chosen."

She smiled, then whispered, "Thank you," snuggling closer, thinking how ordinary he smelled, like soap and man. And how extraordinarily wonderful *ordinary* smelled.

"For?"

"For simply being you." She shifted to look into his eyes, her heart swelling at the tenderness she found there. A good man, he was. *Hers,* he was.

And always would be. Of that, she had no doubt.

"Yeah, well, being me is what I do best," he said with a chuckle, then flipped over to nestle between her thighs, his strength and warmth so welcome. So right.

"I was petrified, you know," he whispered, his thumbs stroking her temples, their mouths barely a breath apart. "That you'd send me packing."

She touched his face, frowning. "Then why did you do it? What made you take the chance?"

He shifted onto his side, propping his elbow on the mattress, his head in his hand. "Because the way I figure it, we each have something the other one needs. Something nobody else can meet, y'know? And I thought—" he shrugged, that cocky grin sending about a million hormones into overdrive "—who the hell am I to buck that?"

A vestige or two of doubt made her frown. "This isn't going to be easy."

"You want *easy*," he whispered, knuckling her hair away from her cheek. "or *happy?*"

"I want *you*," she said fiercely. "And the children and the farmhouse and the chicken-chasing mutt and…" She giggled, even as she blushed. Even as she let her hand tell Steven what else she wanted.

"I see," Steven said, his mouth twitching, then plucked the box from his nightstand, shaking it. "One down, seventy-one to go."

"We'll have to pace ourselves, then," Sophie said, her brow knotted. "Since I don't dare get the poor chemist's wife out of bed again tonight."

He roared with laughter, and she thought there was nothing better in the world, to hear his laughter.

Except, perhaps, for seeing the children again…and eventually holding Steven's baby at her breast…and knowing that she was loved—deeply, truly loved—more than she'd ever thought possible.

The lonely little princess would never be lonely again, she thought, as the most extraordinary man in the world drew her into his arms.

Epilogue

With a satisfied smile, Princess Ivana lowered herself onto a padded folding chair out in the lavishly decorated garden. The wedding had been lovely, hadn't it? Joyous. A fitting beginning to what she was sure was to be a long, wonderful marriage. And no one could call Sophie a Plain-Jane anything today, not in her mother's silk satin Dior wedding gown, not wearing that brilliant smile.

Steven's family was charming, if boisterous. Ivana had instantly taken to them, and to his five wards as well—soon to be his and Sophie's permanently, once the adoption went through. Perhaps now Sophie would have the family she'd always wanted, not the helter-skelter one she'd made do with for so long.

And perhaps, one day, they would add to the brood, as well?

Her granddaughter's life would be fuller than ever. But, now, it was a life of her choosing, and Ivana doubted whether Sophie would ever have a moment's regret.

Sophie and Steven approached, her granddaughter in a graceful slip of a dress and sandals, her handsome groom wearing a plain knit shirt and pleated pants. The children, as

well as that charming Mrs. Takeda, would stay here for a week
while the newlyweds honeymooned at some undisclosed location, before they all flew back to Michigan. The prospect of
having the palace ring with the sounds of children's laughter—
and bickerings, she imagined—filled Ivana with a kind of eager anticipation she hadn't felt in far too many years.

"We're ready to leave, Baba," Sophie said, leaning over to
kiss her on her cheek.

Ivana drew her granddaughter close and whispered, "Be
happy, child."

Sophie beamed and gave her a thumbs-up.

But as the newlyweds walked off, holding hands and chattering to each other, Ivana's gaze settled on her other grandchild, who had so unselfishly kept his own worries from his
sister, so as not to spoil her wedding day.

And she silently wished the same happiness for him.

"Your Highness?"

Frowning, Prince Aleksander looked up from watching his
sister and new brother-in-law leave their wedding reception,
relaxing when he recognized his valet. "Yes, Tomas—what is
it?"

"I have just received a message from that private investi-
gator you hired. He's located Jeff Henderson's widow, Your
Highness."

Alek started. "Where?"

"In a small town in Texas, I gather. Shall I go ahead and
make travel arrangements?"

Alek acknowledged the message with a single sharp nod.

* * * * *

Silhouette®

INTIMATE MOMENTS™
presents a riveting new continuity series:

FIRSTBORN SONS

Bound by the legacy of their fathers, these Firstborn Sons are about to discover the stuff true heroes—and true love—are made of!

The adventure continues in September 2001 with:

BORN TO PROTECT by Virginia Kantra

Former Navy SEAL Jack Dalton took his job *very* seriously when he was ordered to protect Princess Christina Sebastiani from ruthless kidnappers. But nothing in the rule book prepared this Firstborn Son on the proper code of conduct to follow when the virgin princess managed to capture his world-weary heart!

July: **BORN A HERO**
by **Paula Detmer Riggs** (IM #1088)
August: **BORN OF PASSION**
by **Carla Cassidy** (IM #1094)
September: **BORN TO PROTECT**
by **Virginia Kantra** (IM #1100)
October: **BORN BRAVE**
by **Ruth Wind** (IM #1106)
November: **BORN IN SECRET**
by **Kylie Brant** (IM #1112)
December: **BORN ROYAL**
by **Alexandra Sellers** (IM #1118)

*Available only from
Silhouette Intimate Moments
at your favorite retail outlet.*

Silhouette®
Where love comes alive™

Visit Silhouette at www.eHarlequin.com

SIMFIRST3

 Silhouette®

where love comes alive—online...

eHARLEQUIN.com

your romantic escapes

—Indulgences—

♥ Monthly guides to indulging yourself, such as:
  ★ Tub Time: A guide for bathing beauties
  ★ Magic Massages: A treat for tired feet

—Horoscopes—

♥ Find your daily Passionscope, weekly Lovescopes and Erotiscopes

♥ Try our compatibility game

—Reel Love—

♥ Read all the latest romantic movie reviews

—Royal Romance—

♥ Get the latest scoop on your favorite royal romances

—Romantic Travel—

♥ For the most romantic destinations, hotels and travel activities

All this and more available at
www.eHarlequin.com
on Women.com Networks

SINTE1R

NOTORIOUS
Vicki Lewis Thompson

Blaze™

In August 2001
Harlequin Blaze
ignites everywhere...

GOING FOR IT
Jo Leigh

TWO SEXY!
Stephanie Bond

Look for these red-hot reads
at bookstores!

Careful: It's Hot!

EXPOSED
Julie Elizabeth Leto

"Blazing hot! A story so sexually seductive you can't stop reading."
—bestselling author Virginia Henley

◆ HARLEQUIN®
Makes any time special®

Visit us at www.TryBlaze.com

HBINTROR

Feel like a star with Silhouette.

We will fly you and a guest to New York City for an
exciting weekend stay at a glamorous 5-star hotel.
Experience a refreshing day at one of New York's
trendiest spas and have your photo taken by a
professional. Plus, receive $1,000 U.S. spending money!

**Flowers…long walks…dinner for two…
how does Silhouette Books
make romance come alive for you?**

Send us a script, with 500 words or less, along with visuals (only drawings,
magazine cutouts or photographs or combination thereof). Show us how
Silhouette Makes Your Love Come Alive. Be creative and have fun. No
purchase necessary. All entries must be clearly marked with your name,
address and telephone number. All entries will become property of
Silhouette and are not returnable. **Contest closes September 28, 2001.**

Please send your entry to: **Silhouette Makes You a Star!**

In U.S.A.
P.O. Box 9069
Buffalo, NY, 14269-9069

In Canada
P.O. Box 637
Fort Erie, ON, L2A 5X3

Look for contest details on the next page, by visiting www.eHarlequin.com or
request a copy by sending a self-addressed envelope to the applicable address
above. Contest open to Canadian and U.S. residents who are 18 or over.
Void where prohibited.

Where love comes alive™

Our lucky winner's photo will appear in a Silhouette ad. Join the fun!

SRMYAS1

HARLEQUIN "SILHOUETTE MAKES YOU A STAR!" CONTEST 1308
OFFICIAL RULES
NO PURCHASE NECESSARY TO ENTER

1. To enter, follow directions published in the offer to which you are responding. Contest begins June 1, 2001, and ends on September 28, 2001. Entries must be postmarked by September 28, 2001, and received by October 5, 2001. Enter by hand-printing (or typing) on an 8 ½" x 11" piece of paper your name, address (including zip code), contest number/name and attaching a script containing 500 words or less, along with drawings, photographs or magazine cutouts, or combinations thereof (i.e., collage) on no larger than 9" x 12" piece of paper, describing how the Silhouette books make romance come alive for you. Mail via first-class mail to: Harlequin "Silhouette Makes You a Star!" Contest 1308, (in the U.S.) P.O. Box 9069, Buffalo, NY 14269-9069, (in Canada) P.O. Box 637, Fort Erie, Ontario, Canada L2A 5X3. Limit one entry per person, household or organization.

2. Contests will be judged by a panel of members of the Harlequin editorial, marketing and public relations staff. Fifty percent of criteria will be judged against script and fifty percent will be judged against drawing, photographs and/or magazine cutouts. Judging criteria will be based on the following:

   - Sincerity—25%
   - Originality and Creativity—50%
   - Emotionally Compelling—25%

   In the event of a tie, duplicate prizes will be awarded. Decisions of the judges are final.

3. All entries become the property of Torstar Corp. and may be used for future promotional purposes. Entries will not be returned. No responsibility is assumed for lost, late, illegible, incomplete, inaccurate, nondelivered or misdirected mail.

4. Contest open only to residents of the U.S. (except Puerto Rico) and Canada who are 18 years of age or older, and is void wherever prohibited by law; all applicable laws and regulations apply. Any litigation within the Province of Quebec respecting the conduct or organization of a publicity contest may be submitted to the Régie des alcools, des courses et des jeux for a ruling. Any litigation respecting the awarding of a prize may be submitted to the Régie des alcools, des courses et des jeux only for the purpose of helping the parties reach a settlement. Employees and immediate family members of Torstar Corp. and D. L. Blair, Inc., their affiliates, subsidiaries and all other agencies, entities and persons connected with the use, marketing or conduct of this contest are not eligible to enter. Taxes on prizes are the sole responsibility of the winner. Acceptance of any prize offered constitutes permission to use winner's name, photograph or other likeness for the purposes of advertising, trade and promotion on behalf of Torstar Corp., its affiliates and subsidiaries without further compensation to the winner, unless prohibited by law.

5. Winner will be determined no later than November 30, 2001, and will be notified by mail. Winner will be required to sign and return an Affidavit of Eligibility/Release of Liability/Publicity Release form within 15 days after winner notification. Noncompliance within that time period may result in disqualification and an alternative winner may be selected. All travelers must execute a Release of Liability prior to ticketing and must possess required travel documents (e.g., passport, photo ID) where applicable. Trip must be booked by December 31, 2001, and completed within one year of notification. No substitution of prize permitted by winner. Torstar Corp. and D. L. Blair, Inc., their parents, affiliates and subsidiaries are not responsible for errors in printing of contest, entries and/or game pieces. In the event of printing or other errors that may result in unintended prize values or duplication of prizes, all affected game pieces or entries shall be null and void. **Purchase or acceptance of a product offer does not improve your chances of winning.**

6. Prizes: (1) Grand Prize—A 2-night/3-day trip for two (2) to New York City, including round-trip coach air transportation nearest winner's home and hotel accommodations (double occupancy) at The Plaza Hotel, a glamorous afternoon makeover at a trendy New York spa, $1,000 in U.S. spending money and an opportunity to have a professional photo taken and appear in a Silhouette advertisement (approximate retail value: $7,000). (10) Ten Runner-Up Prizes of gift packages (retail value $50 ea.). Prizes consist of only those items listed as part of the prize. Limit one prize per person. Prize is valued in U.S. currency.

7. For the name of the winner (available after December 31, 2001) send a self-addressed, stamped envelope to: Harlequin "Silhouette Makes You a Star!" Contest 1197 Winners, P.O. Box 4200 Blair, NE 68009-4200 or you may access the www.eHarlequin.com Web site through February 28, 2002.

Contest sponsored by Torstar Corp., P.O. Box 9042, Buffalo, NY 14269-9042.

SRMYAS2

Revitalize!

With help from
Silhouette's *New York Times*
bestselling authors
and receive a

FREE

Refresher Kit!

LUCIA IN LOVE by Heather Graham
and LION ON THE PROWL by Kasey Michaels

LOVE SONG FOR A RAVEN by Elizabeth Lowell
and THE FIVE-MINUTE BRIDE by Leanne Banks

MACKENZIE'S PLEASURE by Linda Howard
and DEFENDING HIS OWN by Beverly Barton

DARING MOVES by Linda Lael Miller
and MARRIAGE ON DEMAND by Susan Mallery

Don't miss out!

*Look for this exciting promotion, on sale in
October 2001 at your favorite retail outlet.
See inside books for details.*

Only from

▼ *Silhouette*®
™ *Where love comes alive*™

Visit Silhouette at www.eHarlequin.com   PSNCP-POP